SICK OF BEING ME

Sean Egan was born in London. His first professional writing work was a brief stint providing scripts for the television soap opera Eastenders. He is currently a journalist specialising in popular music and tennis. He has written for, amongst other outlets, *Billboard, Billboard.com, Classic Rock, Discoveries, Goldmine, Mojo4Music.com, Record Collector, Record Mart & Buyer, RollingStone.com, Serve And Volley, Sky Sports, Tennis World, Uncut* and *Vox*. He also writes CD liner notes.

He is the author of four previous books, one of which - *Jimi Hendrix And The Making Of Are You Experienced* - was nominated for an Award for Excellence in Historical Recorded Sound Research by the Association for Recorded Sound Collections. *Sick Of Being Me* is his first novel.

Advance praise for *Sick Of Being Me*

"Sean Egan writes with warmth, humour and gut-wrenching honesty about the gritty, real-life roots of the rock and roll life. From the innocence of the Beatles to the junk-infested squalor of a tragic wanna-be, he tells a moving story that will click with anyone who has stood in front of a mirror playing air guitar." ~ *Gary Valentine, former bassist and songwriter with Blondie, author of 'New York Rocker: My Life In The Blank Generation'*

"A harrowing look at the face of the rock 'n' roll dream you don't read about in standard bios – the insecurities, self-doubt and abuse that both fuel pop star aspirations and lead many of its followers into destitute self-destruction. Told with wry unflinching detail and gallows humour, it's not just the drama of rock 'n' roll, drugs and sex (in that order) but also of failure; the harsh odds stacked against talented and critically acclaimed musicians even making a living at the business; and the fragility of the close bonds that bring bands together in the first place. For Egan's anti-hero, the demons that drive him to find his salvation in rock 'n' roll are the same ones that lead him into the gutter. It might take place in the world of rock 'n' roll and junkies but in his protagonist's struggle to balance his impulses, we recognise more universal battles waged by all of us." ~ *Richie Unterberger, author of 'Unknown Legends of Rock 'n 'Roll', 'Turn! Turn! Turn!' and 'Eight Miles High'*

"Sean Egan's new novel is a brutal but poignant journey into the raw underside of rock 'n' roll. Egan writes with such an authenticity that his characters seem real: they are cut straight from the pages of NME or a sordid chapter in *Behind The Music*. When you put down the book you half expect to find a Coronets CD at your local shop. Few rock 'n' roll novels are as dead-on in their realism and few writers are able to describe both drugs and rock with such vivid and compelling language. This book reads like a cautionary tale: it should be required reading for anyone starting a band, or toying with a life of drugs, for that matter. Where *High Fidelity* and *About A Boy* were light and fluffy, Egan's *Sick Of Being Me* is dark but honest, though it never loses sight of its pure rock 'n' roll heart." ~ *Charles R. Cross, author of 'Heavier Than Heaven: A Biography of Kurt Cobain'*

"Sean Egan tells a dark and dirty tale about the world of rock and roll: the sleazy, desperate bottom of the rockpile where the people who don't 'make it' live. The central character Paul finds he has a natural ability as a guitarist but he doesn't get the breaks. Given a chaotic upbringing by his dysfunctional, penniless parents, his ambition to make it as a musician too soon brings him into contact with hard drugs. He quickly becomes addicted to heroin, a smack habit which creates a battleground of his need to score and his need to play." ~ *John Steel, The Animals*

"Very convincing and authentic both in its depiction of the music scene and the drug scene. The chapters involving the drug dealer genuinely disturbed me: though the book is set in the '90s, he reminded me of several characters I met back in London in the '60s, the time of the Kray twins and many others like them. A very talented writer." ~ *Vic Briggs, former guitarist with Brian Auger's Trinity, Dusty Springfield and Eric Burdon & The Animals*

"If these pages are the script of Sean Egan's passage to manhood he has endured more of the seamier side of life than one should ever be asked to. If it is fiction then he is the possessor of a marvellously vivid imagination which will serve him well as a writer in the years to come. Its gritty realism holds the reader firmly in its thrall with powerfully descriptive paragraphs that trace a boys's rites of passage through the post-Beatle years in which a drug fuelled music scene takes its heavy toll. Gripping stuff." ~ *Frank Allen, The Searchers and author of 'Travelling Man: On The Road With The Searchers'*

Sick of Being Me

Sean Egan

God Save The Queen
Words and Music by Paul Cook, Glen Matlock, Steve Jones
and John Lydon
© 1977 Warner/Chappell Music Ltd and Rotten Music Ltd
Warner/Chappell Music Ltd, London W6 8BS
Reproduced by permission of International Music
Publications Ltd
All Rights Reserved.

Lazy Day
Words and Music by Raymond Thomas © 1969,
Reproduced by permission of Memforest Ltd./EMI Music
Publishing Ltd., London WC2H 0QY

Textual design and cover: Bernie Ross

British Library Cataloguing in Publication Data available

ISBN 0-9545750-0-8

Askill Publishing
PO Box 46818
LONDON
SW11 6WE

PART ONE

One

I'd just about resigned myself to not scoring.

It was one of those days of pain and grimness that were so normal to me then. It was around one in the morning and I didn't have any money. Not even enough for some valium or dikes, supposing, that is, I could have found the only dealer I'd ever known who sold them - not many dealers were going to do themselves out of some business by selling stuff that lessened the pain of withdrawal. There were, though, plenty of dealers who would supply you smack on credit, so long as you paid over the odds when you had money. That was one thing I'd never do. Once you owed a dealer, you never stopped owing.

I was walking home after rehearsals with my band. My nose was streaming. I had my amp in one hand and the strap of the cloth cover of my guitar in the other. There was no point making the effort of putting one of them down to wipe it away. When you're turkeying, you're always leaking. Mucus, piss and shit, twenty-four hours a day. And when you've got a regular supply it has the opposite effect. Someone once said to me that users spend ninety per cent of their lives trying to score and ten per cent stoned. I'd say the average user spends at least 25 per cent of the time sitting on the toilet, staring at the wall thinking, "Please, *please*".

It was cold, and where the wind was blowing against my mucus it was doubly cold. My face screwed up against the chill, I came up to a little supermarket, one I went in occasionally. I hated the owner. He over-charged for everything and never said "Thank you" when you bought something. Looking at a Bird's Eye poster behind the grille over his windows, I felt a surge of hatred for him. In feeling it, I became brave. Or, rather, I got this couldn't-give-a-toss attitude that often overtook me when I was irritated, this feeling that I should go ahead and do what I liked and bollocks to the consequences. Grimy, miserable, sore all over, I decided that I *was* going to score tonight.

The shop was on a corner. I walked round to the adjoining street. There was a side door to the building. I knew it was locked but, after looking around, still pushed at it. I kept walking, my eyes on the wall the door was set in. The wall was very high - three stories - with what looked like a conservatory at the top. I found a small part where it wasn't so high. Between the shop and the next building - a one-story jutting-out of an ordinary house - there was a small vertical gap. The gap started well above my head. It was enough - just - to squeeze my body sideways through. The trouble was there was no way to get up to it. There was an overflow pipe sticking out of the shop wall at my chest height that would make a good foothold but I'd have to be several feet taller to use it. I stood there thinking about it for a minute. When I started feeling it was hopeless, I got irritated again. I swung my guitar off and leant it against the wall, then put the amplifier against the base of the wall and stood on it. Bracing myself with one palm, I swung my leg up and got the sole of my baseball boot onto the overflow pipe. I heaved up and managed to slap my hand into the gap.

Balanced in a squatting posture on the pipe, I carefully reached down for my guitar. I couldn't bring my amp over with me but there was no way I was going to leave my guitar out in the street as well. I grabbed the ribbing of the case between two fingers and lifted. When I had the bottom of the guitar resting on the foot that was on the pipe, I let go of the ribbing on the neck and grabbed the ribbing on the body.

I rose. The sight discernible between the two walls was of another wall about ten or twelve feet away. Between that and me was darkness. I lifted my guitar up, put it in the gap and lowered it over the other side into God-knew-what. I held onto it as long as I could, grasping the ribbing of the head, but it still hadn't touched ground when I finally had to let go. I winced as I heard it connect with what sounded like concrete, scrape along something and then thump down onto the ground. This all served to make me even more irritated and I didn't even think to worry about the noise it had made as I hastily followed it. From on top of the pipe I could lift my left leg and place it in the gap. I pulled the rest of my body up to stand with two feet squeezed into the narrow space between the two walls. I strained my eyes but still couldn't see what I would be descending into. I grabbed hold of the low roof of the neighbouring structure and let myself hang. As my feet stepped carefully down the bricks, the back of my jacket rasped against the supermarket's building.

With my body-weight supported only by my fingertips, I was still treading on air. I let go.

Dropping into darkness is weird. It turned out to be only a short drop but it still made me leave my stomach behind. My disorientation wasn't helped by the fact that when I landed, I literally bounced back and forth between the two walls for a couple of seconds.

Although my heart was hammering, there was no damage done. I wasn't even standing on my guitar. I groped for it and pulled it upright, then slid with it towards what light there was. After about six feet I emerged from between the two walls into the supermarket's yard. I could now see much better. I was in a square enclosed on four sides. There were no lights on in any of the windows. I waited a minute or so to see if anyone had heard me coming over.

To my right was a pair of windows, the kind of which open outwards on hinges. They were closed. I ran my fingers around their edges but the catches were on. I would smash the glass and open the catches if I couldn't find another way in.

Three seconds later I came upon a way to save me doing that. There was a wooden side door. I turned its handle. At first, I thought it was locked. When I squinted closer, however, I saw that it was opening a fraction, then stopping. A door-chain? I put my fingers in the gap and felt for it. There was nothing there, even when I ran them from top to bottom. I pushed again. The door gave a little more. There was some kind of object placed against it inside. Bracing myself with a foot, I leaned in, applying steady pressure. The door moved, though slowly, the unseen object making a muffled scraping sound on the floor as it was forced along. When the gap was big enough, I slipped inside. I peered down but couldn't make out what had been behind the door. I squatted. I saw the words 'Golden Wonder' and realised it was a box of crisp packets. That itself was sitting on a case of peach tins. I'd take some of both when I left. A habit never leaves enough money for food.

The windows I'd been trying to get open turned out to belong to a bathroom. Turning away from that, I saw in the gloom a white banister. Guessing that the shop was downwards from where I was, I clutched it as I gingerly descended one-at-a-time steps I couldn't see. My guess was wrong: downstairs was a kitchen. So I went back the way I'd come, then up another flight. Feeling my way on the landing at the top, my fingertips collided with a wall. I turned to my left and again they came into clumsy contact with a vertical surface, but this one rattled slightly. A door. I found a handle. I pulled but the door didn't move. I tried pushing. It swung in and I was looking at the neon-lit Coca-Cola sign on the shop's cold foods cabinet. I was startled for a moment by the loud humming suddenly surrounding me before realising it was the sound of the Slush Puppy machine. I stepped carefully inside.

Illuminated only by the lamplight coming through the windows and the neon of the displays - the only sound the humming of the machines - the shop felt like the set of a science fiction movie. The surreal atmosphere made me feel excited and giddy. Or at least as giddy as a junkie who hasn't had a hit for sixteen hours and who's got snot running into his mouth can feel.

Immediately, the thought of grabbing a couple of the bags of crisps seemed ridiculous. I was surrounded by food. I stepped quietly over to the cold storage display, leaned my guitar against it and took out a Cornish pastie. Unwrapping it and taking a bite, I moved towards where I knew the till was. I lifted the door of the counter it sat on and walked behind it. The cigarettes were in racks to the back of the till. I found the hook where the carrier bags hung and pulled a couple off, then, in between bites of the pastie, began throwing the cigarette packets in. I cleaned the shelves of everything except four or five packets. In the end, the shapes of the boxes jutted through the thin material of three bulging bags. I threw some chocolate bars from a display on the counter on top of them.

I placed the bags by my feet. The green numerals 00:00 shone from the till's totals display. Even if I hadn't had to squint, bent over, to see the buttons on it, I still wouldn't have known which of them did what. Some had numbers on them, some what could have been acronyms. I pressed the ones with letters. Nothing happened. I tried some of the numbered ones. Still nothing. I placed my entire palm across one half of the bank of buttons. This caused the till to begin emitting a continuous, high-pitched beep. I grabbed the three bags and made to leave. My foot hit a box on the floor and I tipped forward, trotting several rapid, thumping footsteps. I wasn't panicking, though. In my state, I didn't have the energy. I slipped the handles of two of the bags over my wrist so as to be able to grasp my guitar. I had no choice but to move slowly as I went back down the stairs because I had no hand free to guide me. By the time I was out in the yard again I was sure I was going to be caught because I realised I hadn't worked out how I was going to get back out into the street.

I walked sideways up the tiny alley that led to the street-side wall. I could barely see but my hands - weighed down by my cargo - felt no drainpipes or any other possible means of assistance. I walked back into the yard. In the gloom, I spied a wooden box that I could stand on. I put the bags and guitar down and took it over to the alley. It was too big to go in, even turned sideways. I looked around again, walking back and forth across the yard, bent over. The best I could find was an empty plastic plant pot that wasn't quite high enough.

In the end I had to stand on my guitar. I threw the bags of cigarettes over the wall, then, with the guitar's head leaned against a corner where two walls met, I stood on the upper horn (it was a Fender Strat) so that I could grab the top of the wall. It was a situation where I was trying to tread so, so lightly, but, of course, I was having to put all my body weight on it. I winced as I put my other foot on the tip of the peghead. Mercifully, there had been no cracking sounds by the time I managed to throw my fingertips over the top of the wall. I clambered up the wall with my arms stretched tight and my arse stuck out. When I could turn round and sit on the wall, I found the thankful sight of a road still deserted and the carrier bags - some of their contents scattered - lying near my amp. I eased my backside forward and wrapped my feet round the neck of my guitar. Carefully - knowing one slip would mean me having to go down and use it to stand on again - I lifted. It was ridiculous how long this was all taking me.

At last, me, my guitar and the fags were all safely on the other side of the wall. The bags I was carrying swung and banged against my legs as I moved off. I was walking at as brisk a pace as I could manage.

By the time I was six or so streets away, I began to feel safe. As soon as I did, I started thinking about what I'd got. Which is when it occurred to me: what had I got? Some chocolate bars that would save me going hungry for a few days. A load of fags. I had imagined selling them but, now I came to think of it, who did I know that would buy them? And no money. I was so disgusted I actually stopped dead and stood there with my face raised and the bags hanging from my limp arms.

Christ.

I started walking again, but slowly now.

Jee-zus Christ. Nothing was ever as good as you thought it would be.

I put my amp and guitar down and let the bag handles slip over my wrists. I took out two of the fag packets for the filters. I was shaking my head as I picked up the amp and guitar again, but it was a shaking of familiarity more than anything else - this was the story of my life.

I left the bags where they were and walked off to what I had started to resign myself to half an hour before. Another miserable night waiting for morning.

* * * *

I got release from turkey through the best and least harmful way: sleep. It's not something you can just will and, of course, the pains are the very thing preventing it when you want it. I lay in bed for an hour that night, my body shivering and my skin prickly and greasy with sweat. Every couple of minutes I hawked and spat on the carpet. Every ten minutes I had to get up and walk over to have a piss in my sink. But eventually I got lucky. I drifted off and for three hours didn't have to be aware of my body. When the alarm went off at half-five, I still felt like shit, naturally, but I'd moved three hours further toward when I wouldn't feel like shit. I didn't know where I was going to get the money to score but that was a different matter.

I filled my sink up with hot water. The blue enamel it poured into was caked with dirt and piss. I'd be cleaning it tomorrow. Every five days I had a shave and I would wash away the build up of the last four days along with the foam and hairs. My movements were slow and trembly as I ran my sponge down my arms and chest and over my legs. I was well into turkey now, into the stage where your muscles ached so much it was like somebody had punched you all over when you were asleep. I felt so weak that even the smallest effort was enough to make me want to groan. It wasn't enough to make me feel angry, though, because that would take too much energy. I towelled myself as much as I had the heart to. When I put on my clothes, I did at least feel a small sensation of satisfaction, knowing that I'd managed to get rid of my junkie stench.

As I walked down the stairs and into the shop, however, my head started buzzing unpleasantly. I didn't bother to respond to Mr. Case's "'Morning," but just walked over to where my round was marked up.

With my papers loaded into my trolley, I moved off immediately, knowing that if I thought about the next hour-and-a-half pushing it around the streets it would literally be enough to make me want to cry.

For the first few streets, I felt alright. Shortly, though, I was in a state where I was just concentrating on the next letterbox, focusing on making the following few yards to it. Only after delivering each paper did I allow myself to think about the fact that I had to deliver another one. The sweat was by now flowing freely again and I could feel the muscles underneath my ears twitching continuously. When I got to Raynes Court - a high class block of flats we delivered to - I allowed myself to sit down on the stairs for a couple of minutes. I knew that I was now a third of the way through the round. When I hauled myself to my feet once more, my eyes were closed and my lips compressed at the prospect of another hour to go.

On the last four or five streets I had to stop to vomit twice. The first time, I felt my stomach going into spasms. It wasn't painful but the bizarre violent jumping of your innards makes you feel queasy in the brain as well as in the gut: an awful, all-over slithery sensation. I stopped and held my face away from the papers. My stomach felt like it was rolling over itself as the eruption of sick hit the pavement. I vomited again. I waited, hoping for more so I'd know it was all over. When it didn't look as though more was coming, I pushed once more at the trolley. My eyes were streaming and my breath coming in gasps. I was half-blind as I pushed papers through letterboxes. The second wave of vomiting came when I was sitting resting on a kerb in my last-but-one street. There were no giveaway spasms this time. It just stormed up my throat, catching me by surprise. When I brought my head up, a man putting his rubbish out across the street was staring at me. When my eye caught his, he looked embarrassedly away.

* * * *

At about half-nine that morning I went around to the flat of a bloke called Mick. His girlfriend Julie answered the door and told me he was at work. The best guitarist I'd ever met and he was now working in a chemist. While talentless little twerps who didn't even play an instrument got contracts every day. I didn't blame him for giving up. I'd done it a few times. I'd been planning to ask him to lend me some money. 'Lend' meaning 'give' because he knew enough to know any money you lent a user you'd never see again. I was too embarrassed to ask Julie for money so instead I asked her if she had any Valium or paracetamol. She said she didn't, uneasily looking me up and down. Mick saw me quite often so was used to my appearance but my yellowy skin, matchstick arms and legs and permanent look of exhaustion would have been a shock to her, especially as she'd known me before.

She felt sorry for me. She asked me if I wanted a cup of tea. I said yeah, I wouldn't mind. As I did, there was a catch in my throat. Somebody showing me kindness was so unusual. People normally treated me with contempt or weariness, someone who was either poncing money or stoned.

I sat down with her and for half an hour tried to be a normal person. Despite the ever-worsening withdrawals - making me feel I had the most vicious 'flu ever invented - I sat politely in an armchair and chatted about Mick's job, my band, her job. I wanted to stay much longer but I knew I had to get away when I started to shiver badly and could only speak with a lot of concentration.

I decided to go around the nearby pubs and look for half-filled glasses of beer on the window-ledges outside. Alcohol would blur the pain. By now, I knew I'd have to forget about rehearsals tonight. There was no point going in when I wasn't going to be able to play a note.

A miracle happened. I was walking away disappointed from my third pub. The weather was a bit too cold for people to be taking their drinks outside and all I'd got was an inch of beer at the bottom of a pint glass. There was a man with a beard and hair pulled back in a ponytail walking towards me. I recognized him. I'd got into a conversation with him once when he, myself and my band's drummer, Doug, had all been sitting waiting for six hours outside the flat of a dealer. I couldn't remember him telling me his name but he knew mine. He held his hand out to me now, smiling. "Paul, ain't it?"

As I took his hand, my heart lifted. Maybe he had some grass or DFs or something, or at least could buy me a couple of drinks. "Alright?" I said.

"'Ow are ya? Still scoring off the guy in Crompton Street?" As he spoke, I had to pretend not to notice that he had extremely bad breath.

I shook my head.

"Nah, me neither. Pain in the arse."

"I know."

We then spoke simultaneously:

Me: "'Mean, six hours."

Him: "Six hours we were waiting for 'im."

We smiled. Then neither of us knew what to say.

"So...'Ow are you?" he repeated.

"Oh... You know..."

Again, there was an awkward silence. I was trying to think of a way to ask him if he had any downers.

But then he said, "Listen, I've got some stuff. A load of it. Bloke was getting rid of all his 'cos of his girlfriend. Dealer." In a gesture of happiness, he lifted the pockets of his leather jacket with the hands that were stuffed into them. "You want to come back with me and...?"

I thought he couldn't be talking about smack. Nobody ever had a 'load' of it. He must mean grass. That would do me.

"Grass?"

"Nah," he said, smiling slightly. Then, under his breath, "H. Fucking good quality an' all."

My insides started curling in hope. I was praying that the six-hour wait we'd been through together would mean something to him. "Haven't got any money". There was a slight whining tone to my voice.

The mutual six-hour wait obviously did mean something. "No, don't worry. I've got plenty. Come on, I live round the corner." He walked past me.

Stunned, delirious with relief, I followed.

* * * *

He was lonely. That was why he was giving it away. When we got to his flat - which was tidy and decent for a smackhead's - he started treating me as though I was royalty, pouring me a Coke and running upstairs to a neighbour's to borrow an acoustic guitar I could play on. While he was doing that I was at the cooker in his tiny kitchen pouring some vinegar into a spoon and then adding about a quarter of a gram of his smack. The spoon was my own, as was the syringe resting on the counter next to the cooker. I always used my own works and always had done, long before everyone started talking about AIDS, though I'd caught hepatitis from a dirty needle when I'd once got a bit careless. When the smack began sizzling I started getting a bit jumpy. I always did, frightened of allowing too much to boil away. I realised, though, that this time it didn't matter. The stuff wasn't mine and there was more where it came from. That thought made me feel so, so good. I pulled a bowl - clean - out of one of his cabinets and poured the contents of the spoon into it. Then I took out one of the cigarette filters I kept in the breast pocket of my jacket, tore off a piece and dropped it in the bowl as well. I drew the smack up into the needle through the filter.

I hurried through to the living room so as to be sitting down when I jacked up, pulling my belt through the loops of my trousers as I did. I made the torn on my right arm and flicked repeatedly at a vein with my fingernail. My left arm was no good for injecting anymore. I was lucky, though, in still being able to use one arm to inject: I wasn't down to my legs or feet yet. I sunk the needle in and pushed the plunger. Within about eight seconds, a sweet warmth filled me, from top to bottom. The warmth swirled around before moving towards my stomach area and then just sat there, glowing.

* * * *

Out of politeness, I had to stay for a while after the hit. The bloke had shot up after me. When I went into the kitchen later to make us some coffee, I realised from the empty bowl that he'd actually used my dregs. At least the needle in the bowl wasn't mine, so I wouldn't need to find another one.

He sat listening to me noodling on the guitar, nodding his head appreciatively. He was pathetic in his desperate-to-please loneliness but I also felt sorry for him. I remembered how Mick's girlfriend had pitied me earlier. I also remembered how grateful I'd been that she'd actually wanted my company, instead of trying to get rid of me. I was just as lonely as this bloke - his name was Bruce - and for the same reason. We were both boring junkies who spent their days trying to score. I'd used to think I wasn't as boring as the others because I was a musician. I was talented. I had ambitions. But these days I even bored myself talking about how bands I'd been in had nearly made it. Nearly making it meant nothing, not after thirteen years.

"I'll probably give up when I've used this lot up," the bloke said.

"I gave up a couple of months back."

He laughed, thinking it was a joke.

"No," I said. "I keep coming off and going back on."

"Yeah. I went into detox once."

"So did I. Detox is alright but I find it quite easy to give up on my own. Quite quick an' all. I can reduce the dose quickly. Always start again, though."

"Yeah, it's a mental thing."

I felt contempt for him again. When he said it was a mental thing, for him it just meant he needed to escape from life because he was a non-entity, a person of no interest or talent. The vast majority of users I'd ever met were like that. The reason I always went back to smack was because I didn't want to think about thirteen years of working hard and getting nowhere for it. Being a brilliant guitarist and being in great groups but always having to start all over again when they broke up because people didn't want to know about bands who could actually play. I didn't have any choice. He did.

Thing is, I was lonely too. So I kept the conversation going. It was obvious we had nothing in common but at least I could talk about how bad turkey was and moan about dealers with someone.

"When d'ye get into it?" he asked.

"Uni."

"Eh?"

"University'.

"Oh. You been to university then?"

"Yeah."

"My sister went to university. In Plymouth."

What was I supposed to say to that? "Yeah?"

"Yeah."

The conversation died for several minutes. I noodled away on his neighbour's guitar. He knew I played because I'd had a guitar with me that time we'd been waiting outside the dealer's flat. He watched my fingers.

After a while, he said, "You're good, int ya?"

I didn't answer. Everyone who ever heard me play would say how good I was and start asking me if I'd ever tried to get a contract.

But what else could I talk about? The only things in my life were smack and my band. So we went back to talking about drugs, a conversation I'd had so often, with so many different users, that when I said something it was like reading a speech that I knew by heart.

* * * *

Rehearsals went pretty well that night and I wasn't feeling too bad when I got home at about eleven p.m. I'd scored for nothing and I had a friend - or a kind of friend - who I might be able to get free drugs off again. Just as important, though, was the rehearsal. If I'd been to rehearsals, at the end of the day I felt okay. Not head-over-heels happy - I wasn't sure this band was going anywhere and I also tried my very best not to care about it too much, so I wouldn't be too upset if this band went kaput like all the others - but satisfied because the day hadn't been a complete waste spent trying to score.

As I always did, I checked and double-checked that I'd set the alarm before getting into bed. I'd lived above Mr. Case's paper shop for a year-and-a-half. In return for my board, I got up at the crack of dawn 52 weeks a year and delivered his biggest round. It was a brilliant arrangement for a musician, leaving me free to concentrate on the band without having to worry about getting a full-time job. Of course, being a junkie had made it very, very hard to stick to it. I'd managed, though. In eighteen months, I'd never missed a day. Rain, snow, turkey, I'd still got out of bed and done it. I was actually proud of that. It felt... solid. Looking at my life, I could say that was at least one thing I hadn't fucked up.

PART TWO

Two

I suppose I fucked up my life because I fell in love with The Beatles when I was a kid. If I hadn't been so knocked out by them, I would never have wanted to be a musician and wouldn't have gone through all the disappointments and humiliations that go with being one. I'm always tickled by the fact that I was born in 1965. '65 was, it so happens, the greatest year ever for rock music. Dylan released *Bringing It All Back Home* and *Highway 61 Revisited*, the Stones released *Satisfaction*, The Who released *My Generation*, The Beatles released both *Help!* and *Rubber Soul*, the Byrds released *Mr. Tambourine Man* and Holland-Dozier-Holland - via different Motown acts - released *The Same Old Song, How Sweet It Is To Be Loved By You, This Old Heart Of Mine* and *Stop! In The Name Of Love*. Of course, I was too young to appreciate that at the time. I became seriously interested in the Beatles when I was ten years old, when they enjoyed an unexpected new surge in popularity. EMI decided for some reason to re-promote their singles and to release *Yesterday* on single in Britain for the first time. *Yesterday* went top ten and a load of their other singles entered the charts. A publishing company started reprinting their official magazine from the 'Sixties, with a few pages of new material wrapped around it. I loved the whole Beatles package: their look, their charm and their sound. That sound was a life-affirming giddy concoction that no-one has been able to match, then or since. It just filled you with warmth.

One week, I bought one of those re-promoted singles with my pocket money, *Can't Buy Me Love*. That record is one of the ones that sums up the attraction of the early Beatles. Even now, it makes me feel glad to be alive when I hear it. (In those days, I only liked the Mop-top era of The Beatles: I didn't think the stuff they recorded when they all grew beards and stopped touring was as charming. Of course, it was - only more sophisticated. *Hey Jude*, for instance, almost moves me to tears these days.)

I came home from school one day and immediately put *Can't Buy Me Love* on the turntable of our mono player. My mum came into the room.

"Gring-grang!" she said to me.

"Gring-grang!" I cooed back. It was our private, lovey-dovey code.

When she heard the first bars of the song, she said, "Oh no, not this again," even though she liked it.

I played it through twice. When I was turning it over after the second spin to listen to the B-side (*You Can't Do That* - bloody good as well) my dad came home. He had a carrier bag under one arm and when the first strains of *You Can't Do That* emerged from the speaker, a sly smile came across his face. He produced some objects from the bag and affectionately slapped me on the side of the head with them. I shrank back from the mock-blow at the same time as I was reaching out for the objects. Incredibly, it was two Beatles albums (compilations: one called *Hey Jude*, the other *Rock And Roll Music*) and the *Let It Be* single.

"Are these ours?" I shrieked.

"No," he said. Then added, "They're yours."

"Tha-anks!" I got up and hugged him.

My mother's cold voice cut into the scene. "Where'd you get the money for them?"

My dad, his arms wrapped around my shoulders, turned to her and said in a mischievous tone "Nowhere."

"Where'd you get 'em?"

"In a shop."

My mum was staring at him. "Oh - you didn't nick 'em did ya?"

My dad, smiling, just walked over and slumped in an armchair and began to watch the television. I was left standing in the middle of the room with my emotions about the items in my hands having turned from delight to awkwardness. I realised straightaway that my mum didn't care about them being stolen - she often bragged to me about the way she nicked things at work - but that she wanted to use it to start a row with my dad. Which would turn the flat into a place that was miserably hushed and smouldering for several days.

"What d'ya do - just walk out of there with them under your arm?"

"No. Just stuck 'em in me bag. There's no-one there at the back. Piece of cake."

As they tossed barbed comments back and forth, I very, very quietly, looked at the sleeves in turn. The photograph on the back of the *Let It Be* single showed The Beatles in the bearded period. I assumed from that that I wouldn't like it when I heard it. I was still young enough to be amazed that someone's tastes weren't the same as mine and turned to my dad and said "Dad - did you get *Let It Be* 'cos you like it or 'cos it was easy-" I looked warily at my mum. "I mean- y'know... did you..."

"'Cos I like it."

"Oh." I kept my eyes trained downwards on the record sleeve, away from my mum's unamused stare.

* * * *

I stood before the sweets display with my hands in the pockets of my coat. The sweets display of Woolworths consisted of packets of chocolates and confectionary hung on hooks on two large boards. I'd been standing before it, gazing at Maltesers, Treets, Mars Bar family packs and Opal Fruits for twenty minutes, every so often glancing toward the serving till ten feet away. I could almost groan with my hunger. Not for the first time, I thought, *Oh God, just do it! Just take the chance.* I threw my face toward the till again. The girl serving there, for the first time in quite a while, wasn't looking at me. Her eyes were down, concentrating on affixing price tags. My hand jerked out of my pocket toward the sweet board. Just then, the girl's eyes swung up at me. My hand stopped in mid-air. It trembled there. I jerked it out of the air and back into my pocket as I looked away. I found I was looking at a light fixture. Realising that did not look natural, I jerked my face away from it and pretended to be intensely interested in a sign beyond the sweets board reading 'Kitchenware'. I squinted my eyes consideringly at it and said, barely audibly, as if in fascination "Ohh..."

God. *God.*

I might as well go home.

I couldn't help glancing toward the till again. The girl gazed levelly at me. I threw my face away, my arms rustling my coat as they briefly jumped in startlement.

I moved away from the display. I went around it and double-backed, walking, hands still in pockets, toward the entrance. My eyes narrowed and my nose crinkled up. As my mouth tightened, a blast of bitter air shot out of my nostrils. Bloody cow.

Outside on the Arndale shopping centre's buffed stone floor, I wiped away the tears that stung in the bright light. My pace was slow as I considered where else I could go. I'd already been in Martin's, diagonally opposite. The sweets were at a very small counter with a girl stationed directly behind them. The crisps were on a rack in a more secluded area but the man behind the cigarette counter had been watching me with his arms folded as I had hovered there. I couldn't try in Lang's, the other newsagent. It was easy to nick in there but that was where I'd been caught before.

I sat on a plastic bench as people bustled by and the muzak played, my hands still stuffed in my coat pockets.

I was starving. I'd had two biscuits in the morning. That was all. My mum had gone to my aunt Ruth's to see if she could borrow any money, but when she went there she always stayed all day. I hated fighting sleep to sit up and wait for her, my stomach rumbling. That was why I'd come here. As for my dad, neither of us had seen him since the day before yesterday.

A woman pulling a laden shopping trolley passed before my bench, her teenage daughter following close behind. The woman turned, a smile on her face, and murmured something I couldn't hear which made the girl smile herself and slap softly, playfully at her back. As the girl went by, I jealously noticed she carried a Bejams carrier bag from which protruded a packet of Fig Roll biscuits.

Please, please, let mum have got something. Last time, she'd come back from Ruth's without money but a loaf of bread. We hadn't had any butter to put on it but it was still delicious after eating nothing the entire day. I had revelled in the smell of it: putting it up to my face and inhaling as I chewed the first bite. Remembering it now, I could smell it in my mind. My mouth instantly filled with saliva.

Not only was there no food, the television wasn't working. Later on tonight, when all the other kids on the estate had gone in, I would be going back to an empty flat with no company, no food and no television.

I rose. I walked back toward Woolworths. I went in by the door farthest from the counter where the girl who'd been watching me was. Coming around the far side of the sweets display, my heart came to life as I saw the girl's counter was busy. There were now two assistants on it and both of them were occupied serving. I halted before the Opal Fruits. I would have preferred chocolate but I needed to act quickly. I glanced at the till. Neither girl had noticed me. I casually took my hands from my pockets. With them hanging by my sides, I threw another glance. The girl who'd had her eye on me was talking to a customer, smiling. Her roving eyes passed sightlessly across me. I looked at the Opal Fruits. Another glance at the girl. She was still chatting, still smiling, and once more her gaze passed across my face. I was preparing to turn to the board when her brain caught up with her vision and her pupils flicked back to me. Riveted, I stared at her. She stopped chatting and her smile faded. Her expression challenged me to do it. The customer she was talking to turned to see what she was looking at.

A second later I was fingering the Opal Fruit package and my face was feigning interest in the words "Made To Make Your Mouth Water", my lips silently enunciating them. Sweat was pouring out of me and my heartbeats pounded against my throat. Worse than being frustrated yet again was the self-awareness: I looked *stupid*.

As I glumly approached the glass doors of the Arndale's exit, I sucked in air in amazement at seeing that it was completely dark outside. The skies had been bright when I came in.

Car lights shone and people wrapped in coats strode quickly on Lett Road, the half-mile long street leading to the road my estate was located in. It wasn't cold but wind was beginning to whip grit about unpleasantly. Two kids that I knew were sitting on the wall that fronted my estate as I approached. Both gazed at me, neither speaking, despite the fact that I'd been friendly with both of them at times. I stared hostilely at one of them. They were only staring because they were playing with each other today. But in a way, I felt I didn't deserve to be resentful: as they stared I sort of had the feeling that they knew there wasn't any food in my place.

To my surprise, my mum was sitting in an armchair in the living room. She had a hand over her eyes.

"Gring-grang!" I said.

She took her hand away and smiled weakly. "'Allo, love..."

I went over and straddled her legs. "Did Ruth 'ave any food?"

"No, she weren't in." Her voice was heavy. She put the top of her head against the seat-back and looked wearily at the ceiling.

"So..." I hardly dared say it: "Didn't you get nuffin?"

She looked at me without moving, shaking her head, her lips sucked in ruefully.

"What... I mean - nuffin?"

"No," she said softly. "I'll get some money tomorrow. Definitely."

My voice poured out in anguish. "It's no good tomorrow!"

She gazed at me.

"I've only 'ad two biscuits to eat all day!"

"I know," she sympathised.

I tutted and pushed myself off her legs. I walked across to the settee and threw myself onto it. I stared at the opposite wall.

We were silent.

After a few minutes, I looked at her. "What about dad? He might 'ave some money when 'e gets back."

Her expression ridiculed the idea. "He *is* back."

"And 'e 'asn't?"

"Since when 'as 'e 'ad any money?"

We were wordless again. After a few minutes, I swung up and walked out of the door.

There was no answer to my knock on my parent's bedroom door. I pushed it open and put my head forward. The room was dark but with the light from the hall I could see my dad lying fully clothed in a fetal position on the bed. I went inside.

My dad's eyes were closed. I climbed onto the bed and wormed into the crook between his head and knees. Warmth radiated from his body. As I'd thought he was asleep, I was surprised when, with a swish of the material of his shirt, my dad's arm settled around me, air sighing through his nose. I peeked up. His eyes were still closed. I snuggled in deeper.

* * * *

I suppose I had negligent parents, at least in one sense: despite the fact that both of them had jobs most of the time, I often went hungry. So did they, come to that. This was because both of them smoked up a storm and both of them were complete piss artists. Also, both of them had lovers at various times that they needed to spend money on. Not that I realised that at the time. I simply knew that the awkwardness on my mum's face when I met her in the park once clinging to the arm of a man I didn't know and the conversations my dad had from phone booths - me standing by his elbow - in which he used a sweet tone I never heard him employ with anyone I knew, indicated a situation between them that wasn't normal.

Yet in no way was I deprived of love. My mum's love was a healing kind: she was a warm bosom to sink into and an understanding mind that never blamed me if I had problems. My dad's love was more conspiratorial: any problems I had faded away when he was around because his couldn't-give-a-damn attitude - to authority, to unpaid bills, to neighbours who disproved of me begging for biscuits from their kids - made me super-confident. The only trouble was they hated each other. I was constantly edgy whenever all three of us were together at one time, such as the time we were setting off on a holiday to Devon when I was twelve.

My mum and I were sitting in my granddad's Cortina, waiting for my dad to emerge from my maternal grandparents' flat, just across the driveway from ours. After a tedious ten minutes, he appeared. He got inside and slammed the driver's door. With his hands on the steering wheel, he paused and sighed heavily.

"What'd she say?" my mum asked.

My dad reached for the seat-belt. He performed an imitation of my Nan, his tone a squawking one. "'You brought that car back at eleven o' clock. 'Ow much can I trust you, John, 'ow much?'" I could believe the tone. I didn't really like my Nan because she looked down at my dad. That was why I never went to her when I was hungry.

My mum looked away from him at the windscreen.

"Eleven o' clock! It was quarter-to-ten."

"Well you said you'd 'ave it back by half-eight."

"Well if you hadn't wanted to go up fucking Staines I might 'ave."

My mum tutted. She imitated him: "'Fackin' fackin' fackin'.'"

"Yeah, and why am I saying it?"

"It's *their* car."

"Don't I fucking know it."

"Oh..." My mum sounded suddenly weary. She grimaced. "Shut up!"

"I drive your dad every bloody weekend and that's all-"

"Look!" My mum was at a loss for what to say in the silence her voice had gained. She looked away, breathing hard through her nostrils. She turned her face back again. "Look. This is our first holiday in twelve years. It's Paul's first holiday. Let's just... We've only got one week... Let's just enjoy it, for God's sake."

My dad wordlessly twisted the key in the ignition.

On the way to the motorway, we picked up my uncle Reg and my cousins Andrew and Natalie. My aunt Anne was heavily pregnant and had decided not to come on the holiday. Andrew was two years my senior, Natalie a year younger than me. Natalie and I had been boyfriend and girlfriend when my parents and myself had been temporarily living with her family a few years before. It had all been holding hands and cuddling at every opportunity for a brief period and then we suddenly got embarrassed with each other and it stopped.

* * * *

We were all waiting for Natalie to change out of her swimming costume so we could go for something to eat. I was sitting with Andrew on the leather-covered bench in the front of their caravan. The others were standing around outside. Natalie was behind a curtain that screened off the back part of the caravan. Andrew got up suddenly to join the parents.

I looked toward the curtain and called, "Oi, Natalie. I'm peeking."

"You better not."

"I am."

"I'll tell my dad on ya."

"Go on then."

Over the last few days, Natalie and I had become the closest we'd ever been since the days of our romance. We hadn't been together this long since then and we were starting to dare to flirt, although both of us were too old now to unselfconsciously demand kisses the way we had before. Yesterday, when we'd been playing pinball in the kid's room of the local pub, another girl from the caravan site had teased Natalie over her defending me when the girl had got into an argument with me. "You *love* 'im," she sneered. I'd immediately been embarrassed, thinking Natalie would respond with something like "Get lost, do I." Instead, she said, "I know I do. He's my cousin." I'd glowed with pleasure and gratitude. This was part of the reason why the last week had been so happy. It had been a brilliant holiday.

Natalie emerged from behind the curtain wearing matching top and shorts and flip-flops. She looked lovely.

"Unh, you look stupid," I said awkwardly.

"I know you do."

I dug her in the back as she went past. She turned threateningly. I stopped and pulled my body away. She looked me up and down, trying to decide how to retaliate. Seeing that, I hastily shuffled further back.

"Chicken," she said and walked out.

Reg was speaking to my dad as we descended the steps to the gravel. "I wanna 'ave a quick shave before we go," he said, rubbing at a day's growth.

While Reg walked towards the caravan site's toilet facilities, my parents and us three kids went in the opposite direction towards the sea, thirty feet away across fist-sized pebbles.

The five of us skimmed pebbles while we waited for Reg.

I squinted, counting my stone's jumps. "...free, four, five..." I turned to Andrew. "Fiver."

Andrew span a stone out himself. "Not bad."

"I got a fiver the other day," Natalie said.

"No you didn't," Andrew and I said together.

"Yes I did!"

"No you didn't," Andrew said. "Shut up Natalie."

Natalie picked up another stone and threw. "No, you shut up."

"Only one more day, Paul," Andrew said.

"I know". My voice was sad.

Natalie, hearing us, turned to my parents. "We can come 'ere next year, can't we?"

"Can we, dad?" I asked.

My dad was gazing off to sea. "Yeah. Why not?"

The affirmative didn't make me totally optimistic. He frequently promised me things in such a matter-of-fact voice and then failed to deliver. But the fact that he hadn't said no gave me a feeling of hope despite myself, because the last week had been the happiest of my life. "Great!" I said. Then I noticed my mum standing a couple of feet away from my dad, her arms folded, her sunglasses perched on her head, gazing at me. She had a smile on her face. It froze me for a couple of seconds because I couldn't work out what it meant. I had assumed at first that it was a sarcastic one, contemptuous of more pie-in-the-sky from my dad. But it wasn't: she was looking at me fondly. She rarely showed affection to me like that when my dad was around. I was like a competition to the two of them. They would usually each try to get me alone because showing their love for me would often go hand-in-hand with bad-mouthing the other. But the atmosphere during this holiday had been so different. They had relaxed, neither of them putting any pressure on me to love one more than the other. It was partly relief that made me grin back at her.

* * * *

My cousins and myself knew the words to *Lazy Day* by heart now. It was a song by the Moody Blues, Reg's favourite group. We'd sung it every time we'd gone out in the car this last week. We were doing so now, on the way to lunch, with my dad driving, Reg in the front passenger seat and my mum, Natalie, Andrew and me in the back, Natalie sitting on my mum's lap.

Lazy day, Sunday afternoon
Like to get your feet up, watch TV
Sunday roast is something good to eat
Must be lamb today 'cos beef was last week

Our voices automatically rose higher as we went into the chorus, which was in fact nothing but sung sighs. I loved the song. It was very Beatles in a way, an isn't-it-good-to-be-alive song. You couldn't help feeling deliriously happy as you sang it in the company of five others with whom you'd just spent a wonderful six days as you weaved through lush green Devon lanes. We went into the next verse.

So full up, bursting at the seams
Soon you'll start to nod off, happy dreams
Wake up to tea and buttered scones
Such a lot of work for you Sunday mums.

I winced as the chorus came round again. Everybody was singing - sighing - so loud that Natalie stopped and laughed and my mum smilingly narrowed her eyes. When the song ended, everyone either laughed or made sounds of exhaustion. I ducked my head sideways and gave a small, joyous squeak as I deliberately bumped my head against my mum's shoulder. Pulling it away, I saw that she had tried to respond by kissing the top of my head but I'd moved too quickly. I hastily put my forehead to her shoulder and let her do it. When she had, I sat upright.

A sound of amusement from Natalie made me look up. She was sharing a smile with my mum about what we'd just done. I was relieved when I realised it wasn't a smile of ridicule: she had found the moment touching. I looked out of the car window, pulsating with a pleasure I could never remember feeling before.

Three

The door of Carol's flat opened to my knock. Carol lived on the eleventh floor of her block. She'd got a flat from the council because she'd had a daughter - Tracy - four years ago when she was sixteen. She was my cousin, the elder sister of Natalie and Andrew.

"'Allo, babe," she said as she held open the door for me to step inside.

"Wotcha."

"'Ow you been keeping?" Carol closed the front door and stepped into the tiny kitchen to the right where she was sorting laundry.

"Alright." I walked into the living room. I could still see Carol because there was a large open panel between the two rooms. There was a black and white portable television sitting in the open panel, facing into the living room. Tracy was watching it from the sofa.

"'Allo," I said to her in a sing-song voice as I sat in an armchair. Tracy glanced at me then resumed watching the television. "'Allo!" I said again. She still didn't respond. I was hurt, because she'd played happily with me last time I visited. I decided not to play with her ever again. And if she tried to sit in my lap later, I wouldn't let her.

"D'ya wanna cup of tea, Paul?" Carol called.

"Yes please." I noticed for the first time an acoustic guitar leaning against one of the chairs at the table. "Oh - whose guitar, Cal?"

"Mine."

"*You* can't play the guitar." I got up and walked over to the instrument. I stood looking at it with my hands in my pockets. It had a gleaming black body. "Is it alright to pick it up?"

Carol turned from the kettle. "Yeah. Don't put it out of tune, though."

"Eh?"

"Don't touch the pegs. Those white things on the end."

As I didn't know whether I should touch the guitar's strings, I put both hands around the body and lifted. I froze when the body connected with a chair-leg, wincing at the echoing bang that resulted. I exhaled a tortured "Agh!" by way of apology to Carol but her quick glance up at me wasn't a worried one. When I pulled the strap over my head, it was to allow the guitar to hang for playing by the left hand. I wasn't left-handed: it was just that Paul McCartney was my favourite Beatle. I walked over to Carol's Bob Marley mirror and looked at myself. I liked what I saw. I turned toward Tracy, in my pleasure unable to resist trying again with her. "Look, Tracy. The Beatles."

"There 'are, Paul." Carol put my tea in the panel.

"Fanks. Oi, can you play this, Carol?"

"Yeah."

"Can ya? Who taught ya then?"

"Robert." That was her boyfriend.

"Can you play any Beatles songs?"

"Er... Oh - *Day Tripper*, I know."

"Really?" I didn't have the song but knew it well from the radio. "Play it for us?"

"In a minute."

While Carol finished her laundry, I sat in the armchair. The guitar's weight across my thighs felt pleasing. I ventured as far as to lightly stroke the strings.

After a while, Carol came in with her own cup of tea. She put it on the table, came over and took the guitar. "You've got it upside-down."

"Eh?"

She explained to me Paul McCartney might play the bass left-handed but this guitar was strung for a right-hander. Sitting on the settee beside her daughter, Carol pulled a small triangular piece of plastic from where it was wedged under the guitar's bridge. Just as I was about to ask what it was, she - with a quick jerk of her head toward the fingers she had positioned around the guitar's neck - ran it experimentally down the strings.

"Oh," I said in surprise. "Don't you use your fingers to play the guitar?"

"Depends. Some people do." Carol shifted her fingers on the neck again. Then, unbelievably, she proceeded to produce from the strings the lick of *Day Tripper*. Of course, I was used to hearing it played electrically but it was unmistakably that insistent, coiling pattern.

"Brilliant, brilliant!" I gushed. It was awe-inspiring that my own cousin, in the same room as me, was reproducing that sound.

"That's all I know of it," she said.

"That's brilliant!"

She put the guitar down to sip at her tea. "I can teach you that in two minutes. It's easy."

"What - teach me to play it?"

Twenty minutes later the guitar was across my lap again, this time the right way round, and sounds were emanating from it that were easily recognisable as *Day Tripper*. I'd also learnt that the 'bottom' string of a guitar meant the top and that, as you had to press the very tips of your fingers against the strings to avoid touching the others, playing guitar for the first time was painful: Carol showed me the calluses she had built up.

For a couple of years, I had lain in bed at night fantasising about being a pop star. That night, lying under the covers - my fingertips raw and my hands aching due to the fact that Carol's guitar wasn't meant for ones that small - my fantasy was suddenly an ambition. I was amazed at how easy it was to play the guitar. Before this, I would always have thought that trying to learn to play any musical instrument would have been well beyond me, as well as simply boring. And expensive. Yet Carol had told me she'd bought her guitar for £2 from a second-hand shop.

* * * *

Dave, Carol's guitar tutor, was a man in his mid-thirties who had long hair tucked behind his ears, wore jumpers without shirts and when listening to Carol playing would lean forward with his hands together and eyelids down and nod continuously. He had rings on three of his fingers and played guitar with a cigarette hanging from his lips. On the wall above his settee was a framed silver disc Dave had been awarded when he was with the folk group Reminiscence.

Dave just about summed up how glamorous and privileged my life had begun to seem since I'd got my guitar. I had been bought it just three days after Carol had first taught me *Day Tripper*. I'd asked my mum if I could have my main Christmas present early, knowing she would say no but also knowing that asking her in front of my dad would mean he would buy me it. It worked perfectly and he ignored my advice that they were dead cheap in second hand shops and took me to a guitar shop to pick a new one out. It was lucky that an assistant suggested a junior model because I was so excited at the prospect of owning one that I'd forgotten about the pain of trying to get my hand around a large neck. I picked a black Yamaha from the range we were shown. My dad said, "Better try it first", deliberately giving me the opportunity to show off the fact that I could play *Day Tripper*.

After that, I was round Carol's at every opportunity. I would ask her to teach me what she'd learnt after each of her twice-weekly lessons. It worked well because she wasn't too far ahead of me. After a few weeks she brought a message back from her guitar tutor that I should come along with her: he must have been intrigued by this little twerp always telling Carol to tell him to teach her more Beatles songs. One of Carol's lessons was on Wednesdays in the early afternoon, conflicting with school hours, so I couldn't go, but the other one was on Saturdays. I liked Dave as soon as I met him but I also knew that my dad wouldn't. I could just picture him ridiculing his over-serious manner and saying he was a big poof. Dave said that I could come along with Carol to her lessons for no fee. He also promised to teach us some Beatles numbers.

After the initial joy of mastering that *Day Tripper* lick, I was then daunted by how much there was to learn. I was suddenly encountering words like keys, chords and bars which sounded ominously like things you would hear in a lesson at school or read in a book. They sounded boring. After grasping the terminology, though, the rewards were beyond belief. For just a little concentration and practice that was a pleasure in itself, I could flush with pride at hearing myself produce music. 'Real' music - the kind you heard on the radio. I could also throb with a sense of knowledge. I'd never been outstanding at school, but here was something I could be an expert in: the joy I felt at finding, listening to the radio, that I knew that *The House Of The Rising Sun* was in the key of A minor was indescribable.

And then there was the admiration of other kids. Mr. Burns, my teacher, often brought a guitar into school and used it for accompaniment as he taught us songs like *I Know An Old Woman Who Swallowed A Fly* and *Skip To The Lou*. I had been asked by a kid called Jamie if I would play guitar during a short play he and his mates were going to put on in a drama lesson. That day, when I went up to Mr. Burns' desk to get my work marked I said, "Sir - you know your guitar? Can I use it this afternoon in Drama?"

Mr. Burns took off his glasses and looked at me in surprise. "Do you play guitar, Paul?"

I nodded. "Sir."

He gazed at me. He was probably amazed that such an average pupil could be interested in anything artistic. "Well... I think I'd better hear something then." He got out his guitar from where it was leaning against the wall behind his desk and handed it to me. Surprised, I slipped the strap over my shoulder, noticing the neck was a bit wider than on mine. I simply played the latest thing Dave had taught Carol and I: a Rolling Stones number called

Love In Vain (written by Robert Johnson). I hadn't liked the song when I heard it on record, but the undulating figures in it were lovely. Although I still had to look at my fingers, I was good enough on guitar now not to be nervous and played a few bars without errors. I had distractedly heard a couple of voices at nearby tables say admiringly "God - listen" and "He's playing the *guitar*" but when I looked up was surprised to see most of the classroom staring at me. Mr. Burns smiled warmly and congratulated me on my ability and gave me permission to use the guitar in Drama.

I could have cried with pleasure as I walked past the upturned, astonished faces back to my seat.

Dave would bring me down to earth after experiences like that, telling me I should never get lazy. He would say, "You might think to yourself, 'Oh, all my mates think I'm brilliant already so why should I bother getting any better?'" When he started teaching me barre positionings, however, it only made me more convinced that the guitar was wonderfully easy: as soon as I'd grasped the principle, I had more than a hundred chord fingerings at my disposal, as opposed to the handful I'd been aware of before. Yet when Dave stressed practice every day and setting myself targets, he really had no need to worry. I was always amazed how quickly time passed when I was practicing. I lost count of the number of times I'd be noodling in my bedroom for what seemed half an hour and came out to find that hours had gone by and I'd missed television programmes I'd wanted to watch. I also loved the feeling I'd have after a long practice session: a simultaneously mellow and drained sensation.

Four

Dave had stretched my loyalty to the Beatles quite severely in the few months I'd been taking lessons. He'd introduced me to many musical styles unknown to me and persuaded me to listen to artists I'd previously been hostile to in order to learn more, not just about playing guitar but about music generally. I'd been reluctant when he lent me a Rolling Stones compilation and told me to learn *As Tears Go By*. I hated them: my dad had told me they just copied everything the Beatles did. Also, they weren't as 'nice' as The Beatles had been. I was won over, though, because the album contained nothing but classics. I decided that I did like the Rolling Stones but that they'd never been as good as The Beatles had. When Dave introduced me to Bob Dylan with the *Highway 61* album, I was knocked out that music so 'hard' - not built around three-minute pop melodies and not romantic - could be so powerful. The way Dylan vengefully sang "How does it *feeeeel*?" in *Like A Rolling Stone* almost made my hair stand on end.

I drew the line, though, at punk, and so did Dave. When punk first happened - late 1976 - it was genuinely disturbing. The whole movement seemed hateful and vicious beyond belief. The people sporting swastikas or with safety pins through their noses or with satanically pointed black eye-shadow were like nothing ever seen before. I was actually frightened by it. I'd read a newspaper article about how every generation was more vicious than the previous one and about how society seemed to be sinking to lower and lower depths. I was an impressionable child and whenever I thought about that, I would feel a real dread.

Mind you, the name of the Sex Pistols, the band who were the punk movement's leaders, just made me tut with contempt. It was the kind of cheesy name a kid my age would make up to shock. Whenever I heard it, it always made me remember a time a few months previously when I'd been travelling on a bus with a mate and seeing a sign reading 'COXSWAIN' had turned to him and said - in a comment that was really too juvenile even for a twelve-year-old - "Ahh! Cocks!"

Punk was the talk of my school. One day I sat at a dinner table with my best mate - a kid called Hodgsy - and a couple of other boys. There was an unappetising pudding, semolina. One of the kids there hunched over his plate and mimed vomiting contractions.

"I know," Hodgsy agreed. "Enough to make you puke like punk rockers."

We laughed. The papers were always alleging the Sex Pistols puked wherever they went.

"They probably showed this to Johnny Rotten when 'e puked up the uvver day," I said.

"God," one of the other kids - a boy called Wells - came in. "The Sex Pistols are well-bad, int they?"

"Why? They only throw up over people and stick safety pins through their nose."

"Yeah. They only beat up old ladies and that."

"Imagine wearing a safety pin as an earring. God."

After lunch, we started walking to the games field.

"They're gonna set up a punk rock fan club," Hodgsy said. "You pay two pounds and you get a bag of Johnny Rotten's puke."

"Yeah," Wells said. "Johnny Rotten's life story written by himself wiv everything spelt all wrong."

"Yeah," I said. "Duhh, well I woz born on, like, der twentieth of November, like, and, duuhh..."

Hodgsy said "Oh excuse me..." He thrust his body vigorously off the ground several times. "I'm just doing the pogo."

We howled with laughter. "What a dance," Wells said. "It's so hard, innit? Takes a really long time to learn."

"Yeah, it's so complicated. Imagine someone..." Hodgsy jumped up and down again: "Oh, I've invented the pogo!"

"God save the Queen," I began to sing.

They all joined in. Because the record was banned by all radio stations, nobody our age had heard it, but we all knew the lyric by heart from shock-horror newspaper reports. We sang to a formless chant:

"The fascist regime
It made you a moron
A potential H-bomb
God save the Queen"

We grinned wildly, looking at each other as we chanted the next, and best, line:

"She ain't no human being!"

"Just fink," said Hodgsy. "Number one in Jubilee week. There must of been loads of old dears who bought it 'cos they fort it was the national anthem or somefing!"

* * * *

I was in Andrew's bedroom. I had never been close to Andrew. I'd always found him a bit callous and nasty. In fact, I probably wouldn't have associated with him if we hadn't been cousins and hadn't gone to the same school. Things had suddenly changed, though. He had a drum kit. I was sure he'd got his mum and dad to buy him it because he was jealous of all the attention I was getting for my guitar playing. The fact that he always denied it only made me all the more irritated with him. After I'd got over the initial resentment, however, the two of us had become much more friendly than we'd ever been. It was great for me to have a kid my own age to discuss playing music with. Andrew had surprised me by how serious he was about drumming. Like me, he didn't work particularly hard at school, but when it came to the drum classes his dad paid for he never missed a day, and he practiced for at least an hour in his room each night. Not only that, he had a few days ago joined a band.

We were currently standing at opposite ends of the room, throwing his football back and forth. I put a spin on my latest throw and Andrew had to dip hastily for it. It rolled out of his hand and fell. Wincing, Andrew grabbed it as it bounced up from the carpet.

"Don't!" he said. He didn't want his dad to hear. We weren't supposed to play with the football indoors.

"Sor-*ree*."

Andrew bopped me on the head with the ball as he walked past me to put it away. He stuck it in the corner behind his kit. He then sat on the stool and lifted his sticks. I flopped down on his bed, saying "Ungowa!" like Tarzan did in films as I did so, for no particular reason.

Andrew was adjusting his hi-hat. His kit comprised of bass, snare and two tom-toms, a basic set-up, although I didn't actually know that at the time. I did know that it wasn't a Ludwig kit like Ringo's. I let my head drop back and gazed at the ceiling. Andrew launched into a tattoo.

"Yeah!" I said, slapping rapidly at my thighs.

Andrew put the sticks down and placed his palm on the splash cymbal to stop its resonating noise as soon as the pattern was completed. He wasn't supposed to play the drums when his dad was in. I stretched, yawning. I struggled up onto my elbows. Andrew was now adjusting the masking tape underneath his cymbals. I slumped down again. It was quiet for a few moments.

"Why don't you play some Sex Pistols music on them?" I said as a joke.

"Gonna get their album when it comes out."

I looked at him, shocked. "Are ya?"

"Yeah. Snazzy group." He got up abruptly and walked over to his records, stacked horizontally against the far wall. He produced two singles and stepped over to the bed with them. He held one of them before my face. "That's a snazzy record."

I immediately recognized the picture on the sleeve. It had been reproduced endlessly in the media: the Queen's face with the eyes and mouth ripped away and replaced by untidy ransom note lettering indicating the name of the record and the artists. "Oh God!" I reached for it.

"Careful, careful..."

I handled the sleeve delicately. "Is it- It's *God Save The Queen*, innit?" I carefully pulled the record out and looked at the label. "Jesus, it is an' all. Where'd ya get it?"

"In a shop, where'd ya fink?"

I looked at him. "D'you *like* the Sex Pistols?"

"Ye-eah." Andrew showed me another of the singles, this one without a picture sleeve. "*Anarchy In The U.K.* It's French, that. Cost me two quid, 'cos it's banned in this country."

I was intrigued at the thought of hearing their music. "Play it!"

"D'ya wanna hear it?"

"Yeah. Oi, people only say they like the Sex Pistols to be... Y'know. 'Cos they fink that makes 'em stylish."

"No they don't. They like 'em 'cos they're good."

"They can't even play their instruments!"

"Yes they can."

"No they can't."

"Go away, guy. You 'aven't even 'eard 'em."

"You probably like Vik Vomit and The Lumps an' all."

"Never 'eard of 'em."

"Ain't ya? That's a punk group."

"Says 'oo?" said Andrew.

"My mate at school. 'E saw it in the paper."

"There's no such group."

Andrew walked over to his stereo and took *Anarchy In The U.K.* out of its sleeve.

"Oh weddone," I said.

Andrew put the needle on the record and turned. "*This* is a bit of punk for ya."

Roaring guitars suddenly filled the room, followed by Johnny Rotten's insane cackling. When Rotten started singing - his voice sounding depraved and menacing like no other singer I'd ever heard - I grinned in disgust and amusement.

Half a minute into the song, I got up and started jumping up and down. "Yeah! Let's all pogo!"

Andrew, unamused, lashed out with pretend punches and kicks. I collapsed back onto the bed, laughing hysterically. When the song's first guitar break came, I was surprised at how good it was. I covered my surprise up by thrashing on an invisible guitar. "Waaah!"

I did another bout of pogoing as the record ended. The song climaxed with Rotten singing "Get pissed! Destro-o-oy!" followed by an ungodly wail that I recognised as the sound of a feedbacking electric guitar.

I chuckled. "God, guy!"

Andrew lifted the record off the deck. "Good, weren't it?"

"*Destro-o-oy!*"

"No, it was though, weren't it?"

"It's sick!"

* * * *

It was a few weeks later and I was round Andrew's house again. When he put his Sex Pistols records on - *God Save The Queen*, *Anarchy...* and (a new one) *Pretty Vacant* - I listened to them without once pogoing or making wisecracks. I finally admitted to him something that I had known for a while now: "The Sex Pistols are a good band." Andrew gave me such a look of surprise that I laughed out loud. "Well, they are," I said defensively.

"Took you long enough to realise."

"I know."

And they were. They would never touch your heart the way the Beatles did, but *Anarchy...* and *Pretty Vacant* were two genuine rock classics, even if they did have a slightly demented kink. (*God Save The Queen* was the most famous but was a drone.) The reason I'd been afraid to admit it to myself up to now was because of a fear that if I liked punks' music, I might end up like one: I might end up as sick as the kind of people who stuck safety pins through their noses. But the example of Andrew showed me that didn't necessarily follow: he liked the Sex Pistols but he was normal.

I told Andrew that. He laughed. "You spastic!" he said. "You shouldn't believe what you read in the papers about punk, you know."

"'Ow come?"

"'Cos half of it's made up."

"Why - do you know any punks?"

"Yeah - there's one in my band."

"Is there? D'you play punk music?"

"We play anyfing."

"Any Beatles stuff?"

He shook his head. "*Satisfaction*, we do. By the Rolling Stones."

"That's brilliant, *Satisfaction*."

"Why don't you come wiv me tomorrow? Listen to us."

* * * *

The other members of Andrew's group were all older than him. The punk was the guitarist. I noticed him as soon as Andrew and I walked into the living room of the bassist's house. The guitarist had a spiky orange hairstyle and wore a torn t-shirt, studded wristbands, tartan trousers with bondage straps and Doc Marten boots. He was sitting in an armchair with a beautiful-looking cherry red electric guitar - a Les Paul - across his knees. Mind you, all electric guitars looked beautiful to me then: I wanted one, having realised that almost all of my favourite records featured electric guitar, not acoustic.

"Right," Andrew said. "This is my band. That's Trevor..." He pointed to a bloke of about eighteen with short fair hair wearing jeans and a leather jacket.

"What d'ya mean *my* band?" said the punk.

Trevor snorted. "'E's only been in it five minutes."

Andrew, smiling, indicated the punk. "And that's Steve. Steve the hedgehog."

The last was obviously a reference to Steve's exploding hair. I guessed Steve to be around eighteen too. Andrew turned toward a girl sitting on the settee, also about eighteen, wearing a white polo-necked sweater and black trousers. "And that's Jane."

"She's not in the band," said Trevor.

"Yeah," Andrew said. "She's not in the band."

Jane smiled at me. I was shy with girls. I looked quickly away from her.

"There 'are – 'ave a seat." Andrew pointed me to the space on the settee beside Jane. "He's my cousin, Paul," he explained to the others. "'E plays guitar."

"Do ya?" Trevor asked.

I nodded.

"You any good?" Steve asked.

I shrugged, smiling, too embarrassed to admit that I was.

"'E's got a little acoustic guitar," Andrew said. His tone was a mocking one.

Steve smiled. He gazed at me for a while before asking, "What kinda music d'you like?"

I thought of saying The Beatles but remembered he was a punk. Punks always said they hated anything from previous generations. So I ended up shrugging again.

"You don't know?"

I said nothing.

"You don't know?"

I thought of saying I liked the Sex Pistols but got the feeling Steve would think I was crawling to him if I did. I shrugged, smiling idiotically.

There were exchanged glances and hisses of amusement amongst them.

"What kind of guitar you got? Or don't you know that?"

I looked, wearily now, at Steve and looked away again.

"'E don't know."

"Ah, leave 'im alone," Jane said.

"Does 'e speak, Andrew?"

There was silence. I looked up to find that Andrew was looking into Steve's eyes, smiling, his shoulders shivering in mirth. Andrew stopped laughing abruptly and said mock-defensively "Ah, shut up. Leave 'im alone, right. 'E's my cousin."

We all went, including Jane, to the garage. Trevor's bass was perched on a stand in there. Andrew started setting up his kit.

Tools were arranged on shelves around the garage, which blazed unnaturally white with florescent lighting. Jane sat on a kitchen stool in one corner. Steve and Trevor warmed up while waiting for Andrew to get ready, filling the garage with burbling bass runs and guitar doodles. I was watching Steve's fingers on his guitar. Once I started learning guitar, it had amazed me that the people I saw playing electric on television used their fingers to form the same chords as I did yet produced a far more powerful and exciting sound. Even now in the presence of an amateur musician playing in a garage, the instrument just sounded so glamorous. I wanted an electric guitar so badly.

"Alright," Steve said when everyone was ready. "What shall we play?"

"*Pretty Vacant*," I said. It was an attempt to crawl to Steve, but I was desperate for their approval now.

Trevor was gazing at me. He looked at Andrew. "You got a punk for a cousin then, eh?"

"Yeah."

Trevor looked at me again. "Right little punk, ain't ya?" He nodded at my body. "D'you dress like that on weekends, then? D'you wear your gear in the week or something?"

Steve and Andrew wheezed contrived laughter. I, hands in my pockets, walked away from Trevor's eyes to the nearest wall. I was now so self-conscious that I felt awkward leaning against it in case they thought I was trying to look cool.

"'E likes the Pistols," Andrew said.

"Does 'e?"

"Yeah. I got 'im liking them. 'E used to hate 'em before I played 'im their records."

For a terrible moment I thought he might tell them about how I'd been scared of turning into a punk through liking their stuff. But then Trevor asked "Why - what did 'e like before? Barry Manilow?"

"Yeah," Andrew said.

Steve looked up from tuning his guitar. "Did ya?"

"Na-ah," I protested, seething at the way Andrew was showing off to them.

"What shall we play, then?" Trevor said.

"*My Generation*?" suggested Steve.

Again, I tried to ingratiate myself. "Unnh. That's a bit old."

Steve - a punk and therefore supposedly contemptuous of 'Sixties music - said "Why - 'ow old does it 'ave to be?"

Wishing the ground would swallow me, I shrugged.

"C'mon then," Andrew said. The other two turned toward him. "Ready?"

Andrew held his left drumstick up and tapped on it four times with his right drumstick. The three launched simultaneously into sound. At first, it seemed formless. The close walls of the garage made for dense acoustics. Despite the glamour I'd heard in Steve's warm-ups, the noise the three were now making was anything but glamorous. Although I knew Andrew was a good drummer, the sound of his sticks hitting the skins in here was a pathetic slapping. After a few seconds, I could recognize what they were playing as something resembling *My Generation*, a record I knew because Andrew owned it. Their expressions as they played amused me. Despite the cock-eyed rendition, Steve and Trevor had very solemn looks on their faces, while Andrew constantly nodded his head and occasionally snarled at the other two.

After forty-five minutes and several other songs, they took a break. Steve brought in a tray with five cups of tea on it. The other four took a mug each. I thought the last one was mine but didn't go and take it in case it wasn't.

"Ain't you got a singer?" I asked Andrew.

Andrew, sipping, shook his head.

Jane was standing in front of the tea tray. "Don't you want your tea, er..." She turned to Andrew. "What's 'is name?" Andrew told her. She turned toward me. "Don't you want your tea, Paul?"

"Oh. Ta." I moved toward the tray. Jane made to get out of my way but I moved in the same direction she did. We stepped back and forth trying to get out of the other's path. We snorted and said "Sorry," to each other. Finally, I got my tea and brought it away. I felt Steve's eyes on me.

"Oi, Paul," he said. I looked at him. Steve wasn't looking at me but at Andrew. "Have you got a bird?"

I cradled my cup near my mouth, pretending to be waiting for it to cool.

"Eh?" Steve said.

I flicked my eyes at him.

"'Ave you ever been out wiv a girl?"

"No," I said, speaking in hope that an answer would make Steve stop. There was a tone of defensiveness in my voice.

"Why not?"

Everybody's eyes were now on me. I shrugged.

"D'you go to a mixed school or a just-boys school?"

He must know I went to the same school as Andrew. I said quietly "Just-boys."

"Eh?"

"Just-boys," I said louder.

"Ohh," said Steve in mock-realisation. "Is that why you 'aven't gone out wiv a girl? 'Cos of that?" He waited for me to answer. When I didn't, he said "Eh?"

I looked at his mischievous face, shrugged and looked away. Trevor's shoulders were shivering. I turned away from him toward the drum kit. Andrew was sitting hunched over his tea, smiling. As I looked, he turned his face towards Trevor to share his amusement. I sipped at my tea, carefully looking over the cup's rim at nothing.

"Oi, mate..." It was Trevor's voice. "Can I ask you something? You know all the kids in your class at school, right? Who would you say is the best-looking?" I gazed at him. He was smiling. "Eh? Who d'you fink?"

I shrugged.

"D'you reckon it's you? Eh? Are you one of the best-looking kids in your class?"

Steve chuckled quietly. Then he said, "Yeah. Better-looking than you, anyway."

I found myself glancing at Jane. She was smiling slightly. Her eyes shifted from my face to Steve's before looking at the floor.

Trevor got up with a sigh and put his cup down. "C'mon then," he said in indication they should resume rehearsing.

Steve, tea finished, stood and picked up his guitar. "Nah, only joking mate," he said to me. "D'you wanna 'ave a go on my guitar?"

I hesitated, suspecting a trick. It turned out he was sincere. Maybe he was feeling guilty about making fun of me. Within a few seconds, I was standing with his Gibson hanging from around my neck. I didn't like the bulky feel of it quite as much as Dave's more slimline Telecaster which he very occasionally let me play. (Dave was a bit of a snob about acoustic guitars: like a lot of folkies, he felt electric guitars were a bit phoney.) I played the riff to The Kinks' *You Really Got Me*. It growled out pleasingly well from Steve's amp.

"Alright, mate" Trevor said. "*Pretty Vacant*, right?"

"Oh..." I said, realising he wanted me to play along with the band.

"Don't you know it?"

I knew the chord progression, having sat through Andrew's copy a few times and identified it. "Er..." I hesitantly attempted the opening, winding figure for the first time. Like magic, it rose perfectly from the speaker.

"Not *Pretty Vacant*," Andrew groaned. "Sick to death of it."

However, Trevor wanted to do it so we had a bash. I was terrified but also anxious to impress. I played the intro again. Trevor and Andrew introduced bass and drums after the fourth bar, as on the record, beginning the purring, loping build-up. On the switch to where the vocal was on record, I hit a note and ran my finger along the string to replicate Steve Jones's explosion sound. It made me too late to start the rhythm part on time and we had to stop. I was surprised that they didn't seem particularly irritated. We started again. This time, I got the timing right. The noise we were producing sounded exciting to me but it was very disorienting playing along with other instruments. I tried to close my mind to what the other two were playing, but I also knew enough about groups that I had to keep to the tempo being set by the drummer. The tempo Andrew was playing at seemed frankly wrong to me, too fast.

The ending was a bit untidy, my memory beginning to fail me by that stage. I didn't attempt to reproduce the feedback that ended the record. Andrew meanwhile was thrashing around his kit to produce the kind of climatic finish you usually heard on heavy metal records.

"E's not bad, is 'e?" Steve said of me.

"D'you know *Honky Tonk Woman* by the Stones, Paul?" Trevor asked.

"Yeah. *Honky Tonk Women*, it is," I said.

"Eh?"

"It's *Honky Tonk Women*. A lot of people fink it's *Honky Tonk Woman*." I hissed laughter, embarrassed at their gazes.

* * * *

It was later that evening. I was in the bathroom at home, drying my hands and face after having washed them. As I did so, I gazed idly into the mirror above the sink. My gaze became less idle. I inspected my unstyled bouffant of black steely hair; my brown eyes that were so dark they gave the impression of having no iris's and which had unusually narrow, Chinese-like sockets; my large jutting brow; my permanently blotchy cheeks; my small mouth, the centre of whose upper lip protruded slightly over the lower one.

My face was generating more and more attention like that from Andrew's band today. The previous week, I had been walking home from school when I saw two girls my age up ahead and noticed them glance at each other. As they passed me, one of them loudly pretended to vomit.

Things like that had been happening quite often. It seemed... weird. I'd never thought I was good-looking but I hadn't thought I was ugly. I hadn't thought about it one way or the other, really. Up until a couple of years before, neither had any of the kids my age. But now they were becoming interested in girls and in how they themselves looked, and were noticing how other boys looked. And it seemed they thought I was ugly. At first, I'd thought they were joking. I looked at my face and it wouldn't make me think 'Ugh!' All I would see was... me. But so many different kids independent of one another had told me - sometimes brutally and directly, sometimes, like Steve and Trevor, mischievously and indirectly - that I was ugly.

I obscured the sight of my face by rubbing the towel over it.

Five

Arriving home from school one day, I saw my dad up ahead. I ran and caught him up, slapping his back as I jumped dramatically down beside him, and started to walk in step with him. He glanced at me.

"Are we 'aving chips for tea?" I asked. He'd had money the last few days.

My dad didn't react for a few seconds. Then he shrugged his shoulders and jerked his head slightly.

"Can we 'ave?"

He didn't reply.

"Eh?"

"Mm," my dad said, his tone meaningless.

I studied his face. I tried to remember if I'd done anything to make him angry with me. I walked glumly behind him up the pathway of our estate, thinking I was in trouble. Once inside, my dad went into the living room and sat in an armchair. I hovered in the doorway, nonchalantly swinging on the door, but waiting, scared, to see if he had anything to say to me.

"D'you want me to go down the chip shop?"

My dad turned his head. He gazed at me without answering. I was uncomfortable. I looked away from his eyes. I looked back and shrugged my shoulders. "What?" I said defensively. I must have done something, then. But my dad looked away without having spoken. "D'you want me to?" I asked again.

"Yeah, okay. What d'you want?"

Relief flooded me. I stepped into the room and pumped my fist in the air like a footballer. Holding that pose, I said "Cod and chips!" My dad reached into his pocket for his wallet. I stepped toward him.

"We're being chucked out of 'ere, by the way," he said. "By the council."

"Chucked out?"

"Yeah."

My dad held out a five pound note. I lowered my eyelids and looked at it. After a couple of seconds, I slowly reached for it. I looked into his eyes.

"For not paying the rent," my dad said in a weary voice.

"But you started paying them back."

"Yeah, not enough, though."

I stared at him. "But... what're... where we gonna live?"

"Dunno."

I was still staring. My dad sighed exhaustedly and gazed past my shoulder. I looked down at the money in my hands, now unimportant. I looked again at him, visions of sleeping on park benches in my mind. My dad sucked in his lips to indicate that he too was unhappy. But he said nothing to lessen my terror. He merely put his head against the back of the chair and stared at the ceiling.

"When they gonna chuck us out?"

"When they've found us anuvver place."

"Anuvver place? What - to live?"

"Yeah."

"Ohh! I thought you meant they'd just kick us out of 'ere and we wouldn't 'ave nowhere to stay."

"No."

"Ohh. Thank God for that." I went and sat on the settee. "Where they gonna put us?"

My dad shrugged. "Be somewhere worse than this, though."

"How d'ya mean?"

"Well, it'll be in a worse area. State of the place they give us'll probably be worse an' all. A tower block, knowing them."

"Oh no."

We were quiet.

Eventually, I spoke again. "They won't put us in a tower block, will they?"

"Might do. That's what they do wiv people 'oo don't pay the rent. Dump 'em in tower blocks, 'cos nobody else wants to live there."

I tutted. "Flipping gits."

"I know," my dad agreed.

"But... Will they put us high up in one?"

"Could do."

I tutted. "God."

"They're gonna give us a month to leave after they've found us a place. So that's something."

I was dismayed that he found any comfort in that. "But... I mean, if you say you'll pay 'em back what you owe 'em, won't they... Y'know... give us anuvver chance?"

He shook his head. "I said that before."

Neither of us said anything for a while. I stared at the floor.

"You gonna get the chips then?"

"Yeah," I said heavily. I sighed and rose. I exchanged another look with my dad, sucking my lips in. He rolled his eyes to indicate he felt the same.

It was nearly what I wanted.

He seemed a very different person to his usual carefree self. It had finally happened: he'd come up against something that none of his couldn't-give-a-damn displays could change.

* * * *

Our new home turned out to be the worst nightmare we could imagine. The nineteenth floor of a tower block in Battersea. My mum cried when she received the letter telling us and I cried with her - something I wouldn't have done if my dad was around. My mum pretended to the council that she had agoraphobia but it didn't make any difference. I was frightened, genuinely frightened:

Battersea had been to me like Northern Ireland, a violent place that you occasionally heard terrible things about. Now I was going to live there.

The three of us went to view it together. The block was Ethel House on the Ward Estate. It looked as horrible as I'd imagined it: a huge, grey building with rows and rows of windows that were somehow sinister looking. I made a face at my mum. She ruffled my hair reassuringly.

When we went up, the inside of the flat was actually quite nice. It was neat, clean, well-decorated and had a gleaming fitted kitchen. But it was still the nineteenth floor of a tower block in Battersea.

On the way back down in the lift, my mum asked a woman what the place was like. She replied "Oh, I wouldn't recommend anyone moving 'ere. It's like halfway house, there's so many of us trying to get out."

The fact that we were moving and that I'd therefore be going to a new school spurred me into action with regards to a girl that I liked. Her name was Debbie Wells, a girl my age with a bell of brown hair and a pretty, freckled face. I hadn't asked any girls out before. In fact, I'd been surprised that kids my age were already formally going out together, as opposed to just playing kiss-chase or whatever. I'd thought kids only started doing that at sixteen, seventeen, not at fourteen. But now, seeing as I would probably never see Debbie again if I didn't take the initiative, I'd decided to try for my first date.

In Geography on my last day at my school in Putney, I was sitting next to a kid called Neil Winters.

"Oi, guess what? I'm gonna ask Debbie Wells out."

"Oh *yeah*?" Neil said in scepticism.

"Yes, though."

Neil looked up from his book. "You ain't, are ya?"

"Yeah."

"*She* wouldn't go out wiv you."

I hesitated, surprised. "Yes she would."

"She *wouldn't*." Neil went back to his work.

* * * *

I noticed that my friends were being nice to me because it was my last day. I was standing on a corner near the school with Hodgsy and a kid called Stefan. The home-time crowds were flowing around us.

"I'll miss not being able to talk about the Sex Pistols wiv you, Paul," Hodgsy said.

I put my hands on Hodgsy's shoulders and hopped towards him. "Will you miss doing the pogo wiv me?"

He put his hands on my shoulders. "Ooh, yes!" We jumped up and down together.

Stefan laughed. "Watch out, Paul. Debbie Wells won't wanna go out wiv you if she sees you pogoing."

"What you talking about? 'E's gonna take 'er to see Vik Vomit and the Lumps."

We laughed. The fact that Stefan and Hodgsy were indulging me like this, being more generous than they would on any other day, made me happy, but also a little sad. I wouldn't be seeing them much again.

"'Ere she comes, 'ere she comes!" Stefan said suddenly.

We turned. Debbie Wells was walking with a friend in our direction on the opposite pavement.

"Go on then, Hodgsy," Stefan said.

Hodgsy crossed the street, intercepting the two girls before they could turn the corner. He was going to ask for me. I immediately felt my heart pumping and an airy feeling in my chest. I leaned against the hedge of a house, half-wanting to disappear but keeping myself in a position where Debbie could see me clearly. Stefan glanced at me, then resumed watching as Hodgsy spoke to Debbie. Debbie's face jerked about in puzzlement.

"D'you wanna?" we could hear Hodgsy say.

"Who, though?" Debbie replied, her voice irritated.

Hodgsy never had much patience with girls. He flung his arm toward me and barked "Him!"

My lips opened as though my name had been called in class. Instinctively, I started to move my body forward, as if to present myself.

Debbie's eyes alighted on me. "No fear," she instantly told Hodgsy. She walked off. Her friend followed, an eye looking at me out of the corner of its socket.

I pushed myself off the hedge. My eyes met Stefan's. I sucked my lips in theatrically. Stefan, in kindness, sucked his lips in too and looked at the approaching Hodgsy.

"Paul..." Hodgsy said, not realising we'd heard. "Sorry. She said no." I nodded in acknowledgement. "Sorry."

"She ain't got no taste, 'as she?" I said in a weak voice.

"Yeah, sorry Paul."

* * * *

I had only been doing it for a minute or so when it came. Aggrieved thumping from beneath my bedroom floor suddenly mingled with the sound I had been making bouncing my football on the carpet. I stopped, wearily lowering my eyelids. The banging beneath me ceased. "Bastard!" I shouted at the floor. Spitefully, I threw the ball heavily down one more time. The thumping beneath me started again but I was already walking over to my bed. "Go fuck yourself, you cunt!" I stamped my foot hard on the floor, staring at it. I turned and threw myself face-down on the bed. I lay quietly with my face in the pillow for several moments. Then I raised my face and screamed "You fucking miserable bastard, why don't you drop dead you cunt!" before slapping my face into the pillow once more.

I couldn't do anything in this place. I didn't know anyone to play out with in this area so I was stuck indoors all day. When I did try to do something to stop myself getting bored, downstairs would start complaining.

I got to my knees on the bed. I sat with my hands on my thighs and gazed at the blankets. I thought of playing some guitar but there were only so many hours in the day you could play without getting sick to death of it. I sighed heavily. After a minute, I got off the bed. I went to the window and pushed it open as far as it would go - five inches. Squinting against the sun, I gazed down. Nineteen floors below, a teenage girl rode by on a bicycle. The sound of whirring wheels wafted up to me.

Opposite my block was a large stretch of wasteland covered with untended grass. Its yellow-green surface was broken near the centre by the untidy coal-black circle that was the remains of a bonfire. Beyond the wasteland was a disused flour mill. There were slates missing from large sections of its roof and its outer wall was crumbling, loosened bricks lying on the pavement.

The top of my head was resting against the window's glass. They were suicide-proof, our block's windows. I wouldn't blame people for trying to throw themselves out. I thought of Battersea as *Desolation Row* after a Bob Dylan song. It was so different to Putney. I'd lived on a council estate in Putney, but in Battersea the working class weren't just relatively poorer - they were dead common. Everything about Battersea had shocked me. The way little children were cheeky to their mothers and the way their mothers didn't seem to care. The way kids were sent down the chip shop every single night for their tea. The way a kid would just take a piss in the middle of the pavement in the High Street. The way parents would send their kids to have skinhead haircuts in the barbers so that they wouldn't have to pay for another for a long while. I had literally never seen someone with a skinhead haircut in real life before coming to Battersea.

There was a second-hand shop in the High Street that summed up everything about the area to me. It was a place where housewives wheeling prams would buy second-hand shoes which had the dark foot impressions of the previous owner's feet inside and where people haggled over the price of tatty second-hand blankets. Junk shops in Putney didn't sell second-hand shoes and second-hand blankets.

I was lonely. I didn't have any mates in Battersea. Sometimes I fantasised about going downstairs and kicking my ball against a wall and falling into a conversation with another kid which led to a friendship, but I never had the guts to try it for real. Whenever I went out to the shops and I heard the shouts of kids playing on the estate, I would go round the other side of the estate to avoid them. I was scared. The kids in this area were supposed to be tough.

My parents didn't have any friends here either. We didn't know the neighbours. We only knew a couple of people on our floor to say hello to. There was never any opportunity to get to know people. When you came back to the block, you simply got in the lift, pressed your button, got out at your floor and went in. Bang. That was it - all chance of a social life over for the evening.

Mind you, I wouldn't have wanted to know a lot of the people in the block. When I got into the lift when a crowd of people had been waiting, one of them would usually press the floor buttons for everyone else. When people would ask me "What floor?" and I said, "Nineteen, please", those in the lift would turn and look at me and there was always some smartarse who said "Gonna jump?" or "Up in heaven." I hated them.

I ejected spit from between my lips and watched it fall downwards. It quickly flew in and out of sight. I spat again. I turned and looked around the room. There was a plate on the floor which I'd eaten toast off earlier. The knife I'd spread the margarine with lay on it. I stepped over and picked it up. I stood at the window waiting for somebody to pass on the pavement below. After a couple of minutes, no-one had. I held the knife out of the gap, arm fully extended, and aimed at a parked car. I immediately realised it was going to fall short. After a few seconds, there was a distant tinkling as it hit the ground at the foot of the block. I instinctively ducked, hands still on the frame, lip bitten. I rose and looked out. There was no-one about. I couldn't see the knife. I put my forearms on the frame again and rested my chin in them. I lifted my chin for a moment to eject another stream of spit.

* * * *

What made the loneliness even worse was that I hardly saw either of my parents these days. I had long been used to my dad's regular disappearing acts but in the past my mum had always been there to keep me company. Nowadays, she was out every evening. She hated the flat and she hated Battersea. She was forever going back to Putney to see her friends and visit her usual pub. (I had decided never to go back there myself: I couldn't stand the kids on my old estate knowing I now lived in Battersea.) So when I came home in the afternoons from my new school where I didn't yet have any friends it was to an area where I also had no friends and to an empty flat. I was always pleading with my mum not to go out, but she would just smile and cuddle me as if to say that I shouldn't be so silly. One particular night, when I saw her putting on her coat after we'd had our tea, I complained "Ohh... Are you going out again?"

"Yeah."

I tutted. "But you've been out all day."

"Well I wanna go out again, don't I?" she said in a sing-song voice.

I tutted. "I'm always on my own."

"I'll bring you back some sweet-and-sour pork," she said mollifyingly. I pulled my face away as she tried to kiss me. I slumped in an armchair and stared in fury at the television. When I heard the front door click closed, I shouted "You fucking bitch!" Suddenly, I stopped breathing, thinking I had heard a sound in the hall. Panic stricken, I wondered whether I had heard the front door close after all. I stared at the screen intently, trying to assemble an excuse. Nothing happened. Trembling, I got up, pulled the door open and poked my head into the hall. It was empty. I went back into the living room, slamming the door hard behind me. Throwing myself into the chair, I raised my face and screamed "Slag!"

I covered my face with my hand.

I jerked out of the chair and yanked the door open, deliberately letting its handle bang against the wall. I went into the kitchen. I yanked the cupboard doors open one by one, deliberately leaving them gaping. When one swung closed again, I angrily wrenched at it. The force with which I did it almost sent it flying closed once more but I kicked at it to stop it, and kicked at it again as it bounced back. The wood banged loudly as my toe tried to tame it. I flung myself to my knees and pushed the door as far back as it would go and held it there, teeth gritted, glaring at it. I let go of it, but still stared.

I got up. I walked over to the fridge and swung its door open. I turned away, hands in pockets. A few seconds later I turned back and pushed the door closed with my toe in case the food went off.

I went out into the hall and pressed the latch down on the front door so my mum wouldn't be able to get in - although I knew that I'd only put it back up again later.

In my bedroom I had three blank tapes that I'd bought awhile back but hadn't recorded anything on. I broke them open, pulling the tape out, covering the carpet in the brown shiny string. I took the darts from my dart board and threw them to miss, adding to the circle of pock-marks on the wall around the board.

I made a bed for myself in the bathroom. I took my pillow and a blanket in there. I didn't have a lock on my bedroom door, but I could lock myself in the bathroom and not let my mum in when she needed to get in there. I was going to stay in there all the next day. I took an opened can of beans in there so that I wouldn't need to come out. Show *her*. I was sick of being left alone. Especially at weekends. Sometimes I didn't speak to anybody all day on Saturdays and Sundays. It was alright for her, going down Putney to see people she knew. What was there for me to do? Well I was sick of it.

* * * *

I awoke late at night to the sound of the letterbox banging. I lay there a couple of seconds in bewilderment. I jumped to my feet and unlocked the bathroom door. Blearily, I opened the front door to let my mum in. I'd forgotten to put the latch back.

My mum stepped in with a takeaway bag in her hand. "Was the latch down?" She was bleary herself, with drink.

"Yeah."

"'E 'are - I got you some sweet-and-sour pork." She handed me the bag.

"Oh, ta." I took it, smiling. Then I remembered. I drew away from her, saying instinctively, "*No...*" I retreated to the bathroom and locked the door behind me.

Within a minute, she'd found what I'd done in the kitchen. The handle of the bathroom door suddenly rattled. I jerked in shock. There was a thump on the door, sounding like my mum's toe connecting accidentally with it as she, surprised, found the door locked.

"Paul - come out of there."

"No!"

"Come out of there, I said!"

Before I could reply, the handle rattled again. Silence. There was a huge thump on the door that made me gasp.

"Open the door!"

I sat where I was, clutching the sweet-and-sour pork. There was another huge thump. Then another.

"*Open the door, I said! Open it, Paul!*"

I narrowed my eyes, sucked in my lips and huffed down my nose, trying - as if she could see me - to communicate the unhappiness that had led me to do what I had.

"Open it now!"

There was another gigantic thump. The wood creaked alarmingly.

"No," I said in defiance, but my voice was weak.

"*Paul* - open this door right now or I'm gonna break it down!"

I grimaced and huffed air out.

"*Paul!*"

"Al-*right*..."

She hadn't heard me. "Open this door!"

"*Alright!*" I was rising, putting down the sweet-and-sour pork. I flicked open the lock and with a pained look on my face pulled the door inwards. I groped for something to say in justification. I yelped as my mum grabbed my hair and pulled me into the hall. My hand alighted in helplessness on her bust as she held me there, me standing on tiptoes to lessen the pain, hissing.

"You spoilt little bastard!" she said. "You fucking spoilt little shit!" The smell of alcohol washed over me.

She wrenched hard and I ejaculated a short shriek. She dragged me by the hair to my bedroom door and, after pushing the handle down, used my body to shove it open. The door rebounded off the wall into my back as she forced me briskly into the room.

"Sorry, sorry!" I was desperately saying.

She thrust me onto the bed and started slapping and punching at me. Her knuckles connected with my head.

"Ahh!" I put my arms out protectively, crying. The blows continued. I slipped over the edge of the mattress. My mum stopped hitting me to yank me up off the floor and back onto the bed, then let fly again with a series of slaps. She stood upright, hands on her hips.

"Sorry!" I grimaced up at her from behind my shielding arms.

She stooped suddenly and came up holding a bundle of cassette tape. She had given me the money for the tapes. "You little bastard!"

She threw the tape at me and I cried out as she bent over for another flurry of blows. It ended after a few seconds. She walked over to my guitar, which was leaning against a wall. She picked it up by the neck. My eyes stared at her from a face blazing from her blows. I held my breath, thinking she was going to damage the guitar.

"You spoilt little cunt! You didn't smash that up, did ya?" She threw it against the wall. It came to rest on the floor intact. "I wouldn't even be 'ere if it weren't for you!" she said. "Fink I wanna stay 'ere?"

* * * *

I lingered in my bedroom the next morning. When I heard my mum finally go out of the front door, I got up and went and watched television in the living room. She might come back but I had to do something. I couldn't stay in my room all day.

When, to my fright, my mum did return, I kept my eyes on the television. She approached me and stood in front of me. I looked up. She always brought me back a Mars Bar when she went to the paper shop. She was holding one out to me now. I ignored it, looking back at the television. She stood where she was. I looked at her again. She smiled. I didn't smile back but I took the Mars Bar.

After that, she must have stayed in every night for at least a month. Then she disappeared - completely and absolutely.

I came home from school one day and found an electric guitar on my bed. It was a Fender Stratocaster with a gleaming red-and-white body that had a beautiful chemical, pristine smell. There was no amplifier with it. I had been asking for an electric guitar since not long after getting my acoustic guitar. My parents had been unable to get one for me for my fourteenth birthday a couple of months back as they'd been skint, but both had, separately, promised me one for Christmas. And here I was with one sitting on my bed large as life with Christmas four months away.

At first, I assumed it was from my dad - one of his typical spontaneous acts of generosity after having, equally typically, mysteriously come into some spending money. But the note sellotaped to it - and written with a pencil that I kept on my chest of drawers - was in my mum's handwriting. It read:

> Dear Paul,
> I love you. I'm afraid I won't be living with you and
> your dad now. It's not because I don't love you. I'm
> sorry if it upsets you. I love you very much. Here's your
> electric guitar. I hope you like it. Please don't be upset.
> I love you,
> Mum X X X

There are times when your mind has to simultaneously take in two things that are so contrasting, your brain freezes up. My mind was conditioned by the sight of the guitar on my bed - my dream come true - to find something benign on the note. It just couldn't cope with what it did find. After searching the flat and finding it empty, I sat on the edge of my bed strumming on the strings of the Stratocaster and my brain acted like a car that wouldn't start. It wouldn't think - only think about thinking. Fragments of ideas came into it, made no impression on me, and then were replaced by other fragments. I thought about thinking of: whether my mum had left already or just meant she was leaving some time in the near future... whether she'd told my dad... whether it had anything to do with me locking myself in the bathroom... whether she was living with my aunt... how often I'd be seeing her... where she'd got the money for the guitar... whether my dad had helped pay for it... whether I might be living with her some of the time... All of this occurred to me without me feeling any particular emotion at all, and at the same time I was distractedly noting how the Stratocaster (I'd actually asked for a Gretsch, the guitar George Harrison could be seen using in all the stage shots of the Beatles) had double cutaways that allowed access to the 21st fret. Because I didn't know what on earth was happening, I didn't know what to feel.

I was still strumming when I heard a key turn in the front door. I stared at my bedroom door. It opened. My dad stood on the threshold, palm on the yawning door, looking at me. I sat frozen on the bed, staring at him. I could tell immediately that he knew. His manner was strange. He remained standing there, his eyes on me. I didn't dare to move, wanting nothing to happen, neither of us to speak, because I knew now that what was going to happen wasn't going to be nice. Finally he came in. He walked over and sat beside me. He looked at the guitar. His expression showed that he knew about it already. He kept his eyes on it, as though appraising it. For one brief second I felt hopeful, thinking that if he was more interested in the quality of my new guitar than anything else then there couldn't be anything wrong. Then he solemnly put his arm round my neck and looked into my eyes with an expression of regret. I opened my mouth, wanting almost to protest. I swept my face away because I was never comfortable crying in front of my dad.

Six

It was dinner time at school. I'd eaten and was wandering around the corridors. I was moving slowly, lazily, my shoulder against a wall. My nylon parka rasped as I slid along. Mrs. Prince, my teacher, was walking in my direction.

"Paul... Have you got that note?"

She'd been asking me for several days for a note to explain my latest absence. I turned and - shoulder still against the wall - went off in the opposite direction. Her footsteps followed behind.

"Paul, come here please."

I ignored her. Then I saw up ahead of me the headmaster looking at the scene in disbelief.

"You! Boy! Come here."

I took my shoulder off the wall.

As he approached, Mrs. Prince started to speak to him. "Mr. Mackie, I'm trying to get a note off this boy to explain his absence -"

"Do your tie up," Mr. Mackie said to me. I did up the top button of my shirt. My expression must have been as glum as I felt because Mr. Mackie then barked, "Oh, I'm not going to have boys sulking in the corridor. Go and wait outside my office."

Outside his office three minutes later, I quickly pushed myself off the wall I was leaning against as he swept around the corner of the corridor. Wordlessly, he held the door open for me. He sat in his chair and I stood in front of his table, hands awkwardly by my sides.

Mrs. Prince had told him all about me. "Three periods of absence without a note," he now said. "Late three or four times every week. Sometimes by an hour. Failure to turn up at registration at the end of the day. Where were you yesterday afternoon? And the day before?"

"Sometimes Miss don't turn up, so we sign our names on a bit of paper."

"Did you sign yesterday?"

I nodded.

"And the day before?"

"Sir."

"So why are you down as absent on the register?"

"I dunno..."

"You and only you."

I shrugged.

"What about the notes?" he asked.

I was silent.

"You've got nothing to say about them, have you? And why are you always so late all of a sudden?"

I shrugged again. "I live quite far away." A complete lie.

"So? There are buses where you live, aren't there? And trains?"

"Sir."

"You can get here alright, then?"

"Sir."

"Then do it. From now on, you're to come into my office as soon as you get into school every morning and before you go home. And you're not going to be late. I also want to see a note explaining your absence last Wednesday on my table tomorrow. Do you understand?"

"Sir."

"I'm not going to have someone wandering around..." He put on a moronic face: "'Unh, don't care'. Do you understand?"

I left his office reeling. It didn't seem possible that someone whose mother had walked out on him could be treated so badly. He didn't actually know my mum had left me - and neither did anyone else in the school - but I was staggered that God, if He existed, could pile misery upon misery.

When my mum had first walked out - six months ago now - I sometimes fantasised about others feeling sorry for me over it. I'd known of kids whose mum and dad had got divorced but never any who had had one of their parents simply disappear. I imagined a kid turning to another as I walked past and saying, "Oi, see that kid there? 'Is mum left 'im and his mate replying, "Really? Blimey. I'd hate that to happen to me." To which the first boy would say, "Yeah, poor kid. Don't you reckon?" The second: "Yeah."

The thing is, nobody knew. I still had no friends on my estate, nor many at the school I'd joined when we'd moved to Battersea. Although I was friendly with some of the kids, I didn't want to tell anyone what had happened, so I pretended I lived with both parents. Which meant I could never invite anyone home.

Nobody in the family had seen my mum since the day she'd left, not even her own mother. I wanted to feel rejected and despised by her. But I knew that it wasn't because she didn't like me that she'd decided not to see me. She loved me. Which made it logical that she would be in touch. Yet she wasn't. Sometimes I seriously thought of suicide. The only reason I didn't do it was because of the effect it would have on my dad.

Going home from school that day, I now realised that I didn't even have the luxury of not giving a toss about anything anymore. The headmaster was onto me. This was in the days of corporal punishment. Although I wasn't worried what my dad's reaction would be to me getting into trouble at school - he wouldn't care - I couldn't be dismissive of the prospect of being caned.

I threw my keys onto my chest of drawers. The place was empty, as it always was. My dad probably wasn't away any more than he had been before, but with my mum now gone the flat always seemed like a ghost town. My wardrobe was lying face down in the chip wrappings and comics that covered the carpet. I'd tipped it over deliberately a couple of months before and just left it there. As I never went out except to go to school, it wasn't as if I had any real need for it. Meanwhile, the legs of the deskchair

I had flung across the room one day stuck up at an angle in one corner. The sheets on my bed were grey and shiny.

My room wasn't as bad as the other rooms. For instance, except in the area just before the television and behind the door, rubbish covered the entire living room carpet. And if I went into my dad's room in the evenings, switching on the light would provoke a mass clicking and rustling as beetles ran for cover amongst the newspapers and Kentucky Fried Chicken boxes on the floor.

There were beetles in my room too. I didn't mind them too much, but I hated the little wriggling creatures with hairy, segmented bodies that were roughly the same size. They lived in the discarded food cartons in my dad's room and under the bags of rubbish in the kitchen. I felt nauseous when I would accidentally kick over a Kentucky Fried Chicken box and see their white bellies squirming helplessly in three-months-old sweetcorn.

The counters in the kitchen were piled with plates covered in half-eaten, fungus-covered meals, empty food packets and dried puddles of spilt tea. In the corner of the kitchen was a dustbin whose liner had been filled six months before. When you knocked the side of the bin, a black cloud of infant flies would rise from it. They would join the clouds of infant - and adult - flies that danced under the lightbulb and over the rubbish bags. When I was buttering toast during the summer I literally had to wave the knife about to keep the flies off.

There were seven large full black disposal bags lined up against one wall of the kitchen. Each had been sealed with a knot when full but neither my dad nor myself had ever bothered to take them down to the dustbins. The exteriors of the bags were covered with tiny, moving white specks.

I kept the beetle population of the kitchen down by torturing as many of them to death as I could. In fact, I spent almost as much time torturing beetles as playing guitar. Sometimes I would simply put a beetle on a counter and bounce a butter knife up and down on its back until it died. Often its spilled guts would make it stick to the knife as it went up in the air. But I preferred more elaborate methods such as cutting their legs off one by one. They would continue trying to flee no matter how many you cut off.

They would be fazed for a second each time a limb went but then they would set off again, crawling through puddles of their own insides on three, two, even one leg. I also liked putting them on the gas rings. I'd turn the flame up high until the cap was blazing hot, then turn it off and place a beetle on it. Every step it took to escape only hastened its death. It would make a frantic clicking noise before finally keeling over. Another good one was to place a whole group of beetles in the bottom of a match box and then put the box onto a ring with a low flame. I had to have a knife handy to push them back when they tried to climb out. They would frantically run around the sides, all clicking, before one by one erupting into orange flame and expiring.

* * * *

Over the next eighteen months I lost contact with the human race.

It's impossible to get close to anyone when you don't want them to know the most fundamental fact of your life. Conversations with schoolmates invariably strayed close to the delicate matter of domestic events. So I gradually found myself avoiding conversations. And although the rest of our family knew, of course, about my mum disappearing, I didn't want to discuss it with any of them. I might fantasise about kids my age feeling pity for me but I didn't want the real thing from aunts and uncles and especially from cousins. I wasn't just hurt, I was hugely embarrassed by what had happened.

So I stayed indoors. I would only go out to do shopping. Even then, I preferred to do it when it was raining, as there were fewer people on the streets. Alone in the flat, I played guitar like a demon. I didn't have private lessons anymore but I'd taken the music option at school so had three periods of tutoring every week, mostly on acoustic. At home, I played electric exclusively. At first, I'd amplified the Strat by using a trick Dave had taught me: plugging the guitar into the input socket of a tape recorder set to record/pause. Shortly after that, my dad bought me a Fender twin reverb amplifier. He also bought me a new packet of picks, but I actually found I preferred the crisp sound produced by the penny I'd been using in the interim. Although I was unhappy beyond belief, my new lifestyle did me good as a musician. With little else to do except play and think about playing (I insulated myself from the reality around me during school hours by thinking about what I'd do on the guitar when I got home), I developed to a level I never would have if I'd had a more normal existence. At the age of fifteen I was as good as guitarists five years older than me. When I listened to The Jam, I would feel a certain smugness at the fact that Paul Weller's technique was actually not quite as good as my own.

The quality of my schoolwork improved as well. I had to work in lessons. There weren't any friends I could chat or muck about with. The only thing to do was to get on with it. I turned from an adequate pupil to a very good one. I hated receiving praise from teachers, though, because that would make me the focus of attention. Music wasn't actually my favourite lesson. Instead, I preferred subjects that didn't involve a lot of one-to-one contact with the teacher. English was the one I liked best. The feeling of achievement in school and on guitar kept me going.

One day, though, it all got too much.

It was a blocked lavatory that pushed me over the edge I'd been walking on for eighteen months. During a half-term school holiday, the toilet in our flat stopped working properly. An accumulation of the newspapers we used instead of toilet paper meant that when you flushed, it would fill up and then spill over. My dad said that he would get my uncle - a plumber - to have a look at it and to try not to use it 'til then. Then he did one of his disappearing acts.

If I had been less self-conscious I could have just gone out to a public toilet. However, the thought of leaving the flat to take a shit mortified me. So instead I held it in for two days, worried every time I ate a meal that I would need to go afterwards. With my dad still absent at the end of the second day, I could forebear no longer. In my bedroom I found an old school sports bag that I no longer used because one handle was broken. I took it into the toilet. The floor of the toilet was covered with newspapers to soak up the overspills. The water in the bowl came up to the rim. Soggy newspapers floated on its brown surface. The outside of the bowl was speckled with brown. I held my breath as I undid my trousers and tried to avoid touching the toilet as I squatted in the cramped confines on the sodden newspaper carpet. My body swayed a couple of times, making me hiss my breath out at the prospect of touching the toilet or having to fling my hand onto the newspapers, but I managed to maintain my balance. Hurriedly I got the sports bag under myself. My bowels erupted into it.

After wiping myself on some of the newspaper stacked on the cistern, I pushed the paper I'd used into the bag. I poked my head out of the front door to see if there was anybody on the landing. I left the door on the latch, ran down to the rubbish chute at the other end of the corridor and put the sports bag down it.

My dad came home the next day but it turned out he had forgotten about asking my uncle about the toilet. Then, after leaving me some money, he disappeared again. The toilet remained blocked several more days. Whenever I needed to go, I would collect a carrier bag from the cupboard in the kitchen. Then I would go into the bathroom (it was cleaner in there). I would squat with the handles of the carrier bag held against my hips. There was a papery, rustling sound at every dropped stool. I also had to put a bowl beneath my dangling penis to catch the involuntary streams of urine. Afterwards I would freshen the room with some hairspray my mum had left behind.

On the third day of my dad's second absence, I was sitting on my bed playing guitar and I felt the urge to go again. My heart folded in on itself. Squatting over a carrier bag in the bathroom always made me feel so degraded and dirty. I tried to ignore the need, playing on. But it wouldn't go away. I closed my eyes, wanting to cry at the thought of what I had to do. Suddenly the wretchedness of my life swept over me. Everything was like this for me: depressing and horrible. It seemed stupid being alive.

Girls didn't like me because I was ugly. Nobody would ever want to marry me. My mum had walked out and it looked like I would never see her again. My dad was never home. I lived in a shithole in Battersea. Everything bad that could possibly happen to me had happened. When I thought of the future, there was nothing.

Grimly, I took another bag into the bathroom and had another sick-making shit. While squatting there, I decided I'd go to Putney. I didn't want my dad to find me dead. Afterwards I took the bag down to the rubbish chute. Then I calmly put my trainers and anorak on and put some of the money my dad had left me in my pockets. I left a note for my dad:

> *Dear Dad,*
> *I've left home. Don't worry about me. I've got a*
> *place to go and I'll be alright.*
> *Paul.*

I put it in an envelope, marked it "Dad" and left it on the living room table.

When the lift arrived, I bent down and slipped my front door key into the shaft. I went to Woolworths in Clapham Junction and bought a packet of razors. (My dad used disposables.) Collecting my change, I shrugged and said to the girl behind the counter "Won't be needing that..." She nodded and smiled distractedly, turning her attention to the next customer.

On Putney Common I tramped through the bushes for quite a while to find a secluded spot. I was hoping my body would never be found. I wanted my dad to think I was alright somewhere. The day was overcast and the grass was wet beneath my feet. When I thought I'd found somewhere that people weren't likely to pass through, I took the packet of razors from my anorak pocket. Woolworths' red-and-white paper bag fluttered to the ground. The plastic-windowed Gillette packet followed. Then a shower of razor blades: I only needed one.

My fingers awkwardly tried to make a cut across the width of my wrist. I found after a couple of attempts that ginger, lip-bitten slashes weren't going to get the blood flowing. I had to do it harder. I braced myself. The skin of my arm furrowed open. It stung evilly but wasn't enough to make me cry out. A slow seepage of blood began. I swapped hands, gritted my teeth and did the same thing to the other wrist, whipping it across the faint blue lines. I flexed my wrist to make the blood flow quicker and felt nauseous when the milk-white layerings of skin were revealed.

Shrill childish voices suddenly sounded alarmingly close by. I turned and ran off in the opposite direction.

Fifteen minutes later I was sitting on a fallen tree trunk, feeling cold and beginning to realise that the razor blades weren't working. The blood had stopped flowing. I tried some more slashes but they were half-hearted: to make a proper wound would hurt too much. I sat there pondering on what I'd got myself into. I couldn't go back. I'd left that note.

I counted the money left in my jeans. I set off on the half-mile walk to Putney High Street.

I tried to buy a pen-knife in three newsagents but none of them stocked them. I tried in Woolworths. An assistant gave me the now familiar shake of the head. I was just about to leave when the kitchen department occurred to me. I found a small, wooden-handled chopping knife. When paying for it at the counter, I deliberately showed the service girl my blood-caked lower arm. She recoiled with a silent gasp. Pretending to be regretful at inadvertently shocking her, I turned my arm over and dragged the change toward me.

I walked back to the Common. At the spot where the fallen tree trunk was located, I ripped the cardboard wrapper off the blade. I unzipped my anorak and pulled my t-shirt and jumper up. My chin on my chest, I held the blade in front of my stomach.

It was easier than the razor blades. All I had to do was perform one quick stab and it was all over. I took a deep breath. My hand jerked toward my body, then stopped. It was such a brief journey, it was nothing more than a quiver. I exhaled.

I breathed in once more. I gripped the handle of the knife tightly, deciding that I'd do it on the count of three.

Three seconds later, I exhaled, lifting my face skywards. My heart was thumping, the sweat prickling under my armpits. I looked down again and held the knife in position. But the moment - if there had been a moment - had passed. I could only bring myself to stroke the tip of the blade up and down my belly. I sat down on the log and folded my arms against the increasing cold.

Wish I was at home.

No! *Shut up!*

I swallowed. I sat and thought.

Aspirins! I'd read newspaper stories many times about people killing themselves with an overdose of aspirins. I still had some money left.

I had a piss against the tree trunk. I tucked my shirt in. Tossing the knife into the undergrowth, I set off yet again for Putney High Street.

I bought a packet of 24 aspirins in a little supermarket just off the High Street itself. I couldn't face the walk back to the Common. Instead, I went and sat on a bench on Putney Hill. As the traffic whooshed past and the sky darkened to grey, I unwrapped the pills. I was too tired now to worry about my body being found. It was a very melancholy feeling pushing the pills down my dry throat one by one as people walked past on their way back to their - I imagined - happy homes. A couple of times people glanced at me briefly as they went by.

The instructions on the box said that no more than eight of the pills should be taken in one day. 24 should be easily enough to kill me.

* * * *

The empty aspirin packet and its foil lay at my feet. My hands were under my thighs. My legs were stuck out in front of me, crossed at the ankles. All the cars going by me now had their headlights on.

It was fully dark before I rose from my seat and wandered away. Hands in pockets and shoulders hunched, I walked slowly down the hill. This was boring. Could I hurry up and die, please? Was that too much to ask, after fifteen years of shit? I wondered what was going to happen. Maybe I'd just die suddenly - fall over while I was walking along? Or maybe I needed to be asleep for it to work? The thought made me stop. Where could I go to sleep?

Bishop's Park. I'd played in it regularly until we'd moved out of Putney. I could climb over the fence and find somewhere to sleep in there.

A few minutes later, my feet were tapping down the steps of the subway leading to the park gates. The gates were high, spike-tipped and padlocked. I threw my foot onto the handrail of the subway steps, hoisted myself onto a pillar and then gingerly transported myself onto the other side. My trainer soles hit the concrete. I brushed my hands down and turned and walked into the darkened park.

After a couple of minutes of walking around, my melancholy started to fade. The sensation of being alone in this huge, dark place was wonderful, the idea that I could do what I liked, with no-one to tell me what to do. I walked over the flowerbeds. After that, I climbed the fence into the locked nursery and swung on the swings in its grounds. Then I got up on the stage that usually hosted brass band concerts. It occurred to me that I could live here. Sleep in the daytime in the bushes - I knew from all the times I'd been here before that there were many places where I wouldn't be discovered - and come out at night. I would be free. How would I get food? Nick stuff from the High Street. There must be some shops where it was easy. I wouldn't need much.

The question was whether I'd be dead before any of this came about. Were the aspirins working? I didn't feel ill. I felt exactly the same. I would wait and see. If they didn't work, I still had something: I could live here.

Another idea occurred to me. A few years ago I had gone one night around to an estate the council had been building next to mine in Putney, taken my clothes off and ran around naked. I now took my trousers and underpants off and walked through the park, enjoying the cold air against my skin. As I moved down the pathways, my cock was rock hard. I went and sat on a flower bed. The bricks were still damp from the day's rain. The feeling of it against my backside was delicious.

* * * *

Fully clothed again, I walked along the riverside path. I sat on a bench and gazed at the King's Arms pub on the opposite bank. My dad could be in there now. It had been his local when we'd lived in this area and he still went in there. I hadn't thought of that. I could have actually met him in the High Street on my way here.

Unless he'd already been home and found the note. Probably hadn't. He was hardly ever there. No. He was probably over there in the pub, drinking and laughing with his mates. While his son was dying across the river. At least, I might be dying. It was taking a fucking long time if I was.

* * * *

I still wasn't dead.

I was lying down on the bench now, head on my arm, staring sightlessly at one of the mounds of dead leaves piled along the pathway. My bored, resentful mind slowly registered the fact that a small part of one of the mounds was moving. It detached itself and, with a scuttling sound, tore off down the path and out of view. I jerked my head up. A rat! I flew to my feet. I backed away from the mound. Then it occurred to me that I might be blundering into other rats. I hopped about in indecision. Then I tore up the pathway as fast I could go and didn't stop running until I'd reached the opposite end of the park.

When I came to a stop, I was whimpering. I stood with my back against the wall of the neighbouring Fulham Football Ground. This was horrible. Horrible. Jesus Christ, all I wanted to do was die.

There was no way I was going to stay in the park now.

The entrance gates to Fulham Football Club were high but had no tips or barbed wire. I tried to keep the clattering to a minimum as I climbed up via the decorative patterns in the metal because there was a light on in the window of a small house located fifteen feet on the inside. After dropping down, I hurried quietly past it to the nearest terrace where I tapped up to the top of the elongated steps.

Concrete. Not exactly comfortable but it would do. All I needed to do was get to sleep. Then I'd never have to worry about anything again.

Ten minutes later I was back in the park. It was horrible in the football ground. The wind blowing around the wide open spaces made it very cold and I had been put on edge when it occurred to me the place might have guard dogs. When I remembered the caretaker's hut in the park, I made the journey back over the football ground's and the park's gates.

The hut was located behind the public toilets. I had to break one of the hut's window panes with a rock to lift the latch. Reaching my hand through the small hole I'd made and then climbing hunched-over through the frame, I could feel the blood trickling on my wrists again. I groped about in the darkness inside for a light switch. When I did find it, though, it turned out that I had merely started thin leaks in the crusts on my wrists.

The floor of the small hut was bare. There were two square tables, several canvas chairs, two walls of tall, narrow lockers and a cupboard. There was also a sink, where I washed my wrists.

Turning, I noticed that there were two calendars on the walls. Both of them featured nude women. I took one of them down and carried it across to a table. I pulled my jeans and underpants down, sat on one of the canvas chairs and began to masturbate. It was half-hearted, though. This wasn't a normal day.

I pulled my clothes up and returned to the matter of dying. I pulled two chairs together, switched off the light and lay down on them, my legs dangling through the gap at one end. The canvas under my face smelt of grit.

I tried breathing slowly, something which usually helped me fall asleep. My body rose and fell to the leisurely sighing through my nostrils. Gradually, I became aware that there was another noise behind it. I stopped breathing and listened. It was a faint, insistent ringing. At first, I thought it was something electrical inside the hut. It took me a minute or so to realise it was my own ears.

The aspirins. My heart started thudding at the thought that the aspirins could do damage to my body. It was, of course, the whole point, but the plain fact of it hit me properly for the first time. For some reason, I thought then of the mates I'd had when we lived in Putney. They would be amazed at what I was doing now. At what had become of me: trying to get to sleep so I could be released from my life. By now it sounded as though a high wind was whistling through my ear canals. It was all so horrible.

I scrambled off the chairs and flicked the lightswitch on. Fuck it. I was going home. I'd had enough of this. It was the worst day of my life. I didn't know whether I was going to die or not, but I wasn't staying here.

* * * *

I'd been sitting on the doormat since ten. On the bus home, I guessed that my dad would probably be back tonight. He knew that I'd be running out of money for food by now. If he didn't come back, I was in trouble. If he already had been back and had read the note, I was in *real* trouble. Christ, what a mess I'd made of everything.

After I'd been sitting there around half-an-hour, the lift arrived on the landing. My stomach swirled as I looked up but the man coming round the corner was a resident of the flat opposite ours. Although we didn't know his family, he asked me if I was okay.

After another half-an-hour, the sound of the lift door scraping open sounded again. My head rose. My dad was walking toward me. Slowly, I got up. He hadn't seen me yet: he was trying to find his front door key on his keyring. When he stopped to concentrate better and swayed slightly as he peered at his hands, I realised he was drunk. He resumed walking my way. He stopped, startled, when he saw me, saying "Oh!" Then he held out his keyring to me and said, "Find that bloody thing for us, willya?" The smell of beer rode out with his words. I gazed at him. I opened my mouth. I was waiting for him to say something about the note or to ask me what I was doing out on the landing. But he only affectionately swatted me on the side of the head. I closed my mouth and looked for the front door key. As I twisted the key in the lock, he was tiredly rubbing his face.

I turned on the hall light. My dad urgently moved me out of the way, stepping toward the toilet with a "Pissoir, gangway!"

I gazed after him. I closed the front door. I went down the hall to the living room. Each step I took pounded in my head. I felt so exhausted I wanted to stop, turn and go and throw myself onto my bed. With effort, I continued going the way I was. The envelope lay unopened on the living room table. I tried to put it in my pocket but it fell to the floor. I looked at it in dismay for a moment, cringing at the thought of the energy needed to bend over. I leaned forward with a hiss and picked it up.

My body groaning, I walked back down the hall. My dad was still in the toilet. Sitting on my bed, I could smell myself. I smelt of the river. I hissed as each shoe came off. My socks were wet. I peeled them off and let them drop. I ejected air again as I lifted myself to push my jeans down my legs. With a great surge of willpower, I took my anorak, jumper and shirt off in one go, pulling them over my head and dumping them inside out on the floor.

I thought about leaving the light on but my dad might come in if he saw it and then he might ask why I'd been out on the landing. Knowing it was the last effort of the day, I mustered - just - the energy to go over and switch it off.

Seven

I finally decided to face the world again. One evening, during the middle of 'O'-Level revising, I noticed my dad getting ready to go out. I asked him where he was going. He said over to aunt Anne's and uncle Reg's. I surprised him and myself by saying that I'd come as well.

Natalie and I were immediately self-conscious with each other all over again. She wore glasses now but it didn't make her seem less pretty to me. I was amazed that she still felt as awkward around me as I did around her. Since the last time I'd seen her, I'd realised girls found me repulsive. It seemed she just saw me as Paul, her cousin and one-time childhood boyfriend (sort of) and didn't judge me any other way.

Andrew was even more of a surprise. Although he was now at college, I assumed he'd be the same character he'd always been. But as soon as we met I noticed a change in him. He smiled and said "Alright?" to me with a simple friendliness I'd never seen in him before. A few years ago, there would have been a catch, such as that he was setting me up for a practical joke. He had matured. When we went up to his room, we had a long thoughtful discussion about music. Not once did he dismiss a record or act with a sneering "Buncha wankers". He was prepared to judge everybody on the quality of their records. In fact, he was prepared to do that more than I was.

He didn't mention that I now lived in a tower block or the fact of my mum walking out, and I got the feeling that it was because he had the sensitivity to realise he shouldn't.

He had a newer and bigger drum kit set up in his room. He told me he'd left the band he'd been in before and now played with a couple of kids from college. I asked him if they needed a guitarist. He thought for a moment and said "Actually, we might do. 'Mean, we're a three-piece, 'cos we thought 'The Jam 'ave only got three and they're brilliant'. But then we realised they do a lot of overdubs, The Jam, so you can't copy them exactly when you play one of their songs."

I nodded. "All these groups with one guitarist do overdubs. They record the rhythm guitar and then they overdub the lead stuff and the solos. If you listen to Who records, Pete Townshend used to do that an' all."

"You could be our rhythm guitarist if you like. 'Mean, I'll 'ave to ask the uvvers first."

* * * *

I was a bit apprehensive when I took my Strat and amp to the house where Andrew's band rehearsed. The members of the first band he'd been in had been totally unpleasant. But Aaron and Philip turned out to be alright. Aaron was the same age as Andrew. He had red hair and a face full of freckles. He played bass but had only been doing so for three months. Up until then they'd had two guitarists and no bassist because nobody had wanted to play bass. Philip was Aaron's brother. Apart from the fact that he was two years younger, he looked exactly like Aaron. The band rehearsed in their family's living room.

I could see the difference between this band and Andrew's first one as soon as the second rehearsal. The three of them told me they'd decided that as I was the best musician amongst them, I should play lead.

* * * *

I'd decided to take my 'O'-levels so I'd be able to get a job more easily when I left school. I didn't want anything to upset my plans to get plastic surgery.

I didn't need to be ugly all my life. You saw adverts in newspapers about plastic surgery. I'd be leaving school in a few months. If I got a job and saved up, I could look alright in... I didn't know... By next year maybe. I'd love to have a girlfriend. Someone to talk to and cuddle. I was sick of being lonely.

After taking my English 'O'-Level exam one morning, I was on my way to lunch when I heard my name called in the corridor. I turned to find Mr. Richards, my class teacher, walking toward me.

"Your father came in to see you today."

"My dad?" I said in surprise.

He nodded. "He's got a very urgent message for you," he said. Mr. Richards unfolded a small piece of paper and gave it to me. "He came in twice, in fact. He wants you to ring him at this number."

My nose crinkled as I looked at the paper. "He say what it was?"

"No. I knew you were taking exams so we didn't want to disturb you. Do you want to use the phone in the staff room?"

"Eh? Oh no, it's alright. I'm going home for lunch." We didn't have a phone at home but I didn't like the idea of ringing my dad in a room full of teachers.

I popped back to our block to get 10p for the phone call. I stepped out of the lift and reached in my pocket for my front door key as I walked down the landing. I looked up to find that I'd stopped before a front door with a board of wood nailed over it and a padlock strapped across the right-hand side. I turned, going back to the lift. I glanced at one of the doors I'd passed to give me some idea of which floor I was on. I stopped abruptly. The number on the door was the number of a flat on my floor. I swung back and strode toward the boarded door. My pace just as abruptly slackened in devastation.

On the ground floor, I tore out of the lift and raced to the nearest telephone box. I asked the operator to reverse the charges but there was no answer to the number Mr. Richards had given me. I didn't know whose number it was but I recognised the code as Putney. Maybe it was Jim, a friend of my dad's.

I went back to school and borrowed my fare to Putney off Mr. Richards. I sat the afternoon exam in a sort of sickened trance and then took a bus to Jim's place.

Jim answered the front door. "Paul," he said. "Well, well." He hadn't seen me for three years. "Alright? 'Ave you seen my old man today?"

"John? No."

I showed him the piece of paper. "D'you know what that number is?" He looked at it and shook his head. "Can I use your phone?"

"Yeah, sure. Come in."

I went into the living room, which was empty. I fell wearily into an armchair and picked up the telephone on the stand beside it.

Jim's wife, a ratbag called Rowena, entered. "'Ere, I 'ope you're gonna put the money down for that. Don't just plonk yourself down in the chair." She walked out again.

I held the telephone near my face, motionless, eyes closed. After a moment, I opened them and began dialling. A female voice at the other end answered. "Hello, King's Arms."

He was at work. I should have guessed. My dad was a barman at the King's now, his regular pub in Putney. After a few moments, he came on.

"Dad? It's Paul."

"Oh, 'allo. You've seen the flat?"

My voice was almost a groan: "Yeah."

"Where're you calling from?"

"Jim's."

"Yeah? You've told 'im about it, 'ave you?"

"No. I don't wanna, either."

My dad gave a hiss-laugh. "Okay. D'you wanna come to the pub? You're quite near now, aren't ya?"

"Yeah. What's gonna 'appen?"

"I'm gonna get in there, get our fings. I've got the tools."

When the call was over, I took the coins remaining in my pocket and slapped them on the stand beside the phone. It was too much for the time I'd been on it.

* * * *

My dad had recently bought a second-hand car, a hatchback. We strode grimly toward it when my dad had finished in the pub. He was carrying a plastic bag, which I assumed the 'tools' were in. We said nothing as we got inside and he reversed out of the parking space.

After we'd gone a couple of roads, I broke the silence. "Where we gonna stay?"

"Round Jim's would be the best place, I think."

"Unh - no. I ain't staying round there. Anyway, I don't mean that. I mean where we gonna live?"

"There's a bloke comes in the pub who's got a flat 'e rents. 'E's doing it up now - the last bloke just moved out. I'll ask 'im if we can 'ave it."

"Is it in Putney?"

"Yeah."

We said nothing for a while.

"Bastards," my dad eventually came out with. "I only went 'ome to get me glasses. I fort 'Oh no, I'm on the wrong floor'."

"So did I."

My dad put his teeth together and sighed heavily.

I said, "But we 'aven't paid the rent for longer than this before, 'ave we?"

"Yeah. Bastards."

* * * *

The padlock came away fairly easily, the nails being squeezed from the wood by the chisel my dad hammered at. He started on the screws that were keeping the board in place. He forced the chisel behind the board and pounded until the moving wood forced the screws to loosen. He loosened all the screws down the key-side of the door. He then pulled one side of the board away - like opening a birthday card - and the screws on the other side came out, groaning. While he was doing that, I put my key in the exposed lock and twisted.

"The door don't open!"

He was standing the now loose board against the landing wall. "They've probably changed the lock." He came and peered through the letterbox. "Unh. They've turned everything upside-down an' all."

"'Ave they?" I took a look. I could see into my bedroom. I hadn't left the door open this morning. Album covers were lying scattered on the carpet. "Oh no! My records." But even as I said it I was thinking, panic-stricken, about my guitars.

"Out the way."

I stepped back. My dad started on the lock, tapping the chisel at the tiny gap between frame and door.

"D'you reckon they'll 'ave taken anyfing?" My dad was preoccupied hammering the handle of the chisel. "Eh?" I said.

"Dunno."

He tried a shoulder charge. Then he resumed hammering. A few minutes later, a couple got out of the lift. They looked in the direction of the hammering noise on their way to their flat at the other end of the landing. I looked away from them, embarrassed. My dad, of course, wasn't. He tried another shoulder charge, and another one swiftly after that.

After another minute of hammering - the chisel bringing forth slivers of raw white wood from the varnished frame - plus more shoulder-charges, the door gave.

I went in first, hurrying to my bedroom. My guitars - the electric one my mum had bought me and my first, acoustic one that had been a present from my dad - stood untouched on their stands. Thank God. My piles of records, though, had been tipped over. I knelt and started picking up sleeves. As I did, I noticed that the drawers of my cabinet were half open. I stopped and looked round the room. The door of my wardrobe (which was upright these days: I'd started cleaning up the flat not long ago) was open, as were the drawers of my chest of drawers. "Jesus!" I looked up. My dad was manoeuvring the board through the front door into the flat. "They've been going through all my fings."

My dad leant the board against the hallway wall and came in. "They taken anyfing?"

"They ain't taken my guitars, thank Christ. I don't fink they've taken any of my records, eever." I stood up. "They've got no right to do this, 'ave they? They're just supposed to lock us out, ain't they?"

"Yeah, but they probably take a few fings for themselves." He turned and walked out.

I looked in the wardrobe and drawers. There didn't seem to be anything missing from there. Then I noticed that my digital watch - which I kept on my cabinet but didn't wear because its strap dug into my skin - was missing. I found my dad in his bedroom and told him about it. He didn't seem surprised. "They've taken my money box," he said, pointing to the dresser where he usually kept a tin he threw his coppers into. There would have been less than a pound in there. "Stupid," he commented.

I followed him to the living room. In there, it looked as though someone had decided to steal our television - a 14-inch portable - but then changed his mind: it was sitting on the floor near the door.

There was nothing missing in the living room. However, when my dad went to the hall cupboard, he found that the coin box had been ripped out of the electricity meter.

"We'll get the blame!" I said.

"I know."

"Report 'em!"

"I'm going to."

"God. The bastards."

We remained standing there; my dad gazing, hands on hips, at the wall, me gazing at his face, biting my lip.

"I've gotta get my guitars out of 'ere in case they come back." My dad nodded. "Where can I take 'em though?"

"Reg's? In fact, might be a good idea if you stay there 'til we get a place."

We left the board leaning against the inside of the door when we drove over to Reg's. I took my guitars, my record player and all my records with me. I put all my stuff in Andrew's room, which I would be sharing with him. Then we went back to

Battersea and took all the stuff we wanted from the flat. It wasn't a lot. My dad said there was no point taking any furniture as we would be moving into a furnished flat. We left with not much more than a bin-liner of clothes each.

* * * *

Natalie and I were alone in the house. Reg and Anne had gone out to the pictures, taking Paul, their four-year old son, with them. Andrew was doing some college work at a friend's. I was waiting for a programme called *Something Else* to start. The Clash were on it. They were currently my favourite band. They wrote about boredom, living in London and being working class. I felt they represented my experiences more than any other band I'd heard, apart from maybe The Jam. Their guitarist, Mick Jones, was my new hero. While I waited, I was sitting in an armchair playing The Who's *Love Ain't For Keeping*. It's straining bluesiness made Natalie - stretched out on the settee - turn her head.

"God," she said. "You're good, ain't ya?"

"Yeah."

She tutted. "Big 'ead." Then she said, "Bet you're not as good as this bloke. The one 'oo's coming on."

"Mick Jones? Nah, 'e's brilliant."

"Hah!" she said in triumph. "So what do you do wiv your band, you and Andrew?"

"Play."

"Yeah - what, though?"

"The Clash, The Who, everyone."

I got up, took a chair from the table and placed it a few feet from the television, then went back to the settee.

"Whaddya put that there for?" Natalie asked, as I'd known she would.

"To see Mickey-boy. 'E's on in a few minutes."

"God."

"One day I might be as good as 'im on guitar."

"You're really good," Natalie said sincerely. "Better than last time I 'eard ya. Mind you, that was years ago."

"You 'eard me play last night."

She tutted. "You know what I mean. You 'aven't 'ad anyfing to do wiv us for about... free years, 'ave ya?"

"'Ow d'ya mean?"

"Never came round. Your dad did. You didn't."

"I was busy," I joked.

"Oi, do you ever see your mum anymore?"

I shook my head.

"'Ave you never seen 'er since she left?"

Suddenly I wasn't able to make wisecracks. I concentrated on noodling.

"I feel really sorry for you." After a pause, Natalie said "My mate thought her mum and dad were gonna get a divorce once."

"My mum and dad ain't divorced though."

"I know, but I'm just saying."

To change the subject, I looked at the clock and said, "Oh - not time yet. For Mickey-boy."

"You really like 'im, don't ya?"

"Yep. 'E's my hero." As soon as I said it, I snorted, embarrassed.

"Does 'e sing the songs?"

"Some of 'em. 'E sings the ones 'e writes. 'E writes all the best ones." I didn't mention that the ones he wrote were the love songs, as I'd only feel more embarrassed.

"It's time now nearly, innit?"

I looked at the clock. I stood my guitar against my armchair, got up and changed the channel on the television. I took my place on the dining-table chair. The end-credits of the previous programme were rolling.

Natalie made a sound as though she was stretching. She came and sat on the carpet beside my chair. "What does 'e look like, this Mickey, or whatever 'is name is?"

"Er... goofy teef, 'e's got."

"Unh. 'E don't *sound* good."

"It don't matter what 'e looks like, does it? It's 'is guitar-playing and song writing."

The programme started. *Something Else* was doing a retrospective, showing one performance each of the many bands who had guested on the programme in the past. The programme lasted an hour-and-a-half. Forty-five minutes into it, The Clash still hadn't appeared.

"Jesus Christ," I said. "We're gonna be waiting all night."

"They should say what time they come on."

The band on screen finished their number. "They better be next," I said. "Uvverwise I'll smash the telly up."

The presenter introduced the next band. It wasn't The Clash.

"Oh fu-u-uckin 'ell."

"Go on then. Smash the telly up."

"I *will* do in a minute."

With a bored sigh, Natalie leaned her head momentarily against the side of my chair. When she took it away, I found myself reaching for it, gently pulling it back.

I patted my thigh. "Put your head there," I suggested.

She did so, resting her cheek against my jeans. I ploughed my hand through her thick long hair. After several seconds, simply for something to say, I asked "How often do you wash your 'air?"

She kept her cheek on my thigh. "'Bout... Twice a week."

"Does it take a long time to dry?"

"Ten minutes."

"No, I mean without a dryer."

"Oh. About half a day."

"Thought so." I continued gently ploughing with my fingers. I lifted some strands and dipped my head to run my nose along them. "Mmm. Smells nice," I said, although they only smelt of hair. I resumed ploughing. After a while, I let my hand go down and rest on the back of her neck. I clasped it softly.

"Ahh!" Natalie issued from below.

Thinking she was enjoying it, I moved my thumb and fingers backwards and forwards.

"Agh!" Natalie hunched, grimacing. "You're giving me the shivers!"

"Oh!" I stopped, grinning. "Sorry." I moved my hand from her neck and started stroking her hair. "Is that alright?"

"Yeah." She put her face back on my leg.

I gazed at her crown. "Oi, what colour knickers 'ave you got on?"

Natalie didn't reply at first. She took her head away and leaned back, palms on the carpet supporting her. She gazed at me for a couple of moments. I smiled at her.

"I'll show ya," she said. She hitched her skirt up to her hip, twisted her hand inside and pulled out a piece of stretched, pale material. "Those ones."

In the dark, I couldn't even tell what colour they were but I said, "Ohh."

Natalie let the material snap back and pulled her skirt down. She leaned on her palms and watched the screen.

"What time d'you reckon Andrew'll get back?" I asked.

She shrugged. "Ages probably."

"D'ya reckon we got time for a quick one?"

Embarrassed, Natalie made a sound of amusement. I found myself making the same sound. We both looked at the television. I wasn't upset by her reaction: I hadn't been serious. I wouldn't have known how to react if she'd said yes. We watched in silence until The Clash came on shortly afterwards. They performed *Tommy Gun*.

"'Is teef aren't *that* goofy," Natalie said.

* * * *

Three days later, my dad and I moved into our new flat. It was the top floor of a house just round the corner from the King's Arms. Although I'd got used to living in Battersea, it felt so great to be back in peaceful, clean Putney once more.

Very soon, the evening spent alone with Natalie began to seem almost like a dream. We never spoke about it to each other and once I'd moved out there was never an opportunity to re-create the intimacy of that day. But it had given me a tantalising glimpse of the life I could have. I could regularly feel just as confident as I had that night as soon as I had plastic surgery. I would be able to flirt with other girls, ones who weren't just letting me do it because we were cousins and used to be boyfriend and girlfriend when we were little kids.

I left school with six 'O'-levels, including grade A in both music and English. I got a job as a porter in a hotel in Kensington. Out of my £75 wages, £15 went to my dad for housekeeping, £15 was spent on food (the hotel provided free meals) and £5 went on guitar strings. If there was a new record out that I really wanted, I would buy it, but that was rare. The great thing about being in a band was that I was surrounded by people as obsessive and knowledgeable about music as me: anything I wanted to hear, I could almost always be sure one of the others had a copy I could tape or borrow. So about half my money was being put in my post office account each and every week, ready for the day when I'd be able to metamorphosise myself.

Eight

"Where *you* been?"

Aaron was looking at me accusingly as I followed Philip - who had opened the front door for me - into their living room. "We're finished."

"I just got back." I put my amp down and swung my guitar off my shoulder. I saw then that Andrew had already started dismantling his kit. "Ah, you're not packing up are ya?"

"*Yeah*," Aaron said. "We've *done* our rehearsing. You were supposed to be 'ere an hour ago."

I tutted. "I couldn't, could I."

Aaron and Philip were sitting on the settee watching children's television programmes. I was relieved to see Aaron had his bass across his lap. I took my guitar out of its case. I plugged the lead into the amp. Even as I was doing it, Andrew was packing his drums in their cases. He walked across to join the others on the settee. Discordant clanging drowned out the television as I tuned up.

"Shut up, Paul!" Aaron complained.

I ran my penny down the strings again and adjusted a machine head. I turned to the others. "Come on then." No-one moved or even looked at me. I peeled off the riff of *I Feel Fine*. I stopped and looked at them again.

"I fort you finished at 'alf-four, Paul?" Andrew said.

"Yeah, but it takes an hour to get back 'ere, nearly. I 'adn't realised that."

Philip nodded at the screen. "They've all changed, ain't they, these kids." They were watching *Grange Hill*, whose original cast were visibly turning from children into adults.

"I know," Aaron said.

I took my guitar over and sat on the settee's arm-rest. I watched with them for a while. I started playing *Honky Tonk Women*. I was heartened when Aaron joined in. Philip stood up, went over to his guitar and started playing too. Philip and I launched together into the song's solo. We grinned as we each tried to finish it before the other. Philip exclaimed in agony as he hit a bum note and fell behind. Meanwhile, Andrew was shouting at us to stop because he couldn't hear the programme. When we'd finished, Andrew stood up, saying, "Oh, I might as well get me drums out again." He added "You've gotta 'elp me though, Paul. *You* were late."

We had a 90-minute session, playing Who and Black Sabbath numbers, plus a couple of our own songs. I wrote the melodies. Aaron and Andrew wrote the words, which were basically just I-love-you-baby mantras. Phil sang them into the second-hand Shure mic his dad had bought him. He had to lean over as he sang because the stand he'd got, also second-hand, didn't have adjustable height.

I'd learned so much about music from being in a band, especially when it came to arranging. Songwriting I found easy. I took the simple route, settling on a chord and moving my little and index fingers around. The variety of tunes that resulted was far wider than I would have imagined. Although I was the only one in the band who could do this, it wasn't until I'd met a lot more musicians that I learned that this ability was unusual. There were so many good guitarists but not many of them were able to translate playing guitar to creating melodies. For me, they just went hand-in-hand. Arranging, I found a little more difficult. You had to think a little more, endlessly deliberating on shading and tempo. I had a pattern, beginning songs with an instrumental version of the middle-eight and introducing a new sound in every verse to avoid repetition: some guitar triplets, Andrew's ride cymbal, whatever. Yet you couldn't follow that pattern all the time because that itself would be repetitious. Such balancing acts were hard work but I was loving the education involved.

An hour-and-a-half later, Andrew packed up his drums for the second time and we went into the kitchen for tea and toast.

"Christ, I'm knackered," I said. "Fucking job. When you take it, you fink 'Oh, it's eight-thirty 'til four-thirty, that's alright'. But it's not, 'cos you 'ave to get ready, get there, so you 'ave to get up at half-seven. And then it's three quarters of an hour, an hour, getting back. So it's like seven to five-fifteen, five-thirty."

"Shoulda stayed at school," Aaron said. "Then you'd get 'ere by four. Give you much more time to practice."

"You're stupid," I said. "What you gonna use a degree for? Go to a record company and say 'Will you give me a record contract - I've got a degree in Maths'?"

"Well next year I'll 'ave loads more time to rehearse, 'cos you don't do as much work at University. And I get my grant."

"That's nuffin, the grant."

"Yeah, but it's for doing nuffin, innit? *You* 'ave to work to get your money."

Of course, I couldn't tell him that my wages were vital to ensure I lived a normal life one day. So I said "It's boring, being at school," which was also true as far as I was concerned.

"Not at college, it's not. It's more relaxed. You're treated better. Oi, I tell you why I stayed on? Even though I wanted to be a rock and roll star. 'Cos of this fing I read in this Paul McCartney interview. 'E goes that 'is mate was at university or college or whatever and 'e fort 'God, six years to decide what to do wiv my life'. Y'know - get your grant money, only 'ave to do a bit of work, loads of time to practice. And I fort 'Yeah, that's what I'm gonna do mate'."

I looked thoughtfully at the rim of my mug. "I coulda stayed on, y'know."

"I know," Aaron said. "You're brainier than me. Why don't ya?"

I thought of the newspaper clippings beneath my mattress advertising cosmetic surgery. I grimaced, shaking my head. "Anyway, I've done it now."

* * * *

I'd been warned about leaving too much water on the floor. I pressed down on the mop, twisting its head in the squeeze-hole of the bucket. I stepped back and lifted it. The steaming head - moulded into the shape of the hole - still dripped. I put it back in, grimacing now as I leaned on it. There was a sudden crack and I plunged forward, kicking the bucket involuntary and slopping water onto the corridor floor. I regained myself and gazed at the broken mop-handle in my hands.

"Oh for God's sake, Paul".

I turned to find Gerry, a senior porter, walking toward me.

"Haven't you got any common sense?" Gerry took the two parts out of my hands and examined them. He tutted. He spoke his next words in a weary tone. "Go into the kitchen and ask if you can borrow one of theirs."

I felt my hackles rise, the impulse coming to snap a reply at him. My mouth only twitched.

A couple of hours later, I was mopping the fire exit stairs. The hotel I worked in was a four-star one and even the fire exit stairs had to be washed every day. The heat created by the radiators in the stairwell was intense. As usual, I was sweating freely by the time I was halfway through. I took my porter's jacket off, put it on a window-sill and continued mopping bare-chested.

On the next landing, I heard footsteps coming down the flights I'd just mopped. It was Rita, one of the housekeepers. As she passed me, she didn't apologise for treading on the wet stairs. Instead, she said, "You'll have to put your jacket on. Guests come down here."

"Oh. Right." It wasn't true. The guests used the lifts and the main stairwell. I retrieved my jacket.

When she was gone, I dipped the mop-head into the water again. In anger, I thrust down hard in the squeeze-hole. The mop snapped in two.

"Oh *no!*" My wailing voice echoed in the stairwell. I shut up, afraid of being heard. I closed my eyes and bit my lip in anguish. I was close to tears at the thought of having to go and tell Gerry I'd broken my second mop of the day.

* * * *

Later that week, I met the linen porter for the first time. His name was Garcia and he was just back after illness. I was rehearsing what to say to him as I approached the linen room. I had become very shy and withdrawn since my mum had left and it was hard for me to introduce myself to people. In the linen room, I found a short, bald man in his fifties.

"Oh, 'allo. Are you Garcia? I'm Paul. New porter. I started about six weeks ago."

Garcia nodded but said nothing. I changed into my uniform and went to the canteen to make a coffee. I went back into the linen room briefly to place my cup on a shelf before going to clock on. I usually drank my morning coffee in the linen room while sorting out the towels I needed to take to the floor's laundry cupboards. When I came back, Garcia stopped sorting through the laundry.

"This your coffee?" His accent was Italian.

"Yeah."

"Drink in the canteen."

"Eh? Why?"

"Drink in the canteen, not here."

"Why though?"

"This my shop, hokay? You drink your coffee in the canteen." Garcia made a dismissive gesture. "Go on. Go."

I tutted. "Your shop. Fink you *own* it."

"I do own it."

"No you don't."

"No argue with me!"

I tutted again. "You cunt."

"You say that to me outside."

I sighed. Silently, I got my cup.

Garcia's pathetic self-importance was not unusual. When I'd left school, I'd assumed I'd be treated like an adult. Yet every day something would happen at work that made me feel like an infant. It amazed me how seriously people in the hotel took their jobs. As though serving drinks or cleaning rooms or inspecting the toilets was important work, rather than just something you had to do to get your wages. It also amazed me that people had lives where they didn't do what I did: work in the day and go home in the evening to spend time on something of true significance, in my case my band. Then the penny dropped that the two things were connected: whereas I could console myself with the fact that one day I wouldn't have to take orders because I'd be making a living from music, the people I worked with would be stuck doing what they were doing their entire lives. That was why they were so petty: they had to invest importance in their pathetic, humdrum tasks because they had nothing else.

* * * *

Rita and her fellow housekeeper Maria came onto the fifth floor to check a room. I was on my knees polishing the box-ashtray outside the lifts. Rita made to walk past, then stopped and asked me "Have you done that?" pointing to the long narrow mirror set in the wall between the lifts.

"No, I don't do those."

"Yes you do!" she exclaimed. "These have got to be polished every day."

"No, I mean Gerry does those."

"Gerry? Oh that's..."

"Ridiculous," Maria finished off for her.

"Yeah, well I don't make the list of who does what. Gerry does."

"Well..." Rita looked at the wall momentarily, groping for a way out. "Well, we expect people to help out in this hotel."

"I do my job."

"Everyone in the hotel has got to help out! I have to do it, everyone has to do it."

I grimaced in bewilderment. "What're you talking about? Gerry gave me a list of the fings I 'ave to do-"

"Yes - so? I have a list but I don't always stick to it. If I see something wrong, I fix it. I was helping Garcia in the linen room today. It's not my job but I was helping him."

I was shaking my head. "This is... I mean, what're you..." There was a moment of silence. "Rita, you're picking on me."

Rita gasped. "I-am-not-picking-on-you!" she managed to issue in stages.

"Rita, you are."

"Don't be ridiculous. All I said was for you to polish the mirrors."

"It's not my job!"

"I didn't say it was. All I'm saying is that the staff of this hotel should be prepared to help out."

"Help out in what?" I shook my head. "This is..." I shook my head again.

"What do you mean 'Help out in what'? Help out in-"

"Ah, fuck it, bollocks!" I stopped her. "I'm leaving." I turned my attention back to the ashtray. "This is my last week."

Rita was silent and motionless for a moment. She said, "Right," softly and walked away, Maria following.

* * * *

I toyed with the idea of getting another job for a while but I decided against it. I might be ugly, but I wasn't doing too badly in life. I had good mates in the shape of the band, I felt fulfilled through the education involved in playing in a group, plus my guitar-playing was getting better and better. I could wait a couple of years. In fact, by the time I'd gone through two years of college, the band would have improved so much that we'd probably have a record contract by then, from which would come the money for my surgery.

Nine

I awoke at the sound of my dad going down the stairs on his way to work. I lay drowsily in bed for a few minutes, before throwing back the covers and going over to switch the light and the radiator on.

My room was a nice one. It had been freshly decorated just before we moved in. The paper on the wall still smelled of the factory, as did the carpet. The flat was really for one, but my dad was quite happy with his bed in the living room. He was also quite happy at the time he now saved. The King's Arms was literally a minute away.

I had breakfast, then visited the bathroom. While on the toilet, I played my Yamaha. It was good to get ordinary practice in on the guitar because during rehearsals you were concentrating on here-and-now practical contributions rather than technique. Then I sat down in my room for some studying. I was doing a dissertation for my politics course on whether Eastern bloc countries could be described as socialist in the Marxist sense. I'd only taken politics because I couldn't think what else to have as my second course in addition to English Lit, my honours subject. For the first few weeks, I'd found it fairly interesting as I'd previously been so oblivious to politics I only had a vague idea what the difference between the Tories and Labour was. Now that I'd learned the basics, however, I was bored out of my mind.

It didn't matter that much, of course, because I was only at university to save me having to work for a living, not to get a degree, but I still had to make the pretence of effort. Which meant having to wade through *The Manifesto Of The Communist Party.* I could hardly make sense of it, even though every point in it was hammered home three different ways. First, the point would be made, then it would be further explained with a preface of "Or, in other words..." then summarised with an "in a nutshell," and I still didn't get it. The withering away of the state? Faaack off!

* * * *

Walking through the main entrance of the university, I heard a voice call my name. I turned and, seeing Aaron, made to move toward him. I stopped abruptly. Aaron was standing talking to a female of about his age. I caught a glimpse of her gazing eyes - turned toward me upon Aaron's shout - before flashing my face away and turning back round. I tried to nod to Aaron as I turned, but it came out like an involuntary spasm.

My face was screwed up in a wince as I walked toward the stairs. Pri-i-ick! Jesus Christ, you fucking big ugly wanker! You look a total idiot. *She* staring at, anyway?

My English Lit tutor had asked to see me. He was a round-faced, grey-haired man in his forties named Mr. Bond and I liked him a lot. When I first attended one of his lectures, I was surprised at his voice. He had a London accent just like mine. I would never have believed that someone with such obvious working class origins could have such a "respectable", high-powered job. (This was in the days before television shows had working class hosts: the London accent was widely perceived as gormless back then.) Of course, he wasn't totally common. His speech was grammatically correct, containing no double-negatives, dropped aitches or glottal stops. He was a friendly, approachable teacher and knew a lot about rock music, at least up to the mid-'Seventies. I admired him so much that I had started to speak like him. That is I began to talk English as I wrote it in my essays rather than how everyone around me when I was growing had spoken it. When I did drop an aitch these days or came out with an "ain't" I felt embarrassed.

"How's your dissertation coming along?" he asked me when I was seated in one of the comfortable armchairs in his study. I paused. I nodded. "Alright." I was writing about working class novelists, basically because I felt they were the equivalent of The Jam and The Clash - chroniclers of the lives of the underdogs. I wasn't into party politics but it was interesting to see my formative culture reflected in the media.

"You should be about halfway through by now."

"Well..." I'd hardly started it.

"Your heart's not in it, is it?"

I opened my mouth, but I couldn't find anything to say.

"And it's not because you don't have the ability. You contribute well to discussions. You just don't put the effort into written work. Your other tutors have told me the same thing."

We were on such friendly terms that I thought of telling him the truth, that I wasn't at university for an education. I kept it to myself. "I'll... try a bit harder," I said.

* * * *

'BLONDE MODEL - PLEASE WALK UP.'

I gazed at the sign, written in felt-tip, pinned to the frame of an open doorway in Old Compton Street. I'd passed it already but had had to work up the nerve to come back to it. I stepped into the doorway. Inside, there were flights of narrow, uncarpeted stairs. At regular intervals there were notices hand-written directly onto the walls saying 'PLEASE DO NOT GIVE MONEY TO ANYONE ON THE STAIRS' and 'MODEL - TOP FLOOR'. By now my heart was thudding and there was an almost nauseous weightless sensation in my chest.

When I turned round what I thought was the last banister, it was to find one more short flight before me and that, for some reason, made my heart beat even harder. I tried taking deep breaths to calm myself as I hauled my body toward a door that had a mirror-panel at head height and a sign reading "MODEL". I stood before it for a couple of seconds before knocking.

There were sounds of movement beyond the door and a short pause before it was opened on a door chain. To my dismay, a woman in her fifties wearing glasses appeared. I wasn't going to do it with her. I'd just ask the price, then go, pretending it was too much.

"Hello, love."

"How much is it?"

"It's twelve pounds with a rubber, fourteen without. She's busy at the moment though, love."

Oh - it wasn't her, then. Thank God for that.

"Oh - right. How much? Twelve for-"

"Twelve with a rubber-"

By rubber, I thought she meant rubber clothes. I couldn't work out why the kinky stuff cost less than normal. "No, I don't want any rubber or anything. Just... straight."

"Well that's fourteen - without."

"And that's it - no extra charges?"

"Well, you've gotta give me my maid's tip."

"How much is that?"

"A pound."

"And no extra charges other than that?"

She shook her head. "No extra charges other than that."

"And how long do I get for that? Half an hour?"

"Half an hour?" The woman rasped a sound of amusement. "No, for that you'll get about ten minutes, love."

I hesitated. I reached in my jeans for the money.

* * * *

Losing my virginity was a milestone but I felt depressed the entire day, and the next day as well. The thought of what the band would say if they knew made me feel a wretch but what depressed me most was the fact that that was the only way I was going to experience intimacy for the rest of my life.

I'd abandoned the idea of plastic surgery. Well, how could I do it? I'd only recently thought about the fact that if I had surgery to improve my looks, I was going to be snickered at by people who knew me. I'd be the laughing stock of the university and of my family. Of course, I could always go away and start a new life once I'd done it, but that would mean leaving the band. We were getting good. I didn't want to throw away my chance of becoming a star. It was no good being reasonable-looking if I was going to be working class my whole life. If I didn't become a professional musician, I'd be surrounded by people like Garcia 'til the day I was dead. I had to forget all about surgery, even though it meant I was trapped in my ugliness.

The melancholy that thinking that brought on was so awful it made my guts churn. I couldn't ever have in my life what just about everybody else took for granted: being unselfconscious when walking into a room, being able to chat casually with a female, being able to hear laughter without assuming it was aimed at me. Usually, I would blot out the melancholy by practicing on my guitar or by listening to records or else just fantasising about being good-looking and able to have girls fall in love with me.

The day after I'd visited the prostitute, none of those worked. I just didn't want to think. If I'd been a drinker, I suppose I would have just gone out and got smashed. Then I remembered the one thing I'd experienced that could provide the kind of oblivion I needed.

I had followed Andrew and Aaron to London University after going back and taking my 'A'-levels. It was so local that we all still lived at home. During my first week, I'd met a bloke called Derek who was also a guitarist, although he only did it as a hobby. Derek had given me a taste of a joint when we'd been discussing the top ten bits of feedback in the history of rock and roll. (Number one *I Feel Fine* by the Beatles he said, though I reckoned it was the end of *Anarchy In The U.K.*) I'd enjoyed the tingling lethargy it had produced and had also felt cool to have tried grass but I hadn't repeated the experience.

Today, I went round to Derek's digs. When I got there, he seemed amused that I was coming to him for drugs. I felt like a kid at school who was trying to look tough by asking someone for a cigarette. Still, it was just another humiliation that smoking would be able to blot out.

Ten

After more than two years together, we were finally playing our first proper gig. My uncle Reg - Andrew's dad - was driving us to the venue in his van. Andrew was packing his drum-kit in the back as I arrived at their house with my own equipment. A couple of nights before, he'd painted the words "THE RAGAMUFFINS" onto the front of his bass drum. He'd used an ordinary house-painting brush and the slapdash, uneven effect actually seemed appropriate for the name.

"The Ragamuffins" had come from Aaron. We'd often talked about what to call ourselves over the previous couple of years but had never decided on anything. With the first occasion of playing before an audience impending, we'd finally had to make a choice. I liked the name. It sounded like a name from the 'Sixties, back when groups were always "The" something. I climbed in the back of the van and put my amp and guitar in there.

We were one of three acts on at our university that night. None of us were top of the bill. We were all unknowns. I'd never heard the other two groups but felt confident we had nothing to be scared of. I'd now seen six or seven of the university gigs and hadn't seen a single band that was better than us. In fact, they all reminded me of the way we had played about a year ago: they were technically competent but there was always something slightly naïve about them. Although most of the bands were roughly the same age as us, none of them had put in the work we had - rehearsing almost every night for more than two years straight - so lacked a certain slickness. It had come as a bit of a shock when I first realised their unfocused melodies and pedestrian musicianship were the faults we'd had ourselves until fairly recently. This was because within a few months of our band starting, we'd all been over the moon at how good we were. Remarking on how unrecognisable we were after three months or so from the way we'd played together in the beginning, Andrew had said, "It's like a body builder - you build your muscles up every day and you end up like Charles Atlas." It had become a joke - we often referred to rehearsing as body-building. Now we all knew we had actually been awful then. It was a bit disconcerting. As Phil had said "'Ow do we know we're good *now*? We'll probably turn round in a few months and go 'Oh, remember 'ow crap we were then?'"

The two groups we were on the bill with were called Grind and The Slammers. We stood around looking at each other sort of warily as the caretaker explained to us we'd all be sharing the sound system, which consisted of two giant PA speakers either side of the stage and five monitors so we could hear if we were out of tune or off the beat. We tossed coins to decide the order of appearance, everyone naturally wanting to go on last. I thought it was ridiculous that Grind wanted to climax the show. They were a synth trio. They would finish the show with a damp squib. As it turned out, they had to go on first. We were on second.

While Grind were doing their sound check, I asked Andrew to watch my guitar for me and went off to the toilets. Hearing the caretaker explain the sound system to us had really made it hit home that in less than an hour we were going to be on stage playing to a crowd. My stomach was doing handstands. I had to have a smoke. I'd have asked Andrew to join me but I only had two joints to last me the rest of the week.

When I came back to the performance hall after finishing half a joint, the Ragamuffins were setting up for the sound check. Although the doors weren't open yet, there were some people standing watching on the large wooden floor of the venue. Like us, the other groups had brought along friends and family. I didn't feel nervous as they watched while we went through a couple of cover versions to get our levels right, a marijuana mellowness having descended on me. The sound check, though, was a bit of an eye-opener. It started with the EQ-ing, during which the mixing desk op found out which frequencies in the hall caused feedback. The op then had to take notes about what we each wanted to hear on our monitors. None of us had a clue, of course. He explained to me that a lead guitarist needed the bass drum plus a bit of bass and a bit of vocals in his monitor. (I didn't need any rhythm guitar because Phil was going to be on the same side of the stage as me.) It was quite a weird feeling to realise that we were so dependent on someone else: we might play really well but if the levels and everything weren't gotten right by the mixing desk then we could sound like crap.

Nevertheless, as we performed *Long Tall Sally* and *Blitzkrieg Bop*, I was pleased at our noisiness. It had always seemed to me when watching other bands here that the PA was too loud, but it was a thrill to hear ourselves blasting from the man-high speakers. We sounded larger-than-life. It somehow seemed like proof we were a real band. For the first time today, I felt excited.

By the time Grind were due to go on there were about sixty people in the audience, most of them drinking from plastic beakers. The other two groups stood in the wings watching as they played. Grind were as useless as I thought they'd be. I hated, and still hate, synthesiser acts. Not only can I not stand the antiseptic, robotic feel of their music, but also I can't stand people who aren't real musicians being up on a stage. The group were like Depeche Mode, playing flat, mordant songs that all sounded the same. It irritated me when their singer gushed "Thankyew!" as the audience applauded after each number, as though the audience weren't just being polite.

Although watching their set seemed interminable to me, when the singer said to the audience, "Thank you - goodnight" and they started walking in our direction, it suddenly seemed as though it had been very short. Surely we couldn't be on yet?

"You doing an encore?" Andrew asked the singer as he went by.

The ripple of applause following the group hardly called for one, but I immediately hoped they would. Anything to put off starting our set. Now the performance was getting closer, the grass wasn't proving so calming after all.

The singer stopped and looked back at the stage, as though considering. But then he grimaced and said, "Nah, ain't got no more songs."

We were on. I walked to my position, to the right of the centrally placed microphone stand, not looking at the audience as I did. Aaron stood on the left. Phil was shorter than Grind's singer, so had to ease the mic a couple of inches down the stand. He had been elected singer despite a fairly reedy, if expressive, voice because he was the only one who wanted the job. The confidence he had shown when putting himself forward was nowhere to be seen now: his face was white. He said nothing to the audience as our instruments burped the brief sounds that was us each making sure we were in tune. We stood around awkwardly, looking at each other before we realised we were all ready. Phil looked at Andrew. Andrew tapped four times on his drumsticks and we launched into *I Want What's Over There*, a number whose 5th chords gave it the kind of powerful sound appropriate for an opener. I'd only written it a few weeks before and Aaron and Andrew had added a Jam-style protest lyric to it within the last week. Not that I could hear much. Apart from the fragmentary effect from my monitor set-up, the only sound I could hear of the entire group was the bass throb of the venue - another thing about playing live that I'd never realised before. I was too busy trying to play everything correctly to be able to dwell on it. When we'd finished, I felt disappointed at the sound but we got a fairly good round of applause so the audience must have liked it. As agreed beforehand, we didn't pause before starting the second song, *Of All The Things I've Done*, a tune I'd written in A minor and E minor - with an E major/A major bridge in double-time - to make it sound like early Beatles. The lyric - in which a man tells his girlfriend nothing that had happened so far in his life compares to meeting her - was lovely and I'd been amazed that Aaron and Andrew could write anything so tender. Again, we played okay -

no mistakes - but how strange it was to be effectively shooting in the dark.

The gig didn't go badly at all. We played for about fifty minutes, mostly our own songs plus a few offbeat cover versions. We hated note-for-note copies of songs and covers of hoary old chestnuts so we only did versions of obscure songs or songs we thought we could improve.

I was motionless the whole time, standing back and concentrating on my fingerboard. Aaron and Phil, though, seemed to think the audience should have something to look at and strutted around in circles as they played. The audience got gradually bigger as the set progressed and after we'd been on stage half-an-hour the place was nearly full. I noticed that the crowd seemed progressively more enthusiastic after each song. I realised this was because they were gradually getting drunker but I still felt enthused by their reaction. After all, no matter how drunk they were, if we were crap they'd boo.

The strongest impression the gig made on me was the fact of how good a drummer Andrew was. He was the only one of us who didn't make a mistake the entire set. While myself, Aaron and Phil were occasionally hitting bum notes and missing our cues, he was thumping and flailing behind us totally consistently. The noise of his drums was amazingly powerful. Just like the Mitch Mitchell fan he was, he always acted like the drums were the lead instrument and created an amazing span of sound with his patterns. Lately I'd been thinking that we were lucky to have a good drummer because I'd just started noticing how few there were around these days. Turning on the radio, it was striking how many records were ruined by drummers just banging away monotonously on the snare. All the skill had gone out of the art. What made it worse was the way producers mixed the drums high and put a ton of echo on them. If I listened to the *Let's Dance* album by David Bowie, for instance, I literally got a headache.

We finished our last song, *Don't Let Them Grind You Down* - another Jam/Clash-style number - and Phil awkwardly said "Cheers, g'night". Handclaps started rippling through the hall and as we walked toward the wings they ballooned into an impressive loudness, accompanied by some mild whoops and a couple of whistles. The four of us gathered together, beaming and sheened with sweat. Natalie, Reg and a couple of Phil's mates were suddenly around us, smiling and patting our backs.

"Better than the Rolling Stones!" Reg said kindly.

Eleven

'At a time when promoters are reverting to their age-old habit of perceiving the punters as fools whose money it is their duty to part them from, it is hugely refreshing to see the Aloha staying true to the spirit of its punk roots with bills constituting quite staggering value for money. We were not only treated to another immaculate performance by the Malcontents (am I the first to notice, incidentally, that the target sticker on Gavin's guitar is one whose type could formerly be seen quite prominently displayed on Paul Weller's Rickenbacker? Another example of the Mal's notorious plagiarism?) but were also privileged to witness a set by one of the seemingly countless excellent young-gun ensembles scraping a living around London.

'The Ragamuffins come on as strong as the Sex Pistols but also insist on their right to unburden themselves in as sweet a manner as Paul Simon. Their buzz-saw riffs are the stuff of which the air-puncher's dreams are made but as likely as not to be swiftly followed by a declaration of loyalty to a lover. The only exception is the apparently obligatory slice of misogyny - entitled 'Shove Your Lies' - and, significantly, this has the most lumpen of their melodies. 'Golden Days' - an all-acoustic affair - is a quite ridiculously affecting look back at childhood, evoking memories of joy at the prospect of the home-time bell, cheese-on-toast for tea and scoring the most goals in a kick-about with yer mates. Most of their songs are political in a non-political way: Thin Lizzy licks and don't-underestimate-me lyrics - the vague, leather-jacketed anti-authoritarianism that has been the stock-in-trade of every really great band from the Stones onward. One of them is even called - yes - 'Don't Let Them Grind You Down'.

'Now that Strummer has played his bum hand with the ghastly 'Cut The Crap' and Mick Jones is preoccupied writing glorified jingles on his beat-box, the road is open for another bunch of seething white trash to become the band The Clash once were. My money is on The Ragamuffins.'

It wasn't bad for a first write-up.

The review had appeared in the Live section of the *NME* four months ago. I carried it around with me in the plastic pocket on the inside of my study binder. I also had four more copies at home. I must have read it eighty or ninety times since the day it had been published, which I could quite confidently say had been the happiest day of my life.

Ten months since our first gig at university, we'd finally been noticed by the music press. And with a vengeance. Support acts usually got barely a mention, let alone dominated the article. I'd used to fantasise about the band getting such a review, used to daydream about a critic enthusing over my playing (those buzz-saw riffs he referred to, although played by Phil, were mine, and even *Golden Days* was one of my rare lyrics) and comparing us to a great band like The Clash.

Everything had changed overnight. We were going places. We'd got our foot in the door. We'd known we were good, but having a review like that made it official. It became easier to get gigs now that we could show that review to venues. After that, we rapidly began climbing from fourth on the bill to third to second and now we were headliners most of the time. It didn't mean that much more money as we'd used to use the headliner's PA system but were now having to spend money hiring PA gear. However, we were making a name for ourselves. We could also send the review into record companies when we'd saved up enough to make a demo. In fact, it was possible record companies could send A&R men to one of our gigs because of the review.

Going to rehearsals made me glow with happiness now. The atmosphere amongst us was fantastic. We were all so optimistic. We were going to make it. Yet we worked even harder than before. If we had a problem or a disagreement with a song, we were much less likely to start bickering. We were willing to graft at something until it was right and everything almost always ended in smiles.

* * * *

As Aaron returned from the lavatories, the enormous hubbub of the two hundred people packed into the White Horse came into the dressing room with him. The large room, which both bands on tonight's bill were sharing, was almost directly behind the stage. The dressing room's lino-ed floorspace was almost twice as big as that of the stage. There were a few empty chairs scattered around in the room, a grimy sink with a clouded mirror over it and, at the far end, cartons of cigarettes stored in a locked cage. Aaron closed the door and the hubbub was muffled again.

He came over to the table at which Andrew, Andrew's girlfriend Monica, Philip and myself were sitting. Instead of sitting down, Aaron stood over us and asked "'Oo's Chris Smallwood?"

I was feeling relaxed because of the joint I'd smoked earlier. "Give up," I said.

Aaron looked at Andrew. "'Ave you 'eard of 'im?"

Lips stuck out, Andrew shook his head. "Why?"

"Tony just told me this bloke out there is an agent for bands. Reckons 'e can get us better gigs and that." Tony was one of the pub's barmen.

"What - 'e's out in the bar?"

"Yeah."

We all considered the fact silently. Then Aaron said, "Shall we go and talk to 'im?"

"An agent?" Phil said. "An agent takes a cut of the fee."

"Yeah", Monica said. "You need all the money you can get for your demo tape."

"Yeah, but he can get us more gigs. For better money."

We sat and discussed it for a while. After a few minutes, Aaron decided to go out and show this bloke our *NME* review. The rest of us treated it as a laugh, dreading to imagine the reaction of this big-time agent to a manic ginger-nut ordering him to pay close attention to the next act.

We went out to do our set, which involved having to walk through the audience - the dressing room was at the back of the venue - and then stepping up onto the stage, which was constructed out of upturned beer crates with wood panels laid over the top. We then kept Chris Smallwood, and everyone else, waiting for five or six minutes while Andrew made sure his drums were miked up properly. He was such a good drummer that he was entitled to his perfectionism but a few of the crowd down at the front of the stage were getting restless.

"Come on drummer!" a bloke in a leather jacket shouted.

Phil's voice suddenly boomed like that of God around the pub: "*Yeah, come on drummer*".

The comment, hugely amplified by the microphone he had spoken into point-blank, actually made me jump. I tutted and said "Prat." A member of the audience noticed what had happened and laughed. Finally Andrew was ready.

I noticed members of the other band standing near the front of the stage, drinks in their hands. On his stool, Andrew banged his sticks together and we launched into *Break It Down*. It was the newest song we'd written and my favourite because I felt for the first time that I'd achieved what I set out to do in writing a number that sounded like an anthem. It had the usual 5th power chords but now I'd learned to thread them together for a streamlined sound instead of the crashing but disjointed style I'd been coming up with so far. Aaron's and Andrew's lyric was the usual stuff about how the working class should never take shit from anyone.

We'd dropped all of our cover versions from the main set except a hard rock version of the Mamas and The Papas' *Monday*

Monday. (I'd nicked the idea from the heavy metal rendition of *The Loco-Motion* by Grand Funk Railroad.) We didn't really need to do other people's songs anymore. It made the set quite a bit shorter but we did cover versions for the encore. We needed to save something these days as we never used to get encores.

Maybe subconsciously it was because this agent guy was in the place but that night the Ragamuffins were on fire: not a note wrong, with Andrew rampaging around his kit, Aaron playing fluidly, me peeling off runs and flourishes like Jimi Hendrix reincarnated and Phil living up to his role as front man: totally extroverted in his singing and playing and creating a real rapport with the audience. Phil's guitar playing was unrecognisable from six months previously, although that wasn't all down to technique. He'd realised that using a Fender Telecaster - one of the brightest guitars there was - and a Fender twin reverb amp - one of the brightest amps - made for a ludicrously 'toppy' sound. When he swapped it for a Les Paul, with its lovely fat tone, it really made a difference both to him and the overall sonics of the group.

It was one of those nights where everything falls together. The crowd seemed in a good mood, the PA was great, the acoustics in the venue were perfect. We were grinning at each other on stage, amazed that this bunch of idiots were being cheered to the rafters by the audience but at the same time knowing we deserved it.

After the gig, I slipped off to wash down my sticky torso in the toilets. When I returned to the dressing room, I found the other three still drenched with sweat standing around a man in his early-forties with shoulder-length black hair.

"Paul," Andrew said. "This is Chris." He paused, then beamed "Our agent!"

* * * *

Despite our acquiring an agent, I decided to get a part-time job. It was true that Chris started getting us more gigs - before long we were doing five, six, sometimes seven gigs a week - but it didn't mean I had any more money in my pocket. For one thing, the payment for most of the gigs we were doing was a split of the money taken at the door. This was all very well when we were playing in places where we were well known, but some of the gigs we did were dire. One night, at a pub called The Swan in Barnes, we had an audience of nine people. The audience was probably more embarrassed than we were and clapped self-consciously loudly after numbers; I just stood there staring at my fingers waiting for it to end. For another thing, every penny we were earning from gigs was being saved for our demo. We were going to make a good one, in as good a studio as we could afford, and spend as much time on it as necessary. All of us could name albums in our collections that would have sounded much better if only more time had been spent on the production and we weren't going to make the same mistake with our demonstration tape.

I wanted a job because I wanted to go to prostitutes. Despite the melancholy feeling I'd been left with the first time I'd tried it, it was now a regular thing. Whenever I thought about seeing a live woman naked again, and being able to touch her, my mouth went dry. I just couldn't resist it. So I got an early morning job cleaning in a hotel. I didn't tell my dad about it because he probably would have started asking for rent. He'd only recently realised I was serious when I'd said that I was only going to uni for the grant money. I was quite shocked that he hadn't been amused. Maybe it was because he was now the manager at the King's Arms and had forgotten about the irresponsible life he'd lived before.

The job involved cleaning the toilets, emptying the rubbish and tidying the area round the bar of the hotel. I was dismayed to find when I started, that there was a girl called Donna a couple of years younger than me also employed there as a cleaner. Inevitably, I felt awkward around her. It was made worse by the fact that she enjoyed my obvious discomfort. When I humped the bins past her or came out of a toilet loaded down with my cleaning equipment, she would often call across to the other, older, cleaning ladies, "Look at Paul - Speedy Gonzales!" or, in exaggerated mateyness, "Alright, Paul?"

One day, a couple of months into the job, she started taking the piss out of me during tea-break. I was putting my usual three sugars in my mug. She was standing beside me waiting for the sugar bowl.

"Ooh, 'e likes 'is sugar, don't 'e?" Donna said to the cleaning women gathered around a nearby table, reading their papers and smoking their fags.

I kept my eyes on my cup. Because she had ensured that everyone's eyes were now on me, my movements were stiff and awkward as I put the spoon back in the sugar bowl. I picked up my cup and went to move toward the saloon bar where I always took the chance to do some studying on my own. Donna's body was in my way. She was still looking at the other women, smiling, inviting them to share the joke. I stopped, huffing in exasperation at the obstacle she was deliberately making of herself. After a couple of seconds, she was still merely standing there. Irritatedly, I shoved her out of the way with my hip and walked past. I felt her hand slapping me hard across the back at the same time as my ears heard her loud tut.

It literally happened before I knew it. I spun round and, as though watching somebody else, I saw my hand throw the cup of hot tea in her face and my fist rap her across the nose. She reeled away from me, eyes closed. Then a hand was wrenching at my shoulder from behind and I was forcibly turned to see Eddie, the manager of the hotel, snarling at me. I thought he was going to hit me and cringed. Instead, he took hold of the front of my jumper and dragged me through the bar. He propelled me through the side entrance and my knees buckled under me as my feet hit the pavement. I was throwing an arm up protectively as I rose but it seemed Eddie's fury had already abated. He was standing before me with his hands on his hips, out of breath, shaking his head.

"Paul..." he started, then stopped to recover his breath some more. He shook his head. "What're you doing?"

I was shaken both by the fact that I hadn't planned to do what I'd done to Donna and by the explosion it had caused in Eddie. He usually had a chirpy demeanour. My voice was high-pitched in indignation as I replied. "You ask her! She's always doing that. Always taking the piss outta me. Why should I just take . . .

stand-" I was spluttering. "Why should I just stand there and take that?"

"Well you could just tell me about it. You don't have to do that."

I had an impulse to answer him but as soon as I did I was thinking about having to explain to him that the reason she ridiculed me was because I was shy and awkward and ugly. I turned and walked back in to collect my study material. I found Donna walking across the floor of the bar toward me, her tear-streaked face contorted in anger. Sharon, one of the bar-staff, was trying to restrain her.

"Listen, you!" Donna said. "All I did was-"

I moved past her and through the bar and started picking up the pages from my binder where they had fallen on the floor when Eddie grabbed me. I saw that some of them were covered in footprints. Hearing Donna coming up behind me, I quickly grabbed the pages - scooping them in an untidy bell between my arms - and turned. Before she could reach me, though, Sharon had pulled her away.

"You bastard!" Donna screamed at me.

"Fuck off!" I said, angry again after seeing the state of my university work. Behind her, I saw Eddie hovering. He was merely standing with his hands on his hips, looking reluctant to become involved in the unpleasantness again.

Suddenly, Donna grabbed the knife that the bar staff used to cut lemons. She waved it at me. Sharon struggled to grab it.

I wasn't concerned, knowing it was bluster. "Come on then - stab me."

"I will!"

One of the staff behind me said "Paul, go 'ome."

"Come on then - I'm standing right here!"

"I fucking will!"

I spat in her face. Instantly - so quickly it surprised me - she spat back. I stood there. It seemed there was nothing I could do now to secure the victory. I turned and walked toward the main entrance.

* * * *

I lay in my bedroom staring at the ceiling for at least an hour. My emotions swung between anger and self-disgust. On the one hand, I was furious at the way she'd deliberately made me feel small. She'd brought it on herself. On the other, my actions frightened me. I'd gone berserk. It had only lasted a couple of seconds, but during them it seemed as though I hadn't had any say in what I was doing. I could end up killing somebody if that happened again.

When my eye caught one of my guitars in its stand, it made me remember how happy and confident I'd been over the last few months. Since we'd got that review in the *NME*, I'd felt that life would never be quite the same again. That no matter what unpleasant things happened to me, I'd always be able to comfort myself with the fact that I had a future in music. I was now realising that that wasn't quite true. Because even if we got a contract and were successful, I'd still be the same awkward, shy, ugly person who girls like Donna took the piss out of. What then?

All this was something I usually tried not to think about. I didn't really need to. At school, kids had constantly reminded me of my ugliness and the fact that females would never be interested in someone like me. At university, it was different. The intake was not a cross-section of society - it was made up of people slightly more intelligent and sensitive than most. They didn't come up to you and mischievously ask if you considered yourself good looking.

Brooding about it now, however, I realised politeness was all it was. I'd been kidding myself. Just because people weren't taking the piss out of me to my face, that didn't mean they weren't doing it behind my back. It was just that they were more subtle about it than the likes of Donna were. I was a big joke to everybody. Maybe even to Andrew, Aaron and Phil.

* * * *

When I got round Derek's later and he told me he didn't have any grass, I could have groaned with frustration. I wanted oblivion today of all days.

"Nah, don't use it anymore, mate," he said as we stood in the hallway of the house he lived in.

"Shit!" I said, not caring that my disappointment sounded disproportionately great.

"Tell you what I have got, if you're interested?"

"What?"

"Smack."

I opened my mouth. At first, the thought of using heroin was extremely unattractive. But within a second, it started to seem less so. Why not? I'd never had it before or seen anyone else taking it, but the word conjured up images of seediness and despair. I wanted to do something as nasty and extreme as take heroin. I knew enough about it to know it wasn't instantly addictive, so I wouldn't be doing any lasting damage.

"How much?" I asked.

"Four quid. Share mine."

I had the money, but it was expensive. I haggled. "Can't afford four quid."

He considered a moment. "Well, I tell you what, you've never had it before, have ya? You won't need that much. Say, three quid."

I hesitated. It was still too much money. Then, in a flurry of self-disgust, I decided I liked the idea of blowing my cash on something so stupid. "Alright."

I had assumed that heroin was a drug that you injected. While I was still wondering when Derek was going to get a needle out, he was holding a lighter underneath a piece of tin foil that was resting on a spindly, metal object that looked as if it had come from a chemistry classroom. Sprinkled on the foil was a thin layer of off-white powder that looked like stained sugar.

"Pass us that pad."

We were kneeling on the carpet in his room. I reached for the lined A4 paper, of the type that we all did our essays on, lying nearby and handed it to him. He passed the lighter to me.

"Keep heating it up."

While I kept the yellow flame licking at the underside of the foil, Derek was looking at the writing on the top page of the pad. Obviously deciding that it was stuff he needed to keep, he tore off the top sheet and floated it onto the far side of his bed. Then he tore off another sheet and started rolling it up into a long thin tube. I noticed him glancing at the foil as he did so and looked back at it myself. The powder was now dissolving into a gleaming brown liquid and a thin wisp of black smoke was spiralling from it into the air.

"Right, that's enough," Derek said.

Uncertainly, I took my thumb off the depressed lighter button. "No, keep doing it," he instructed. He bent over the small metal stand and lifted up one end of the foil, making the liquid flow down one side. "Don't inhale from those bits," he said, nodding at the black specks and lumps the liquid had left behind.

"How come?"

"Make you sick."

He put the rolled-up paper between his lips. With the tube's end almost touching the foil, he sucked at a dancing black wisp. He remained like that for a few seconds. Then his eyelids rose and he pushed himself back on his heels. I took his blank expression and his wordlessness to mean satisfaction. He handed the tube to me and took the lighter. Quickly - in case he noticed and got offended - I turned the tube round the other way so my mouth wouldn't touch the part his had dampened.

"Just breathe it up?" I asked. He nodded. As I bent forward, I was hit by the burning smack's unfamiliar sickly-sweet smell. I sucked on the tube as though drinking a milkshake. Instantly, the unpleasant fumes hit the back of my throat, making me gag. "Fuck!" I turned my face away, almost retching.

"Quickly! Don't waste it."

I turned back, eyes watering, and inhaled again, this time a bit more cautiously. When I handed back the tube to Derek for his turn again, I hadn't noticed any effect. I held the lighter under the foil once more while he inhaled in what seemed to be great pleasure. Watching him, I wondered why he hadn't just rolled two tubes if he was worried about wasting the stuff. I reached for his pad to tear off a sheet for myself. As I did so, I became aware of a gentle sensation of warmth all over my body, as though the rays of a mild sun were caught under my skin. Something else it reminded me of was the pleasure of holding in your own shit -

the kind that brings a little smile to your face. Amidst this internal glowing, I rolled a tube with my free hand. Then I leaned over the foil and sucked again, this time with real enthusiasm, at the black smoke.

It was gorgeous. Ten times better than grass. Better than sex. It was a lovely, tingling mellowness that felt so nice I could have cried. As I lay with the back of my head against Derek's bed, the lighter having dropped out of my hand, I could hear myself repeatedly breathing a soft "Ahh" of ecstasy.

I tried to stay as still as I could to take it all in.

There is nothing - nothing - as pleasurable as smack. I knew after that first hit that if I could have taken this stuff every day and continued to experience the same intensity of pleasure, I would be happy for the rest of my life, even if I had to stay working class, even if I could never be in love with a woman, even if I could never be a rock and roll star.

Twelve

I had got another part-time job, this time working as a general office help in a computer firm. The hours were flexible, so I could fit them around my lectures. Today, I was standing in the post office waiting to weigh some parcels the firm wanted sent. There were two middle-aged women before me in the queue discussing homosexuality.

"Ah tell you sumfink," one of them declared in a loud voice. "People can do what they like in their own 'omes, but if one a' them came near mah grandchildren, I'd shoot 'im."

Her friend was clearly more mild-mannered than her and made non-committal noises.

"They should never 'ave made it legal," the woman continued. "Bloody perverts. Only encourages 'em."

"Well, there's good and bad in everyone," her friend suggested. "They're not all bad."

"Lillee, I've known a lot of 'em. Ah've never met one I would trust."

This was exactly why I wanted to get away from the working class. They had no intelligence, no kindliness, no subtlety. Or originality - listening to these two was like listening to two characters out of a cartoon. Andrew and Aaron made me laugh with the songs they wrote. As far as they were concerned, the working class were the cat's knackers, oppressed heroes. Because

I came from the same background as them - in fact, a poorer one - they assumed that I'd have the same opinions as them. It was bullshit. Working class men were gruff, nasty morons barely one step up from apes. Working class women were like the loudmouth in front of me: people who thought they knew it all when in fact they knew nothing. I particularly hated middle-aged working class women. They were so pompous, genuinely believing in their own incredible wisdom, which they treated the world to in rasping 10,000-cigarette baritones that grated on my ears.

I was still disgusted when I got to rehearsals that night. We were rehearsing at Andrew's place now because Aaron and Philip's neighbours had complained about the noise.

"Fuckinell," I said to Andrew as I put my guitar and amp down.

"What?"

"The working classes are revolting."

It was a long-standing joke between us. He smiled. "Why, what's up now?"

I told him about what I'd heard. "Shit for brains," I said.

He was sitting on his stool setting up his kit. "They can't 'elp it. It's a lack of education."

"Oh, I see. It's all the fault of the fascist Tory party's education cuts."

"And the fascist Labour party's education cuts."

"Jesus Christ. You're more left-wing than Ken Livingstone." Livingstone was the current tabloid left-wing bogeyman.

"Paul, capitalism is bankrupt."

I quoted The Beatles at him. "If you go carrying pictures of Chairman Mao, you ain't gonna get nobody's help any how".

"I don't go carrying pictures of Chairman Mao."

"If you go carrying pictures of Ken Livingstone-"

"Look..." There was a tone of seriousness in his voice now. "You've got a lot of privileges that most working class people 'aven't, right? And so 'ave I. We're getting an education. We get a grant, we're being taught at the expense of the state. So we'll be able to get good jobs if we don't make it."

"We won't need 'em."

"Yeah, but if we don't make it-"

"We will make it."

"Yeah, I know, but just supposing we didn't. We'll at least have qualifications. We'll be able to get good jobs and 'ave fairly good lives. Live in nice 'omes..."

"Oh yeah," I sneered. "Nine-to-five jobs, taking orders from people." In my mind, a picture of Garcia of the linen room at the hotel sprang up at the mention of conventional jobs, as ever.

"It's better than what we've come from. The point is, most working class people don't get the chances we are. We've got two chances: the chance to be rock and roll stars and the chance of getting good jobs with our degrees. Most working class people never get either. So you shouldn't look down on 'em like that. Their lives are really frustrating."

"It's their own fault."

"What - it's their own fault they were born poor?"

"No, but it's their own fault they stay poor. Anyone tries to be a bit intelligent in the working class, and everyone laughs at them. You say something intelligent and it's, 'Oh listen to smartarse'."

"That's 'cos they feel... Y'know. Insecure. 'Cos they're not intelligent themselves, 'cos they didn't get a good education."

I made a dismissive sound. "They had the same education as you and me." I was pleased when Andrew appeared stumped, unable to make a retort. I continued, riding my triumph. "Look at my dad. He did fuck-all all his life, never even fed us, and now he's managing a pub. Soon as he stopped pissing about and started trying, got his pub manager's diploma and that, his life got better."

Andrew waved his hand at me, as though too disgusted to speak.

Aaron and Phil arrived soon after. Their faces were grim as I opened the front door to them. I realised why when I looked down and saw a jiffy bag in Phil's hand.

"Oh no," I said.

Phil wordlessly handed it to me as he and his brother walked past with their equipment. My heart was thumping as I opened the flap of the envelope and pulled out the sheet of paper inside. On a page headed "A&M Records Ltd." was the message:

Dear Ragamuffins,
Thank you for your letter of 23rd February. We listened to your demo with great interest but unfortunately we do not feel sufficiently enthused to be able to offer to sign you. Please find your tape enclosed. We wish you luck in finding success with another company.
Yours sincerely,
Michael Harris
(Head, Artists & Repertoire)

The black, sick feeling I had was only comparable to the way I'd felt the day I had been moved to attempt suicide. The feeling of rejection and amazement and bewilderment made it feel as though time had stopped. Like life couldn't continue. I had experienced the feeling three times before. This was the fourth time a company had rejected our demo. Each time, though, it got worse. If one sent it back, you could put it down to a single individual having lousy taste. But now no less than four people had basically told us that our music was no good. Four people had effectively informed us that all those hours of rehearsal, that great review in the *NME*, those appreciative crowds at our gigs, those three days recording our demo - and the three hundred pounds we'd spent on it - meant nothing.

I felt like crying and if I hadn't had to walk back into a roomful of people I probably would have. From the fact that Andrew was now sitting slumped on the settee staring at the wall instead of perched on his drum stool, it was obvious he'd been told. Aaron and Phil were sat down too, neither of them unpacking their instruments.

I slumped next to Andrew, sighing heavily. I hated my sigh. I hated it because it couldn't express how badly I felt. I felt like not caring anymore. I felt like saying, "Forget it - let's give up". The fact that I couldn't say that made it all the worse. I couldn't give up. The conversation I'd just had with Andrew about the working class suddenly seemed a sick joke. Barely seconds ago I'd been so cocky and so sure of my destiny.

Andrew had taken the envelope from my limp hand and was reading the letter. "Same as the others," I said to him. Our other three rejections - from CBS, EMI and Polydor - had been worded in an almost identical format to the A&M one. The only slight difference was a handwritten P.S. on the bottom of the EMI letter: "Stick with it - you have potential."

Ha. When you got a rejection, the last thing on earth you felt like doing was sticking with it. How could you? If somebody tells you you're not that good at something, you don't take heart from it and rush to do it some more.

Our demo had been recorded in a tiny basement studio in Soho owned by three blokes that Chris, our agent, knew. He'd got us a discount: if we agreed to work at night, when the studio wasn't in demand so much, we could record it for one-third price. So for three nights running we worked from eleven p.m. 'til six a.m., with Chris doing the producing. The studio booth had the classic mixing desk that we expected from rock documentaries and photographs - banks and banks of switches and buttons and faders - but the recording area itself seemed nothing special at all, almost like the inside of a derelict building. It had a bare, scruffy lino floor. Its walls were covered with egg boxes, which I had thought was for sound insulation but which was to absorb high frequencies so as to improve the acoustics. It was very small, hardly any bigger than my bedroom. There was a grand piano in one corner - which we weren't allowed to touch - and that barely left room for our equipment.

Chris told us to record bass, drums and rhythm guitar first, with lead guitar and vocals to be dubbed on afterwards. Phil was happy about that because he felt he couldn't sing his best and play guitar at the same time. Chris had never produced, as such, but he had controlled the sound desk at many of the gigs of bands he represented. We had a bit of help from one of the tape operators there who, on his way home, noticed we didn't really know where to start. He set everything up, arranging the microphones, including two 'ambient' mikes which gave recordings a grittier quality by picking up all the other sounds in the room, even though they were barely perceptible. He stood small metal reflector sheets next to mine and Phil's amps because this gave the guitars a more penetrating sound. Andrew was packed away behind screens to stop the drums bleeding into the other sounds. All this took an incredibly long while - especially miking the drums, which consumed what seemed to me a ludicrous amount of time for what was less than one quarter of the sound element - and meant that half the first night was wasted as far as we were concerned: we'd thought we'd be recording almost from the first minute of studio time.

On the second night, I actually played a lot of the rhythm guitar parts myself. I pointed out to Phil that we needed the best demo possible and that it would be better if I did the parts he always found difficult. He didn't have a big problem with it. I even ended up re-writing bits of songs, taking advantage of the opportunity of handling all the guitar parts by adding arpeggios and progressions that would have been too complicated for Phil. I could feel our numbers becoming richer as we went along. I even used a bit of Wah-Wah on one track - there was a Crybaby pedal lying around - but in the end we didn't use it because I'd really drenched the track in the effect and it distracted too much from the song.

Phil didn't start laying down his vocal tracks until the last third of the third night and we started to panic that we were running out of time. We made it - just. Phil completed his last take while the band who'd hired the studio for the next day were slouched in the armchairs in the control booth.

But the demo still wasn't ready. None of us were happy with the way it sounded. The drums were too far forward, the harmonies were buried and there was a slight flatness about the whole thing. On top of that, Philip had stood too close to the microphone half the time so there was a lot of popping. We'd always agreed we'd only send a demo out when it was perfect and it wasn't by a long shot. Chris told us he'd pay for the three blokes who owned the studio to give it a proper mix with his own money. We were all grateful because he was only our agent so he had nothing to gain from paying for it. He must have felt guilty.

When the tape came back, it was transformed. What had been a slightly murky and bitty sound quality was now glossy and consistent. Andrew's drumming was powerful and striking but didn't deafen like on the original mix. My overdubbed guitar solos rang emphatically. Philip's singing was given every special effect you could think of including echo for atmosphere on the slow numbers and occasional double-tracking. His voice sounded so sophisticated that I could hardly believe it belonged to the bloke who I every day saw fart and burp. They also put reverb here and there. It was a subtle touch but it got rid of that slight dryness and flatness of 'real' sound. The whole thing sounded crisp and powerful. Chris, who heard countless tapes of aspiring bands, said it was one of the best demos he'd known.

And then came the rejection. Within a week of sending it to CBS, our tape came back with a short, bland letter of disinterest. It was a real shock. Over the past few months we'd never had anything but praise, whether from crowds at our gigs or from friends. Des West, who'd signed the letter, hadn't been impressed by the product of three nights of incredible hard work. Nor was he impressed by the photocopy of the NME review that we enclosed. Nor the accompanying letter that Chris had got his wife to type up:

IS YOUR MONEY ON THE RAGAMUFFINS?

The enclosed rave NME review is merely the first stirring of what will become THE RAGAMUFFINS phenomenon.

With only a few months on the London gig circuit behind them, widely respected music journalist Denis Hutching was putting his money (and his reputation) on these four young guns becoming the successors to The Clash. A listen to this demo tape will make it obvious why.

Take the power riffs of The Clash and Thin Lizzy, add the melodic sense of The Beatles and the social conscience of The Jam and you have THE RAGAMUFFINS. Whether they are playing material that can get the whole venue moving like 'Don't Let Them Grind You Down' or showing that they have

the ability to write a sure-fire number one single with
'Golden Days', THE RAGAMUFFINS are the answer
to the emptiness afflicting the modern music scene.
There then followed the band's line-up, a list of gigs we would
be playing in the near future and a listing of the songs on the tape
(nine - all originals). The tone of the letter seemed pathetic now.
It was so confident and boastful.

"They can't 'ave listened to it," Aaron now said.

None of us said anything. We'd all said that before. How could
they? The tape was good.

Silence reigned for a couple of minutes. I broke it by saying
"Fuckinell..."

"We're gonna be another of them bands 'oo get rejected by
nearly everybody before becoming famous," Phil said.

His expressed sentiment didn't have the desired effect - not
even on himself, I was sure. It had comforted us the first three
times we'd been rejected but today it wouldn't work. Yes, it was
true that no-one had wanted to know The Beatles until Parlophone
but what Phil was saying was now beginning to sound like an
excuse. An excuse for our lack of talent. And yet we had talent.
That was the infuriating thing. We had more talent than a lot of
the acts signed to CBS, EMI, Polydor and A&M and actually
making records. We just didn't understand it.

I pulled my guitar onto my lap and started thoughtfully playing
some runs. It made it worse. As I sat there watching my fingers
moving expertly on the fingerboard, my own classy playing
seemed a joke. I started bitterly slashing against open strings.

"I could understand it if they rejected us about... a year ago,"
Andrew said. "'Mean, we weren't really ready then."

Because it was something fresh, something that hadn't already
been said over and over in our previous post-mortems, I found
myself responding: "Yeah..."

"We were crap then," Aaron said.

"Well, we weren't crap," Andrew said, "but we weren't as
good."

I said, "Mind you, even then we were better than Tough Love",
mentioning a band signed to A&M.

"Yeah," Phil said with heavy irritation.

"I mean," I continued. "A year ago, a lot of the time I was writing really pedestrian stuff. Y'know: A-B-C-B. And then I realised: 'Hold on - if I heard this on someone else's record, I'd be bored by it'. So I started writing better stuff. I could start looking at what I was doing properly, being more critical of myself."

"Yeah, we all 'ave," Aaron said. It was just as true in his case. He'd worked hard on bass. He wasn't just providing bottom anymore. His lines were melodic and interesting in their own right. We really had become a good group.

"Still, there's loads of other companies," Andrew said.

"If we keep sending it out, someone's bound to accept it," Aaron said.

"Yeah, keep on doing it 'til they give in."

We all snorted at that.

After a further period of silence, Phil said "Don't really feel like rehearsing - do you?"

My guitar on my lap, I said, "Nah..."

"What shall we do?" Phil asked.

"Play twenty questions?" Aaron suggested.

It was a game we had to while away the hours spent waiting in dressing rooms.

Because it was something requiring high spirits, I was surprised when Andrew said, "Alright, I've got one".

"What?"

"'Ave you ever been caught trying to nick a skin rag?"

The question made me laugh. "Yeah!" I said.

"So 'ave I," Aaron admitted.

"I'll tell ya mine, right," Andrew said. "I kept nicking these dirty books from this Pakistani shop. I used to run in, grab 'em off the top shelf and run out again. There was only an old woman there. But she musta told her son or something, 'cos one day - I think it was the third time I did it, third or forth - one day I went in there, grabbed one, ran out and when I looked round this bloke was coming after me. 'E just goes..." Andrew beckoned in demonstration with a finger. "Y'know - 'e was just walking, and smiling at me."

"What'd 'e do?"

"Nuffin. Just took it off me and goes 'You shouldn't be reading such things'."

Aaron and I then told our stories of being caught trying to steal pornography when under-age. We had a good laugh at our bungling, all agreeing it would have been *sooo* embarrassing if we'd been reported to our parents for it. By the time we'd finished, there was a new atmosphere in the room. It wasn't quite happiness. In fact, it was more like the exhausted, fragile feeling when you've been crying. But, just like the sensation after a cry as well, we also felt purged and able to turn our minds to what we were going to do next.

Eventually, we even started playing. It was a lazy jamming session, not a proper rehearsal, but it was better than just trooping home without having bothered at all. By the next evening we were playing another gig. Because it was one of our regular venues, the crowd - familiar with our material - was receptive and appreciative. As I stood there listening to the applause and the whistles and even a couple of hollered requests (for *Don't Let Them Grind You Down* - everybody's favourite, apparently), the previous day's agonising seemed a distant memory. These people liked us. It put it all into perspective. We were good. It was just that the record companies were taking longer than them to realise it.

Thirteen

"You ruined the whole gig!" Aaron barked at Philip.

Philip tutted. "'Ow can I ruin it? It was crap already."

We slumped our sweaty selves into the armchairs in the dressing room of The Rat Cage.

"No it weren't."

"Yes it was."

"It was going alright 'til you started sulking."

"I'm sick of this! It's a waste of time. We should be making a record by now, 'steada playing in front of people who aren't even listening."

The Rat Cage was a small venue beneath a bookmakers with tables on one side and a space for people to dance on the other. We were playing there for the first time so the place hadn't been as full as some of our more regular venues, but there were still about sixty customers. We had noticed straightaway that the table set-up led to less attention. The seated punters would chat with each other and occasionally throw glances at the group.

"Fucking shit!" Philip said. "We're standing up there like pillocks and they're all chatting each uvver up. 'Cept when we finish and then it's..." He mimed somebody deigning to notice a song was over and clapping their hands in a patronisingly light manner. "Might as well not fucking bovver".

Aaron and Phil had nearly had a fight on stage tonight because Phil had stopped taking it seriously after a while, not playing properly and doing things like singing "You're all a bunch of cunts," to the tune of *Don't Let Them Grind You Down*.

"Well that's not my fault. And it ain't Paul's fault or Andrew's fault. Why should they play properly while you're just pissing about?"

"Why should any of us?" Philip said. "I've tried my best before. I've worked my balls off. It don't matter. No-one gives a shit. Don't matter how hard we work."

Aaron made no reply. I knew why. Because we were all starting to feel like Phil. It was the frustration of so many rejections. We were like a tape sending machine. Get the jiffy bag, get the stamps, get the introductory letter (or the bullshit letter, as we called it), get the tape, send it to the next company on our list. A few weeks later (sometimes longer) back it comes and we do it all over again. Like dummies. Like fucking robots.

Plus a review in the *Melody Maker* a month before. In fact, it had been a review of the Video Stars, the band we were supporting, but we had been mentioned in passing: "A lumpen collection of Clash wannabes describing landscapes through which wander hilarious Tetley-bittermen cartoons of the working class".

* * * *

Two days later, we played a headlining gig at Land's End, a pub in the West End. We hadn't played it much before, but the crowd liked us. We also got our usual good reception at The Oak, one of our regulars, the day after. But travelling home on the tube both nights (Andrew's dad needed the van for work; we were going back to pick up the PA the next day) we were subdued. It wasn't the same after a good gig now.

The train was crowded and Philip and I had to sit on our amps. I got a stab of pain from the interested glances of the other passengers. I'd always basked in the fact that they clearly found a clutch of young men with guitar cases and amps a bit intriguing. How disinterested they'd be if they knew of the mundanity of our lives. It was amazing how quickly everything had dribbled away. All our optimism and high spirits. A few months ago we'd been so confident and happy.

It wasn't just our attitude that had changed. Our friends and families seemed to have a... contempt for us now. They'd ask us how things were going, whether we'd heard from the latest company we'd sent our tape to, and when we told them of yet another rejection, although they would commiserate, there was something different in their faces. You could see they felt we were kidding ourselves. That they thought we should accept that we weren't good enough. Once, I'd been talking to Derek and had made the point that a lot of bands who did get signed weren't as good as we were. He had looked at me and glanced away. My heart skipped a beat. The disdain in the look was shocking. I couldn't stop thinking about that. It kept coming back. It made me see red because Derek was - just like all the others who now had contempt for us - one of those same people who had been impressed before when they'd heard our tape and seen us live.

At Parsons Green station, a man with long, styled, dyed blonde hair got on. I was sure I'd seen him somewhere. Before I could work out where that was, he was approaching Andrew and Aaron, smiling broadly. He hadn't noticed Philip and I because we were at ground level.

Andrew smiled back at him, offering his hand to shake. "'Allo. What're you doing 'ere?"

"I was going to ask you the same. Just done a gig?" Glancing around, he now noticed the other half of the group below him and smiled at us as well. I remembered him. He was one of the blokes who owned the studio where we'd recorded our demo. I'd only seen him fleetingly while we were there.

Andrew nodded. "The Oak."

"Oh yeah, I know it. Go well?"

Andrew nodded again.

The bloke didn't seem to notice his peculiar lack of enthusiasm about it. "I've seen your name about. Seem to be doing well for yourselves."

"Yeah..." Andrew belatedly replied.

"Any luck with the record companies?" When Andrew grimacingly shook his head, the bloke said, "Never mind. Keep trying."

The bloke got off at the same station as us. It turned out he was going to the Half Moon, a local pub, to see a band. He invited us to go with him. None of us were enthusiastic until he mentioned that he knew the landlord was looking for new groups to put on. Andrew said he'd take his gear home and then meet him up there.

It was totally unlike me, but I decided to go with him. I just didn't feel like another lonely, quiet night indoors. I didn't want to study because I was getting more and more pissed off with uni. I hadn't envisaged being there this long. So I dumped my gear in my room, smoked a joint, had a shower and went round to Andrew's to meet up with him and Aaron. Unsurprisingly, Philip had decided not to come with us.

The band at the Half Moon were called Nocturne and they were nothing special at all. All minor chords and Goth hairstyles and second-hand Banshees riffs.

"Fucking crap," Andrew observed over the din.

We were sitting at a table at the back, Andrew, Aaron and the bloke - whose name I had now learned was Barry - with beers before them, me with an orange juice. A sea of leather jackets and exploding Siouxsie Sioux hair separated us from the group.

"Not much cop, are they?" Barry agreed.

"They'll probably get a contract soon, then," I said.

Barry was amused by that. He turned to me. "Who've you had rejection letters from, then?"

"Everyone."

"You name 'em, we've had rejections from 'em," Andrew said.

"Really?" He seemed surprised. "Have you tried the independents?"

"We're on the independents now. We've tried all the majors, so now we're trying them. We're going down and down."

"Well the indies often sign acts the majors have passed up."

"Yeah," I said "But you don't make any money with the indies."

"It's a start."

"We don't wanna start at the bottom, though," Andrew said. "I mean, why should we? We're a great band. Better than this shit..." He nodded at Nocturne. "They probably *will* get signed soon. Bands like them are getting signed while we get reject slips. It's..." He shook his head.

"What do they say to you, when they turn you down?"

Aaron, Andrew and I all spoke at the same time: "Nothing." All of us were feeling too down to find the synchronism funny.

"They never tell you anyfing," Aaron said. "Just 'Sorry, but no'."

"I mean," I said. "If we're crap, we just wish they'd tell us. At least we'd know then."

"Some of 'em just send a photocopied letter," Andrew said.

"Yeah. They keep you waiting months, some of 'em, and then they can't even be bothered writing a proper letter."

"They might as well just say 'Fuck off, we don't give a shit'," I said.

"It's frustrating, I know," Barry commiserated.

"It makes us so angry," Aaron said. "Y'know - being turned down when they've got bands who're total shit on their label."

"I mean, you've 'eard us," Andrew said. "You know we're good."

"'Mean", I said. "We must be one of the best bands who've recorded at your studio. Bands without a contract, I mean."

Barry nodded. "When I was mixing you, I thought 'Sounds a lot like The Clash'. Not quite as good as The Clash, but much better than most of the other bands who want to sound like them."

"We reckon we're more like The Jam than The Clash," Andrew said.

"Yeah. You've got four or five very good songs. The rest of 'em, I thought, were... I don't know... They sounded like inferior versions of those four or five songs. But you've got the nucleus of a good repertoire."

We were all a little taken aback by that. None of us said anything for a few moments. Then Aaron articulated what I was sure we were all thinking: "'Ow d'ya mean? I mean... Inferior versions of..." He shrugged in puzzlement.

"Well, you're not the finished article. You've got a lot of talent but your stuff gets repetitive after a while. I was thinking 'I've heard this one before' by the end of the tape."

Again, we were surprised into silence.

"Well..." I finally managed. "Audiences don't seem to think we're repetitive."

"Hmm," Barry said.

"Anyway," Aaron came back at him, a hint of aggression in his voice. "The same record companies that turn us down've got bands without any good songs. Let alone four or five."

"Yeah," I said. "I mean, even if it was true, so what? It's..."

"Oh, I agree with you," Barry interrupted. "You're a signable band. No doubt about it. I've heard far worse get signed. But it's pot luck. It really is. That's why I tell people 'Don't get into this business'. If a kid asks me should I try and become a musician, I say no. It's not a case of: if you have talent you'll be signed. Not at all."

"What is it then?"

"Oh, loads of things. You might get signed because a company is looking for a group who play your particular style of music. And you might not get signed because they've already got a couple of acts like you. Or they see you in a pub when they're out one night and like you. Demo tapes don't seem to work. They do listen to them, but I can hardly think of any bands I've known who've been signed because of a tape they've sent in."

"Jesus Christ!" I said. "How're we supposed to get anywhere then?"

* * * *

When I got home, I felt worse than I had before I left.

It was like my life was in limbo. I was just hanging around, waiting to become successful. Until then I had nothing to do.

Drugs were the only thing that let me forget everything. It was grass occasionally - such as tonight, because I had only needed it to get rid of my shyness - but mostly heroin. Grass made you paranoid, so it was really no good to me anymore. I was chasing two or three times a week. Never enough to become an addict. Just enough to transport me to a point where I didn't have to think about my life.

Needless to say, tonight was one of those nights I needed it. I got my gear from beneath my mattress. It was kept in the tobacco tin Derek had supplied me with the second time I'd scored off him. Today would be the first time I'd ever used smack on two consecutive days. I'd been very careful not to become an addict. Today I didn't care. It couldn't harm me just this once.

Fourteen

I walked into Haley's Hi-Fi Centre and approached the desk. There was a man of about thirty attending it who I didn't recognise from my previous visits. He was eating what looked like chilli from a small polystyrene carton. I showed him my repairs receipt.

"Hi. Come to collect my stereo."

He took the slip of green card from me and called up the stairs that ran over his head. "Workshop! E127 downstairs, please."

"Can you test it for me before I take it please?" I asked.

"It'll be alright," he assured me, spooning up another glob of chilli.

"No, I mean, it's been in before and they told me it was fixed but when I took it home it still had the same problem." One of the speakers had packed up on the system which I shared with my dad.

"It'll be okay. 'E's fixed it now."

"Yeah, but... Can I just check it before I go?"

He shook his head. "No. I'm not setting it all up."

I stood there watching him as he continued eating. I opened my mouth. After a couple of seconds, I said "Why not?"

"'Cos it's just too much hassle". With that, he dismissed me by turning slightly away and focusing all his attention on getting some more chilli onto his plastic spoon.

I was so angry, I could have smashed the shop up. Yet I did nothing. There wasn't anything I could do. I couldn't ask again -

it would sound like grovelling. I couldn't make a scene - I was too shy. And I certainly couldn't beat him up. Instead, I did the only thing I could do: walk over to the stairs to collect my stereo system from the teenager descending them before meekly departing the premises.

* * * *

I hated life. I hated it so much. A life where you were nothing because you had no money. It even came down to the level of the poxy local Hi-Fi centre. Who gave a shit if a 21-year-old bloke with a London accent and a cheapo £70 stereo was dissatisfied with the service he received? What was he going to do? Sue? It really rammed it home that the world could do anything it liked to you. That you had no power to force it to respect you.

Oh God, I wanted a record contract. I couldn't go on like this. I shouldn't be here. I shouldn't be stuck in a world of pettiness and meanness. I had talent. It wasn't being conceited to say that I deserved more. I did. As somebody not only with a guitar-playing talent and a song-writing talent, but also on his way toward a degree, I definitely did not deserve to be taking shit from some wanker in a Hi-Fi shop.

We were still sending out our demo, six months after Barry had pointed out we might be wasting our time. What else could we do? Stop? There was no other route you could go down. A&R men visiting our gigs was something that was not really in our hands. So we had a meeting about it and said to each other something along the lines of "Well, just because Barry's a producer he doesn't know everything. Lots of bands have been signed on the strength of their demos. Anyway, he didn't say it *never* works." The trouble was, we were already down to the dregs. The two-bit little record companies who could never make you stars because they didn't have the money to promote their releases properly. Last month, we'd actually sent our tape to No Future records, a tiny outfit named after a line in *God Save The Queen* by the Pistols which only recorded bands who were in the second wave of punk that was currently upon us. We weren't punk but we were thinking maybe they'd make an exception in our case because of the quality of our stuff and because we were influenced by the Jam and The Clash. And then we'd make one album with them and maybe a major would hear it and realise how good we were and sign us.

But No Future records wrote back with the same response we'd had from all the other companies, major or indie: "Dear loser, Thank you for your letter of blah blah blah. After giving your material careful attention blah blah blah We would like to wish you luck in blah blah blah". It felt really bad coming from No Future records. They hadn't got an act that knew more than four chords. It was us doing them the favour by offering ourselves, yet they wrote back with exactly the same superior manner as CBS or any of the other majors.

You'd think we'd have got used to the feeling of rejection now. You never did. It got worse and worse. Every time a jiffy bag came back from a label, I was depressed the whole day. It was always at the back of your mind. You could be working hard on a project at uni or having a laugh with somebody in the canteen or having an enjoyable wank, and then you'd remember: another rejection today. Each time was worse because we were running out of labels to be rejected by. What did we do when we'd tried them all? The bleakness you felt was something that couldn't be alleviated in any way. This was supposed to be our future. Every day it appeared more and more that we didn't have one.

I put the stereo system down in its usual place on my chest of drawers. I didn't bother lifting the speakers that lay face-down on its Perspex lid. I didn't want to try it out. I knew that I just couldn't take it if the speaker still wasn't working. It would ruin my day totally.

I fished out the tobacco tin from beneath my mattress. There were a couple of strips of whitish powder along the tin's sides. It wouldn't have been enough a couple of months ago, but I wasn't chasing anymore. When Derek had pointed out to me that it would be far less expensive for me to inject - like he now did - than to chase because you needed less smack, I had initially dismissed him. I knew I was intelligent enough not to become addicted whatever the means of introduction, but the thought of injecting was disturbing. I just didn't like the idea. It seemed somehow dirty and drastic. My reluctance disappeared almost immediately when I lost my job in the computer place. (It was another example of working class pettiness. I was told to clear up a dog turd on the front step. Cleaning wasn't my job.) I then had only my grant money and gig money coming in but still needed smack so that - for brief periods - I wouldn't have to think about my life. So within days of being unemployed, I was reasoning to myself that Derek injected and he seemed perfectly healthy.

What I hadn't been prepared for when I started injecting was just how much better and faster the sensation was. Chasing the dragon was lovely but shooting up was like being hit with ten orgasms at once. It was unbelievable. Now, as I turned my back on my shitty little stereo with its speaker which probably still wasn't working and heated the spoon I'd piled the contents of the tin into, I felt so grateful at what I was soon going to feel. The joy that was coming up didn't seem like it belonged in my life. It felt like I must be stealing it from somebody else's.

* * * *

I took my Strat from its stand and slid it into its cloth case. I slipped my fingers under the wide plastic band that was the handle of my amplifier and lifted. The occasion for moving my equipment from my room was, as always these days, a gig. The Ragamuffins didn't rehearse anymore. The ostensible reason was that over the past couple of months Andrew had had to concentrate on his finals, but we would have found some other reason not to if that hadn't been the case.

When I got to Andrew's house, Monica, his girlfriend, came to the door. She smiled and held it open. I liked Monica. She knew I was shy and always seemed conscientious in not making me feel uncomfortable. Whenever I looked up and found myself looking into her eyes, she would quickly flick them away. When I fantasised about being in love with a woman, I would almost always think about her.

It looked like the other two hadn't arrived yet. Andrew was sitting on his own in the living room watching television. He looked up when I came in. He greeted me with an "Alright?" which had a strange quality to it. He then kept his eyes on my face instead of turning them back to the TV. Being self-conscious me, I thought there was something wrong with me: that I had food on my chin or simply that he'd just realised how ugly I was. He looked at the carpet as he opened his mouth to say something. Despite the fact that he kept his eyes on the floor for a couple of seconds, he hadn't said anything by the time he looked back. Finally, he started "Paul..." Then nothing.

"What?"

"I'm gonna leave the band."

I was so relieved that his strange manner wasn't caused by me that the meaning of what he said didn't make any impression at first. "Are ya?"

He nodded. It was the solemnity about the nod that caused me to get my head around his words. I stared at him. He turned the corners of his mouth up in an apologetic semi-smile.

"What... How d'ya mean?"

"I've..." He shook his head. "Y'know. I've 'ad enough." His voice was very heavy.

I felt a presence behind me. I turned. Monica was standing there with her arms folded. She was looking noncommittally at the floor. I turned back to Andrew. I found I couldn't even dare to say what I knew he meant. "Of what?"

"You know what."

I looked from him to Monica and back again. Monica's eyes, responding to my attention, shrank as though she was anxious I know she had nothing to do with his decision.

"Jesus Christ, And."

Andrew turned silently back to the television. I stood staring at him. After a few seconds, I sighed heavily. I started to say something but stopped when I realised that whatever came out would be so much like begging that I would embarrass myself in front of Monica. He seemed a different person. What he was saying was completely at odds with what he'd said over the past couple of years. Like me, he wanted to be a rock star because he wouldn't have to take orders and he wouldn't have to get up early in the mornings and he wouldn't have to live in the same environment as the kind of morons who read *The Sun*. In fact, he had once said something to me about working class life that was so spot-on that I was surprised that I, with all my venom about the proletariat, hadn't thought of it: "The reason working class people are so unhappy is because they know that their life now is as good as it's ever gonna get." That, to me, perfectly summed up the aching misery in people that I'd first seen when we moved to Battersea: the grim, grey, dreary state of mind of those who had nothing and always would have.

"So what are you gonna do?" I demanded. I didn't know of anything else he was talented at.

He shrugged. "I've got my degree."

"So?"

"So I can at least get a job with good money."

"Unh," I said in contempt. "And you think that'll be any good? You have to take shit from people but you'll be alright 'cos you get a lot of money for it?"

"Who says I'll 'ave to take shit from people?"

I was astonished. "You do!"

"Paul, we can't go on like this anymore. It's a waste of time."

"We've gotta keep trying."

"We've *been* trying! We're not getting anywhere. We can't try harder than we 'ave been."

I felt Monica moving behind me, politely leaving the room. I was angry because he was deliberately forgetting our agreement that there was still hope. For instance, lately we'd been discussing saving up to make another demo tape that represented how we'd improved in the time since we'd made the first one, giving ourselves a new name in the process so that the companies we'd tried before wouldn't automatically dismiss it. "We can't give up! We're a great band!"

He was getting angry now too. "I know we are! But it ain't doing us any good. What's the point of being a great band? No-one's interested."

"No-one in the record companies," I said, thinking of the devotees who would be in the audience we were playing to tonight.

"See?"

"What?"

"You admit the record companies ain't interested in us."

I tutted. He knew I hadn't meant it like that. "We can try with the new tape."

"We've tried all the record companies, for fuck's sake! What's the point of going through that all over again?"

The awful feeling crept into my brain that he might be right. The image of a second wave of rejection letters certainly made me inwardly wince. The self-doubt he'd made me feel made me angry. "Oh, you're just... You're fucking..." I spluttered. "You're letting them win. You're letting them make you believe we're not good enough when we know we are."

"I know we're good enough," he said. "But if they won't sign us, we can't force 'em."

I went home and sat on my bed and played guitar. For several hours, I watched my expert, fluid fingers peeling off runs. As I did, it was the strangest, weirdest, most heart-breaking feeling. How bizarre it was that all the talent in the world could mean nothing.

* * * *

Andrew may only have been the drummer, but his departure led to the band completely unravelling.

It was a psychological blow more than anything. The four of us were close in a way that we weren't with anybody else. We had developed as a unit, agonising over arrangements and rejoicing as we gradually realised we were becoming something significant. Lately, our lack of success had brought about an even deeper solidarity: we felt like four people against the entire world as we tried to ignore the scorn of those who felt we should give up. When one of us suddenly turned his back on the solidarity and ambition that had kept us going, it was as though he had pulled a plug and everybody else's enthusiasm drained away. It was worst for me, in a way, because Andrew was my cousin, he was the oldest of us and I had joined the band last. The idea of just auditioning another drummer to fill the hole he'd left seemed barely thinkable. It had been as much Andrew's band as anyone's. It somehow spoiled the whole idea of the Ragamuffins that someone was dispensable. Plus of course, we weren't going to find a drummer as good as him quickly.

In time, I suppose, I would have got over that mental block and been willing to get a replacement drummer. Before that could happen, though, Aaron left. He had his degree now too and, although he didn't say so, was probably thinking it would be better to do what Andrew was doing and use it to get a 'proper' job. That just left myself, a shy gawky guitarist too self-conscious to write lyrics, and Philip, a non-writing guitarist and the first of us to have become unenthusiastic about the group. It was over.

Fifteen

I started feeling ill during an English Lit lesson. I'd noticed a sensation of airiness when I'd got up that morning, a kind of very faint frothing under my skin. I then assumed it was connected to the drowsiness that I for some reason wasn't able to shake off all day. Now, at one in the afternoon, the laughter and chatter of my fellow students as they discussed Norman Mailer suddenly sounded harsh and hostile. It seemed as though they were trying to make me feel agitated with their deliberately raised voices. Yet when I looked at them, their concentration was on the tutor, not me. And in turning my head, I abruptly realised how tired I was. My body felt battered. The bones in my legs seemed to be grinding against the muscles they were wrapped in when I made even the slightest movement.

I closed my eyes for a few seconds, then opened them and tried to concentrate on what was being said. I listened intently to a girl talking about the character of Lieutenant Hearn in *The Naked And The Dead*. The next thing I knew, I was realising that several minutes had passed, the girl was no longer talking and I didn't know what she had said when she had been. Puzzled, I sat up straight in my seat. My skin seemed to be trying to make the same upward movement as my body. I thought I felt hundreds of tiny feet rushing up my body toward my face. I opened my mouth in distaste. I realised then that I was covered in a coating of sweat. It made the self-repulsion even more intense.

My first assumption was that it must be 'flu. But 'flu was never this bad. I got scared then, thinking it must be pneumonia. If it was, I had to go to a doctor. I rose from my seat and collected my books together. The only person in my line of sight as I left the room was a female student who, absorbed in the discussion, only glanced at me briefly as I departed. Walking down the corridor, I had to stop and lean against a wall.

Emerging into the fresh air, it occurred to me that my doctor's surgery wouldn't be open until five o' clock. The thought of having to wait until then to even find out what was wrong with me, let alone get any medicine or pills to make me feel better, was awful. I made my way to Derek's house, moving at a snail's pace, wincing every time I put a foot forward. I had no money on me but I was hoping he might have some grass that would get me through to five. When I got there, there was no answer to the doorbell. I didn't know what to do. I stood on the doorstep, my body throbbing with my illness. I sat down on the step, gingerly brought my knees up and put my forehead on them, my arms hugging my shins.

I don't know how long I waited there, but every second was agony. At first, I was raising my head and looking for any sign of Derek two or three times a minute. Pretty soon, it became too painful: my head seemed the weight of a cannonball. So I kept it rested on my knees and, eyes screwed shut, prayed that he would turn up in the near future. I started talking to myself, thinking it might help me feel better, muttering "Come on, come on, come on," to the absent Derek. Every so often I would groan in agony, not caring if passers-by heard. My mutterings sometimes became near shouts, me barking, "Come on for fuck's sake!" at my jeans.

I saw someone's trainers between my feet. I snapped my head up. A blast of disappointed air escaped my mouth when I saw it wasn't Derek. It was a long-haired bloke in a green jumper who I didn't recognise.

But Derek was behind him.

Both were gazing at me. I pushed myself up, back skidding against the wall behind me.

"Alright, Paul?" Derek said, looking at me curiously.

"Derek," I gasped. "Think I've got pneumonia."

His lips parted. "Christ, you look ill."

"Have you got some grass?" My voice cracked.

"Yeah, come in." He took hold of my arm to help me through the door.

I was dismayed at the thought of having to climb the stairs to his room so when we were in the hallway, I clutched his arm and asked, "Can you bring it down to me?"

"Er, yeah okay. Shouldn't you see a doctor, though?"

I shook my head. "Tonight. He's not open."

"Well, you could go to hospital-"

"Please!" I cut him off. "I need something!"

"Okay, okay. Sit down." He led me over to the stairs. "Won't be a sec. I've got some smack, if you want that?"

I nodded in gratitude.

Derek came thumping back down the stairs about twenty seconds later. He sat on the stair beside me, a tobacco tin in one hand and needle, spoon and lighter in the other.

"Oi, Dez..."

Derek looked up at his friend's voice.

"'E taken smack before?"

"Yeah, loadsa times."

"Fink 'e might be turkeying."

I looked up, not because I understood what he'd said but because he was talking about me. The bloke kept his eyes on Derek's face. I turned to Derek.

"*Ohh*," Derek said. He looked at me. "No wonder."

"What?" I whined, not comprehending what was going on, eager to inject.

"You're an addict, Paul."

* * * *

Sitting in the waiting room of my doctor's that evening, I couldn't get my bearings.

The emotion most to the forefront was fear. There was something seriously wrong with me. I was still convinced it was pneumonia. I couldn't be a heroin addict. I wasn't taking it regularly enough. I could also take it or leave it. I was far less able to do without regular cups of tea, for instance. It was quite true that my symptoms of illness ceased after the hit I'd been given by Derek earlier but I'd noticed in the past that when I had a cold, I felt much better after taking smack, so that proved nothing. Pneumonia, however, was bad enough. I knew that people sometimes died from it.

I was aware, though, that I would have to tell the doctor I was a user. You couldn't omit to mention a thing like that to a doctor when you were worried about your health. The thought of telling somebody I took heroin made my heart thump. Derek was the only one of my acquaintances who knew. I would have been embarrassed for anybody else to know. Grass was one thing but people who took heroin were perceived as inadequate and stupid. Maybe they were: I'd been extremely surprised to find out today that Derek knew almost nothing about addiction. He had advised me to go to a doctor again after giving me the hit to find out if I was addicted. Being a recreational user like me, he didn't know what the symptoms of addiction were. To think he'd always seemed such an authority on drugs to me.

On top of all this was a certain pleasure. In a way, I liked the idea of telling somebody I was a heroin addict. I was sitting there fantasising about the thoughts that might be going through the doctor's head when I told him. He would probably be horrified at what must be the deep unhappiness that led somebody to be a user. The thought of another human being feeling concern for me made my insides glow a little bit.

My name was called. I rose and walked down the corridor and knocked on Dr. Harris' door. I'd only even seen him once before when I'd asked about getting a tetanus jab. He was a white-haired man who had seemed somewhat distracted.

"Right, what's the problem?" he said when I sat in the chair beside his desk.

In the waiting room, I had decided to tell him, to begin with, only of the symptoms I'd experienced earlier and then get around to my drug intake. Now, though, it seemed a ridiculously convoluted approach and I found myself bluntly saying, "I think

I might be addicted to heroin." It wasn't quite what I meant, of course.

He was visibly surprised, his pallid face quivering. He didn't say anything, though, merely waiting for more information.

"Er..." I continued. "Well, I'm not sure I am. I thought I had- I mean, earlier today I felt really ill." I shrugged. "I thought it was pneumonia, but..." I tailed off.

"You take drugs?"

"Yeah. Not regularly, though."

"What do you mean 'not regularly'?" he demanded.

I suddenly realised that his manner at our previous meeting wasn't distracted - more like austere. This wasn't the sympathetic reaction I'd expected. "Well, not every day. I've always been careful not to become an addict."

"Mm," he said. "When was the last time you took heroin?"

"Today." I told him about how I'd taken a fix to get over my feelings of illness. I also described the symptoms for him.

"And when was the last time you took heroin before that?"

"Er... About two days ago. Nearly two days ago." I had difficulty working it out because I didn't keep regular days. I napped a lot to escape the boredom and loneliness.

"And before that?"

"Uum..." I thought hard. In the end, I worked it out when I recalled a television programme I had seen shortly before I'd shot up. "Monday," I said.

"Three days ago."

I nodded.

"So you've taken heroin three times in the last three or four days. That sounds pretty regular to me."

"Well, I-" I started, thinking he was asking me how I afforded it. Then I realised what he was getting at. "Well, I don't take it every day."

"But you *do* take it every day. You've just told me. When was the last time you took it before Monday?"

"Er... Saturday, I think. Yeah - Saturday."

"Saturday evening?"

"Yeah. Well, night. About four in the morning, it was." It had been one of those nights I'd got up to catch up on my studies after my nap had accidentally turned into a proper sleep.

"So, in fact, it was Sunday." He was gazing at me. He said nothing for several seconds, as though waiting for me to say something. Eventually he said, "That sounds like every day to me."

I opened my mouth to point out he was jumping to the wrong conclusion. I closed it when I realised there was no other conclusion you could come to.

He turned to his prescription pad and searched for a pen. "You know what to do, don't you?" He turned his face toward me and fixed me with his pale, hard eyes. I didn't know what he meant so said nothing. "You stop," he said. "Immediately. You stop taking drugs and you don't start again."

"Well, yeah..."

"It's up to you, not anyone else," he said as he wrote something down on the pad. He tore off the top sheet and handed it to me. "Take three of those a day until the bottle runs out - and keep off drugs."

I looked at his tiny, cramped handwriting. "What is this stuff?"

"Valium. It'll help you sleep when you stop taking heroin. You'll feel very agitated when you come off the stuff, very tense. That'll help you get through it."

* * * *

I was gobsmacked. I was in and out of his office within five minutes. It was just as if I'd come in to complain about a cold. Because he had confirmed that I almost certainly was an addict, I actually left the surgery more scared than when I came in. After getting my prescription filled, I went straight round to see Derek. His friend, who was called Dave, was there.

"Is that all 'e give ya?" Dave exclaimed when I showed him the bottle of Valium. "Jesus Christ."

"He said it's to help me sleep."

"Well that's no fucking good, is it?"

I started getting even more scared. "Why?"

"You're supposed to get methadone. That's not gonna 'elp with withdrawal."

"Have you been an addict?" I asked hopefully.

"Nah, but everyone says it. You take methadone 'cos it's not quite as bad as smack and get yourself off it."

"Oh *no*. You mean... I'm still- What happened today..."

"You're still gonna go froo what you went froo today," he confirmed.

I looked at Derek. He turned to Dave. "Can't 'e go back and get some?"

"What - from that doctor? No. If 'e give 'im valium, 'e ain't gonna turn round and give 'im methadone."

"But... doesn't 'e 'ave to?" Derek said.

"Nah. It's bad. If a doctor don't wanna help an addict 'e don't 'ave to. Don't even 'ave to see 'im, let alone give 'im anyfing."

"You're joking!"

"What am I gonna do then?" I said, panic rising.

"Get anuvver doctor."

"But... They don't have to help addicts, you said." I noted mentally that I was suddenly referring to myself as an addict.

"Some of 'em do. You just 'ave to find the right one. I'll tell ya what, I'll ask this bloke I know. 'E should know which ones to go to."

"Is he an addict?" I asked.

Dave nodded.

"Will you ask today?"

"Er, I dunno. Dunno when I'll be seeing 'im. Soon as I see 'im, though, I will."

"What am I gonna do 'til then?" I demanded, reeling at the thought of several more experiences like the one this afternoon.

"Keep taking smack. It'll only be for a few days."

* * * *

When I looked properly at my bank statements for the past couple of months, I realised what an idiot I'd been. Although I'd gotten a part-time job washing up in a restaurant kitchen after the Ragamuffins split up, I'd already spent the equivalent of a fifth of my grant for the academic year, which had only just begun. I hadn't even been thinking. Every time I withdrew some money, I'd assured myself that my wages from my job - which were paid directly into the account - would cover it. I hadn't looked properly at the statements when they'd come. I'd really had my head up my arse. Since the band had split up, I'd pushed any inconvenient thought to the back of my mind.

Realising that, I immediately determined that I was going to take a totally aggressive attitude to my addiction. I was going to get better as soon as possible. The thought was very appealing: actually taking a situation by the scruff of the neck instead of wallowing in the misery and apathy that had been my life over the last year.

However, my determination faltered a little when the doctor that Dave found for me, rather than prescribe me methadone, suggested I become an in-patient in a drug detoxification unit.

"It's usually the best thing," Doctor Goldman - a kindly, overweight, fiftyish man - told me. "The lifestyle of a heroin user is far more addictive than the drug. You need to get away from your environment, be totally cut off from your influences. It's no good going in for your treatment every day and then coming out and socialising with the same old people again. You know - ones still taking the stuff."

"Oh, no," I assured him. "I don't know any other... addicts. Well - one. Well, he's not even an addict. I mean... I'm a student. I'm not..."

"Oh, I see. Well, even then, there's something of a drug culture with students. Soft drugs. I wouldn't want you taking marijuana instead of heroin."

"No, I wouldn't," I said, although I couldn't see any harm in grass.

"Well, okay. But that is the crux. You have to want to get off drugs. And you have to have something to replace it with. Everyone who comes to me who wants a referral to a detox unit wants to come off but the vast majority come back a couple of months later asking for methadone. You're a student, so you've got a head start to some extent. Most addicts have lives which are rather empty. You've got something to apply yourself to."

What he was saying made my insides curdle. It was causing me to remember that, in fact, I didn't have something to apply myself to. At least, not something that meant anything to me.

"My suggestion to you is work hard on your studying but, also, try and make a real effort on your social life. A social life away from drug users. Take up a hobby, whatever. It's basically a matter of getting yourself into a position where your life is enjoyable enough for you to not be conscious about the quality of it. Instead of thinking 'This isn't much fun'. That's when the temptation to escape from it with drugs comes back."

I couldn't do any of the things he was suggesting. I couldn't improve my social life because, apart from the fact that I was too shy to be able to initiate friendships, I was obstructed by lack of sexual experience. If I made friends, the subject of a girlfriend would come up sooner or later, leaving me embarrassed and vulnerable to teasing. As for hobbies, making music was the only one that interested me and that was the last thing that would make me feel happier, what with all the shit that went with *that*. Still, I wasn't disheartened. Dr. Goldman seemed to think my addiction was more serious than it was, despite the fact I'd told him all the details. I felt a bit of a fraud using the word "addict" to describe myself, as though I was trying to glamorise my behaviour. I'd become addicted totally by accident - in fact, in a farcical way - and I had immediately consulted a doctor. I knew I wasn't a 'real' addict. So I was confident that I wouldn't have such a hard time staying off it after treatment. All I really needed was the right advice.

* * * *

About three days after I'd seen him, Dr. Goldman left a message for me at the number I'd given him (the Kings' Arms). It was to ring him up. When I did, he told me that he'd got me what I wanted: an out-patient place at the area's Drug Detoxification Unit starting the following Tuesday.

The detox unit turned out to be not a part of a hospital, as I had thought, but a building that looked like an ordinary residential house. The staff there were as understanding and helpful as Dr. Goldman had been. Before the drug treatment began, I had to attend a meeting with a counsellor. She was a woman called Val in her late-forties with large pink glasses. It turned out to be much more uncomfortable than I'd envisaged. She wanted to know the precise details of my life. Although she was sensitive about it, I was squirming as I revealed to her the fact that I was a failure as a musician, that I had no girlfriend (she also asked me if I was gay), that I had no social life, that I hadn't seen my mother in seven years and that I hardly knew the father I lived with.

"Well, Paul, you're basically a classic case," she said when I'd finished. "In virtually a hundred per cent of cases, people who take heroin are taking it to replace something that's missing in their lives - even if they don't really know it's missing. What's usually missing is a sense of fulfilment in their emotional lives and, less frequently, their professional lives. It's interesting that in your case it seems to be both. You've had disappointments in both areas. What I hope to do is help you step away from your life and see it from a different point of view, because once you start seeing it from a different point of view you'll find that your problems really do seem less bad."

I was already feeling bored and pissed-off. What was she going to do - get me a record contract? She didn't understand what the Ragamuffins had meant to me. Nobody did.

After the Ragamuffins had split, I simply tried not to think too much. If my mind touched on the subject of what I was going to do with my life, it immediately flinched away. I told myself I would concentrate on university for the time being. I could come back to the subject of how I would become a professional musician later. I didn't really know what this resolution meant. I suppose at the back of my mind I was hoping that things would have magically sorted themselves out in the time I wasn't thinking about them. What I did know was that it meant I didn't have to think about my situation until I'd finished my course - another year.

Something else that made me want to get the treatment over with as soon as humanly possible were the other patients that I met in the waiting room. On my third visit, I heard two blokes who looked in their late twenties complaining about the treatment course.

"It's a joke", one of them was saying in a Scottish accent. "I'm on a gram-and-a-half a day and they're giving me the same dose as this guy here who's doing a fifth that."

I gathered he was talking about methadone. The medical side of our treatment consisted of a week of methadone and two weeks of clonidine.

"It's ridiculous, isn't it?" the Scottish bloke demanded of the other man.

The other man - an exhausted looking bloke with ginger hair and a smattering of freckles - raised his palms and shrugged. "I've been into detox four times, mate. I just wanna... I mean, you know. I'll just do what they tell me. I was on a gram a day. I was injecting in my dick." He turned his face my way as he sensed my head swivel toward him. I looked quickly away. "I've 'ad it up to 'ere wiv it."

"Aye, but how are you supposed to give up when they don't give you the proper help? The social workers took our daughter into care. You think I don't want to get off? They just never give you a proper chance."

Jesus. I was appalled at these people. They were stupid. I didn't belong among them. I would never take heroin if I had a child.

As for the medical treatment, I didn't find in it the shortcomings the Scottish bloke was complaining about - although it wasn't until years later that I realised it was because my habit was nowhere near as bad as his. The only thing to cause me any problems was the Clonidine. Methadone was a liquid that tasted like shit with a lime tang but it wasn't too bad. However, as soon as the unit started me on Clonidine, I began feeling ill. It wasn't bad enough to keep me away from uni but it was bad enough to make me miss whole chunks of lectures as my head span and I tried to fight the feeling that I needed to get ready to be sick. Val had warned me I might not feel too good on it but I hadn't expected the effect to resemble heroin withdrawal symptoms. The whole point of Clonidine was that it was taken to *relieve* the withdrawal pains.

* * * *

It seemed a very intense three weeks. The tedious daily trips. The collecting of medicine which I had to take in front of the staff to prove I wasn't selling it on. The sessions during which I had to go over details of my life that I had never discussed with anyone before. And the glimpses into hell that were the conversations I heard amongst the real junkies.

Yet once it was over, it almost seemed like a dream. No-one in my life knew that I'd gone to a drug detox unit - including Derek - so there were no reminders of my experiences around me. It had been an unpleasant necessity that I could now forget about.

I had had a scare. I wasn't going to do it again. I felt similar to the way I had after my suicide attempt. I had gotten out of my depth and had been a fool.

PART THREE

Sixteen

"Hello, I'm Jennifer". The woman smiling at me was a tall blonde of about thirty with an Irish accent.

"Hi," I mumbled, recognising her as the lady who had delivered a guest lecture on J. D. Salinger to myself and my fellow course students that had ended fifteen minutes before.

She put her plate down on the canteen table where I was reading *'Scuse Me While I Kiss The Sky*, a biography of Jimi Hendrix, while eating a plate of chips.

"I see you're a Hendrix fan," she said.

"Yeah," I said after a pause. Why was she talking to me?

"I'm a huge fan of Jimi," she said.

I was surprised. "*Are* you?"

She nodded. "Even a lecturer's allowed to like Jimi Hendrix." I realised from her manner why she was talking to me: she was simply open and good-natured. It didn't matter to her that I was ugly. "What's your favourite song by him?" she asked.

"*Little Wing.*"

"Yeah, that's one of my favourites. It's beautiful."

"Yeah, but it's too short. I tell ya, there's a better version of it, a live version, on this album-"

"*Hendrix In The West*," she finished for me.

I looked at her in amazement. "How'd you know about that?"

"I don't think there's anyone who knows more about Jimi Hendrix than me."

"Blimey," I said. It just seemed so amazing that someone like her would know something like that.

"Are you enjoying your course?" she asked, putting some salad into her mouth.

"It's alright…"

So what do you want to do? Be a writer?"

"Nah, a rock and roll star."

"Do you play guitar?"

I nodded.

"I bet you don't play it as well as Jimi Hendrix."

"Nah," I admitted to her, smiling.

"Never mind. Not many people do."

"No-one does," I said.

"I used to do a bit of singing back in Northern Ireland."

"Did you?"

"Oh yes. I used to sing in a band. We'd play in pubs and at weddings and places like that."

I told her about the Ragamuffins and the rave review we'd had in the *NME*.

"Really?"

"Yeah, but we split up in the end. Couldn't get a contract."

"Oh, we weren't a band like that. We just did oldies. You write songs yourself?"

"I write melodies. Not words."

She gazed at me. "You're an interesting person to talk to."

I looked down, embarrassed.

"Come round my place one night. Bring your guitar with you and I'll sing."

If I'd had time to think about it I wouldn't have said it but I responded, "Okay. What… Tonight?"

She paused, surprised. Then she smiled and said, "Okay. Ring me first though, because I do one-to-one tutorials, so I might have someone there still."

* * * *

I was euphoric for the rest of the day. I couldn't concentrate on my work. I was just waiting for the hours 'til eight to pass. I wasn't kidding myself: I knew this woman wasn't interested in me sexually. But even to have a woman want my company - or at least not to object to it - was wonderful. At eight, I ran out of the house to the nearest phone box and dialled the number she'd written down for me.

"Hello?"

"Jennifer? It's Paul."

"Oh." Her voice didn't rise in the way I had expected. "Hello Paul."

"Can I come round then?"

"Well, I don't know..."

I closed my eyes. I knew it. I knew she'd change her mind. It was too good to be true. "Why not?" I asked quietly.

"Well I've had a hard day. My last client was nice but I feel tired."

It occurred to me to politely commiserate but I was so crushed with disappointment, I was unable to speak. There was an awkward silence on the line.

She became more embarrassed first and broke it. "I mean, I just feel like taking a bath and relaxing."

I opened my mouth to reply but couldn't think of anything to say. Again, there was a hugely pregnant pause.

"I know I said you could come over but I didn't know what a bad day I'd have..."

"Maybe I could make you feel better?" I said.

She affected a laugh. "Well, I don't know about that. The only thing that would tempt me would be a bottle of wine and a *Standard*."

"Well, I've got the *Standard*."

She was amused. "Have you?"

"Yeah."

"Well, listen. If I change my mind, I'll give you a ring, okay?"

"Haven't got a phone."

"Oh."

For the third time, there was nothing but the static on the line.

"Oh, okay," she relented. "I'll have my bath while you make your way here."

I arrived at her door with my *Evening Standard* and my acoustic guitar. We smiled at each other. In the living room, I leaned my guitar against one of the sofas and handed her the *Standard*.

"Thank you."

She was wearing a blue, satin dressing gown. As she read the front page headlines, she asked if I wanted tea. I offered to make it. I went off to the kitchen, which I'd seen on my way in, and made two mugs. I put them on the coffee table in the centre of the floor.

"Thank you. Do you live on your own, Paul?"

"With my dad."

"Have you not got a mammy?"

"Nah."

"Is she dead?"

"Dunno. Haven't seen her for eight years. She left us."

"Oh, that's terrible. And you haven't seen her at all since then?"

I shook my head.

"My God."

She decided to switch the television on. She seemed to have forgotten that she was the one who'd suggested I bring my guitar. I was anxious for her to hear how good I was on it. However, a programme was on - which I had never seen before - that I found interesting. It was *The Rock And Roll Years*, a weekly chronicle of a past year featuring the hit records of the time. The featured year this week was 1976 and at the programme's end was the infamous "fucking rotter" Sex Pistols interview in which they had horrified a live tea-time audience with the kind of language you never heard on the box back then.

"I hope you don't make music like that lot," Jennifer said.

"The Pistols? Don't you like them?"

"Don't tell me you do?"

"Yeah, they're great."

"Ach, they're nothing but swine."

"Better than Jimi Hendrix," I teased.

"They are not!"

"Nah, not really."

She finally looked at my guitar. "Can you play any of his stuff?"

"Well, kind of, but it's a waste of time. He was unique. You can't play it as well as he did."

"Yeah, that's true. Sometimes I listen to his stuff and it makes me laugh how good he was. Go on, get your guitar. I haven't had a proper sing in ages."

The next couple of minutes were spent trying to find a song she knew which I knew the chords to. We finally settled on *Here Comes The Sun* by The Beatles. I had to play it in a higher key to match her voice. It was a lovely voice: high and clear with great sustain. Listening to her beautiful tones made me remember how harsh and reedy - if soulful - Phil's efforts had been. I played the descending spiral that closes the song and looked at her. "You should be a professional singer!"

"I was, but there was no money in it."

"No, I mean you should try and get a record contract."

"Ach, there's loads of girls with voices as good as mine."

"Are there?" I said sceptically.

"Oh yes."

I got up to have a look at her record collection, which was stacked on the floor behind the television. Whenever I was in someone's home I ended up inspecting the spines of their albums. She had pretty good taste, even if it was mostly greatest hits collections. The only artistes she had more than one or two albums by were Hendrix, the Rolling Stones and Elvis. The only vaguely punk material was the first Stranglers album.

"Not much Beatles stuff, then?" I said, looking up at her.

She was standing over me with her hands in the pockets of her dressing gown. I tried to keep my eyes off the glimpses of bare thigh at my head height. "Ach, I've heard that stuff to death by now. I mean, it's good, but you get sick of it."

I was there the entire evening and we spent most of it talking about music. When we weren't talking about that, we were discussing her job. She'd been teaching English Lit for five years. A lot of her stuff was freelance, teaching foreigners at home (often Japanese about Jane Austen). She really won me over when she explained she did this - and singing before it - because she wanted to be her own boss and didn't want a nine-to-five routine. I was surprised that someone so good-natured – innocent, in a way – could have such strong opinions about something like that.

Walking home at one o' clock that morning, I realised it had been the most enjoyable evening I'd had in years.

And a few days later she gave me the biggest thrill since that rave review in the *NME*. My dad told me someone had left a message for me at the pub. I recognised the number he handed me as hers. (I'd given her the Kings' Arms number when she'd asked how she could contact me, although I didn't dare to hope that she was being anything more than polite.)

"Jennifer? It's Paul..."

"Oh hello Paul."

"Er, you left a message for me."

"Yeah," she said. "I don't know if you want to come round?"

Seventeen

In the six months I'd been working at Strings, I'd developed more on the guitar than in the whole of the time I'd been in the Ragamuffins. When the band had been going, I was basically composing and rehearsing 95 per cent of the time. Now I once again had the time to experiment on the guitar. I was getting heavily into trills, hammer-ons and pull-offs, developing a more expressive and decorative style. What else was there to do on a slow day in a guitar shop when you were surrounded by gleaming Stratocasters, Gibsons and Rickenbackers?

Strings was a large shop in Denmark Street that I'd often bought my guitar equipment in when the Ragamuffins had been playing a gig in the West End. I had applied for a job here after taking my finals. I hadn't had the luxury of worrying about being too shy to meet a whole load of new people: for the first time in my life I needed a full-time job to stay afloat. The manager was a mellow guy with a Zapata moustache called Steve who reminded me of Dave, my cousin Carol's old guitar tutor. Steve was a guitar freak and wanted somebody who could really play working as an assistant. At my interview, he asked me briefly about university and then gave me an old Gibson and asked me to play something. I was surprised but managed to play a decent rendition of the solo in Thin Lizzy's *Whiskey In The Jar*. Steve was impressed and a couple of days later rang the King's Arms to leave a message that I'd got the job.

I was one of six regulars there and I got on with them all. With the exception of Adam, who was a year older than me, all the guys were in their thirties or forties and all very friendly. My job was to assist people looking for a guitar. Steve liked me to play the instruments - especially the expensive ones - in demonstration, as he felt that young players would be more likely to buy if they heard me on them: "They'll get the idea they can make it sound as fantastic as you do". Before long, I found I was much less shy. It was probably partly the fact that the job meant I had to talk to people, partly that I was in a position of relative authority, partly that the atmosphere was very pleasant. Mostly, though, it was due to Jennifer.

"D'you wanna go to lunch, Paul?"

I looked up from my seat on an amplifier near the big plate window. Steve was leaning, bored, on the till counter, a can of Pepsi in his hands.

"He's been on his lunch break all morning, hasn't he?" said Adam, standing nearby with one hand in his jeans pocket and the other holding a Lilt.

"We all have," I said.

"Go early, if you like," Steve said.

I swung the Stratocaster off my lap and went and put it back on its stand. Picking up my own can of Pepsi, I made my way to the payphone at the back of the shop.

"Hello?" Jennifer's voice answered.

"Jenny, it's me. I've got a long lunch break. There's nothing happening here. Thought I might come over if you haven't got anyone there."

"Ach, you may as well. I'm bored shitless sitting on my own here."

I caught a cab home. A full-time job and sharing rent and food money meant I could do it without worrying about the cost. Jenny was lying on the bed reading when I got in. As usual, she was wearing one of her tracksuits. She glanced briefly up from the page. I sat on the mattress and leaned over and kissed the top of her head and the back of her neck.

"Have you not had anything all day?" I asked.

"No. I had an appointment but he didn't turn up. I hate that."
She reached up and affectionately stroked my hair. I kissed the
hand she was doing it with.

She was everything to me. From the beginning, I'd found
myself readily telling her things I had never told anyone before,
whether it be about my suicide attempt or the fact that I realised
how ugly I was. I loved it. Being able to have discussions about
things that I'd previously thought of as dirty secrets that would
only lead to embarrassment and misery if disclosed was such a
relief. It made me feel free and happy.

Jenny got up and sat on the side of the bed. "So what do you
want to eat?"

"Your pussy."

She smiled and put her arms round me. I buried my nose in
her neck and hugged her tight. We sat like that for a couple of
minutes.

"You're going to be late back," she said. I let go of her. She
rose and said, "I've got some cold chicken. D'you want that in a
sandwich?"

"Okay."

When she made to move toward the door, I leaned forward
and stopped her by grabbing her hips. I pulled her tracksuit
bottoms down to reveal a pair of black knickers. She looked at
me over her shoulder. I pulled the knickers into the cleft of her
bottom and started kissing her smooth cheeks.

"You don't have time," she said.

"Yes I do. Just. Anyway, Linda and David are coming round."

"So?"

"Well, they'll be here not long after I get back. So this'll be
the last chance we get until tonight."

That made her think. "You're right as well." She turned and
sat down on my lap, looking at the floor thoughtfully. I abruptly
tipped her over onto the mattress and climbed on top of her while
she lay there chuckling.

We made love doggy-style. Beginning slowly, we built to a
frenetic pace that had my thighs and her buttocks separating a
couple of times a second with a sweaty rasp. Then we slowed

again, trying to spin the ecstasy out. All the while my fingers were doing as she'd taught me: caressing her clitoris or twirling around her nipples. She had come twice before I finally let go, ejecting an elongated, uninhibited moan and burying my face - snuffling - in her now sticky neck.

We remained as if statues for a couple of minutes, savouring the glowing in our loins and enjoying the heat radiating from the other. Eventually I pulled out and flopped on my back onto the mattress. She reached for my hand as she turned to lie facing me on her side. I clutched hers with both mine and turned my cheek until it nestled against the top of her head.

I wanted to lie there in that mellow quiet forever. Instead, I waited another couple of minutes before swinging off the bed.

Jenny was looking at the clock when I came back from my shower. "You've no time to eat now."

"I'll get some chocolate on the way. Got to save my appetite anyway."

She walked me, naked, to the door. We had a lingering cuddle and pulled away from each other slowly, gradually, still holding onto each other's hands when we were at arms' length.

I caught a bus back, wanting to feel the sun shine on me through its upper deck windows and thinking that a dash back in a taxi would ruin my blissful mood. It was highly unlikely that I'd be sacked as Strings was such an informal place of work but even if it hadn't been I'd still not have felt any urgency. I didn't let things like that worry me anymore. They didn't seem important. Nothing really did. When you knew that at the end of the day you would be going home to the pure heaven that was living with a totally sympathetic and totally wonderful person, it seemed pointless to give a toss about anything else. Whatever happened to me, I would still have her. Being working class didn't seem such an issue anymore. Nor did being ugly. Jenny seemed genuinely surprised the first time I spoke to her of my ugliness. She said that it had never occurred to her that I was ugly. I realised, of course, that this didn't mean I wasn't ugly but if she was attracted enough by me to reach orgasm, why should it be important that others found my face comical or repellent?

* * * *

I was sitting on the sofa noodling on guitar when Linda and David, friends of Jenny, arrived. Jenny, cooking in the kitchen, answered the door and I heard the three's voices in the hallway before David walked in. The two women secluded themselves in the kitchen, which was usually the case.

"Alright Paul?" David sat beside me.

"Hi."

"How are you?"

"Not bad. And you?"

"Oh, the usual. Still working at that guitar shop?"

"Yeah, for the moment."

This was the kind of small talk that a few months ago I wouldn't have been able to maintain. Once again, it was due to Jenny. I didn't particularly care for David. Neither did Jenny really – he just came with Linda, who'd been her friend since she first came to London. David had a superior, slightly sneering opinion about every subject. The very fact that I could bring myself to converse with him was another indication of how far I'd come.

Jenny had made chicken. As we sat eating, David was coming out with his usual know-it-all comments. He was the kind of bloke whose sentences seemed to all start with "I", and the very way he enunciated the word - "Ayyy" - made you want to hit him. "I must say, I like your chicken, Jen. You've done it with spices, haven't you?" He turned to Linda and said "Better than just sticking it in the oven and saying 'It's ready' when it starts smoking."

"Ever thought of doing the cooking yourself?" Linda said. "If you're that bothered about it."

I got the feeling they'd had an argument before they'd come over.

David turned to Jenny and me to share his amusement at her irritation. Embarrassed, I looked at my plate.

Jenny showed them out at about half-eleven. She came back into the living room where I was on the sofa watching television. She lay down and put her head in my lap. The evening had gone slowly because Linda and David were so crisp with each other, but I still felt good. I was well-fed, it was a warm, pleasant evening and I was with the person I loved.

Stroking her hair, I looked down at her. "Who do you love best - me or me?"

"Someone else," she said, smiling.

"Linda and David don't seem to love each other anymore."

"She's pissed off with him. He's gone off sex."

"Has he?"

"Hmm."

"Well that's one thing you can't complain about with me."

She smiled again and reached up to rub her hand roughly over my cheek. "No, you randy bastard."

I took hold of her hand and kissed it. "I love you."

"I love you more."

We decided to turn in. Jenny went to use the bathroom first. I sat with my head leaned indolently on the sofa back, watching but not concentrating on the television screen. Another blissful day was winding to a close. There'd be another one tomorrow. Life was good. These days I scoffed at the way I'd used to think that the only way to be happy in life was to be a rich musician. Yes, I would like to be wealthy and yes, I still intended to try to get a record contract one day, but there was no sense of urgency anymore. If it never happened, it wouldn't be the end of the world. No song I'd ever written had given me as much pleasure as Jenny.

Eighteen

I next met David about two-and-a-half months later. Steve had asked me to drop off a guitar to an address that was on my way home. The address turned out to be a restaurant with an American South theme. Apparently, they had live music at night and the manager - who had placed the order for the guitar, a Stratocaster - was part of the band. I asked a barman to fetch him and sat on a stool while I waited. Looking at the beer bottles lined up in front of me made me think of the Kings Arms and my dad. I hadn't seen him since I'd left home and moved in with Jenny. I had thought of going round to visit but felt uncomfortable at the idea. We'd had nothing to say to each other when we were living together. What was the point of going round when we'd only make each other awkward? He must have felt the same way about me too. Our only contact had been to exchange Christmas cards.

"Hello there, Paul."

I turned my head.

David was sitting alone at a small table behind me.

"Oh, hi."

I felt embarrassed because I knew that he and Linda had split up, though logically there was no reason for me to be. He didn't seem embarrassed. He motioned me over, friendlily saying, "Take a seat."

I went and squeezed behind the table with him. We made small talk for a minute before we were interrupted by the manager coming for his instrument. He seemed happy with it and signed the docket. When he was gone, David asked me whether I wanted a drink. I didn't drink alcohol but decided to stay and have an orange juice with him because he looked a bit lonely.

"How's Jenny?" he asked.

"Oh, fine."

"What about Linda? She got a new boyfriend yet?"

"I don't know actually," I said truthfully.

"And you?"

"Not bad."

"Had your circumcision yet?"

My mouth dropped open.

"I thought you were thinking of getting one?"

I was - my foreskin had always been a bit tight and it was becoming an issue now that I was getting so much sex. But how the hell did he know? "What - I -" I spluttered. I tried to hide my embarrassment and bewilderment with a smile. I looked around. There was no-one within hearing distance.

"Oh, Linda told me," David answered the question I hadn't managed to get out.

"Linda?"

"Yeah, they were always talking about us on the phone. I used to listen to her. Going into all the intimate details." Seeing the expression on my face, he tried to ease my embarrassment. "Women are always doing that. They have to talk about every little thing. They were always talking about what positions we were trying. Giving us marks out of ten once."

I knew that wasn't true.

David seemed to get slightly offended by my sceptical expression. "Yeah," he insisted. "I'm telling you - that's what they're like. Like - you were asking Jenny to try anal sex, weren't you? But she didn't want to."

Time seemed to stop. I was sitting frozen in my seat, unable to speak. I knew for a fact that Jenny would never be so treacherous and callous. Yet the details he was coming out with were true. I felt sweat prickling on my neck and across my back.

Even someone as insensitive as David found himself uneasy at my discomfort. "Sorry. I didn't mean to..." He stopped, not knowing what to say. "I mean, what does it matter anyway? We all do it. We all have sex."

"Yeah," I said. My voice cracked.

David tried changing the subject. "So what was that guitar you gave that bloke?"

His tone was injected with so much false interest it made me furious. I was angry with myself for the embarrassment that he was trying to save me from, angry at him for causing it, and I was livid with Jenny. I rose from my seat. I tried to say "Seeya," but my lips only parted fractionally and nothing came out. I was too upset to care and simply acted as though I had managed to say something, turned round and walked out.

Walking home, it was as though I was in physical pain. I was literally wincing. I just could not believe it. There was something so special between Jenny and me. We always wanted to be together. We hated upsetting each other. We told each other things we'd never told anyone else. That she gossiped about what I did in bed with her just didn't fit in with that. It felt as though I'd been conspired against.

As I went up the stairwell of our building, I was shaking. I was rehearsing in my head what I was going to say. I was going to tell her what a fucking bitch she was, ask her how she'd bloody like it if I did it to her.

My heartbeat was throbbing in my throat as I twisted my key in the lock. As I closed the door I could hear Jenny moving pans in the kitchen. I walked over and stood in the doorway. She was cooking. She looked up from the piece of spaghetti she had been preparing to taste and smiled. Suddenly, the image of the vicious nasty conspirator that had been in my head for the last twenty minutes was gone. She was the real Jenny again: the good-natured, caring person I'd been living with for eight months. I didn't know what to do now. I stood there staring blankly at her as she blew on the spaghetti strand and gingerly put it into her mouth. I felt drained. I leaned on the doorframe.

"D'you love me?" The question came out before I realised I was going to ask it. Unlike all the previous times I'd asked, I wasn't sure of the answer.

Her mouth was full. She nodded. "Mmm."

I pushed myself off the doorframe and turned toward the living room.

* * * *

I was subdued all evening. My insides were swirling non-stop. I was totally disoriented. Our relationship seemed completely different now. It seemed cheapened. Even false. I didn't understand how a woman who loved me so much could talk about me behind my back as though I were somebody who meant nothing to her. Not just once, apparently, but regularly. How could she do that? And yet I didn't want to confront her.

Jenny asked me what was wrong. I smiled and said nothing and she was reassured. But when I continued to answer in monosyllables to her comments about her day or what was on the television, she asked again. This time, I was irritated and my anger of earlier came bubbling up. "Nothing!" I snapped. Then I calmed down, because I didn't want to have to explain the reason for my anger. "I'm... tired."

That night was the first night since we'd met when I didn't feel like sex. She wanted to do it and I couldn't think of a reason to say no but my erection was slow in coming and just faded away after I'd been on top of her a couple of minutes. I slumped on her body, embarrassed. I lay there, not saying anything, and felt her head move as she tried to look into my face. I kept my nose against her shoulder. Once again, I felt that terrible swirling in my guts. I could have cried with the feeling of humiliation as I realised everything that I had thought was private and precious in my life had been the subject of ribald discussion between Jenny and a woman who was not that much more than an acquaintance to her. And yet, that pain made me remain clinging physically to Jenny. After all, I normally went to her for a cuddle when I felt bad.

Jenny was stroking my back. "Do you not feel like it?"
I fell asleep on top of her.

* * * *

I just didn't know what to do. Whenever I thought about what I'd
found out, I was seething. The thing that occurred to me most
was the number of times I'd heard Jenny complain about men
who made boorish sexual remarks about women. I had agreed
with her. I hated that type of leering nastiness. But she had done
that to me. She'd been giving me marks out of ten.

What she'd done seemed to make our love a joke. Surely she
realised that when you loved someone, you didn't put them in a
position where they were being laughed at? A position where
pricks like David knew all about your dirty laundry. She was
such a hypocrite. I could just imagine her reaction if she found
out that I had, say, talked about the tightness of her vagina with a
male friend.

And yet, however many times I fantasised about confronting
her with all this, I didn't say a word. If I did, we would never be
the same. Occasionally, I relished the idea of her being stricken
with remorse but I also knew I didn't want her to feel guilty.
Even though there were times when I literally hated her. And
there was another reason I didn't say anything. I was embarrassed.
How did you broach such a subject? It would be excruciating. I
just wanted to forget the whole thing, pretend that I'd never had
that talk with David. But how could I? How could I go on as I
was with Jenny, knowing that five minutes after she told me she
loved me with a straight face she could be on the phone to Linda
comparing my prick-size with Linda's boyfriend's? I wasn't her
fool. I wasn't somebody to provide her with amusement.

All of this was going through my head almost every second of
the day. I couldn't concentrate on anything else because nothing
else mattered as much. Being in love had been the most important
thing in my life but I had found out that it might just have been an
illusion. At work, everything seemed stupid and unimportant. I
suddenly became irritated that Steve expected me to give a toss
about how many guitars I sold. It was his business, not mine. I

wasn't on commission. It was a real effort to be polite and friendly with anyone. Particularly Jenny. I tried to keep away from her.

On the second night after my talk with David I was, once again, subdued. Jenny realised there was something wrong and got irritated when I wouldn't tell her what. It led to a mini-argument and we ended up not talking for the rest of the evening. The next evening, in order to avoid her, I went to see my dad. It was an uncomfortable meeting. Both of us, it seemed to me, were anxious to try to recapture something of the spirit that had existed between us up to the time I was about thirteen. It was no good. We had nothing in common anymore, and even though he had bettered himself by becoming a pub manager, he still had an affected cavalier attitude about everything in life. It had seemed quite swashbuckling to me when I was young but now it just seemed typical of ignorant working class bravado. It was a depressing evening. I went home thinking how much more pleasant it would have been if I'd spent it with Jenny. This was stupid. What did it matter if she had spoken about our sex life? Was it really so important? But the thought quickly died. Thinking of what she had done made me feel that sulphuric acid was running from my throat down to my guts. She had pissed all over my trust.

On the third day she clearly decided she'd had enough of my cold and monosyllabic behaviour. She'd come into the bedroom where I was broodily playing my Yamaha and asked what I wanted for dinner.

"I'm not hungry."

She remained in the doorway, looking down at me. I pretended not to notice and continued picking.

"How long is this going to go on?" she finally said.

I ignored her.

"What's the matter with you, for God's sake!"

I looked up. All the withering ripostes I'd been rehearsing in my head for days hovered on my tongue. But embarrassment made my lips tremble and only a puny wheeze emerged. I looked back down.

She strode over and plonked herself on the bed next to me. She looked intently into the side of my face but I wouldn't meet her eyes. "Look-!" She grabbed the neck of the guitar and pulled it toward her.

Infuriated, I resisted and my elbow banged into her face. I froze, horrified and on the point of apologising, but she didn't seem particularly concerned about it.

"What have I done to you?" she demanded. "Why are you treating me like this?"

"You're a fucking slag! You fucking bitch!" My voice was anguished. I got up and left the room, afraid of crying in front of her. Guitar in hand, I went into the living room and threw myself onto a sofa. I put the guitar across my lap but only to try to make out I was preoccupied when she inevitably followed me in. When she did, she was calmer. She walked slowly over and quietly sat down on the same sofa but a few feet away.

After a few seconds of gazing at me while my fingers - clumsy with nervousness - ran through standard blues licks, she asked, "Why am I a slag?"

Her reasonable tone disarmed me. "Because you are," was all I could manage.

There was another pause before she said, "A slag is a woman who sleeps with more than one man."

"I know."

"Well... I haven't."

"I'm not talking about that!"

"What are you talking about then?"

I said nothing.

She gazed at me in silence again. I was squirming, wishing I hadn't said anything in the first place. Now that the confrontation had come, I just wanted to forget about it.

She sighed. "Are you going to tell me?"

"Why don't you ask David?"

"David?"

"He knows all my personal details." I looked at her. "Because you told Linda."

"Told Linda what?"

"Everything! That I wanted anal sex. That I was going to get circumcised."

Her parted lips froze. I looked away from her face back at the strings.

"Well..." She started, and stopped. Then: "I mean, is that all?" I looked at her.

She flicked her eyes away from mine. "I mean, I thought you were worried I was seeing someone else."

It felt like my heart had crumbled into a pile of ashes. Her dismissive attitude amazed me. She was obviously embarrassed but that was as far as it went. The fact that she wasn't immediately remorseful made her seem as hard as nails. I swung my head back to pretend to concentrate on my guitar strings, suddenly feeling without hope and friendless.

"Is that what's upsetting you?" she asked. "It's... not that much to be upset about, is it?"

I was so emotional that I couldn't speak.

"Sorry..." she offered.

The weak, trailing apology just left me convinced she wasn't the person I'd thought she was.

I sat there playing guitar and she sat there gazing thoughtfully at the carpet. After a few minutes, I couldn't stand it anymore and went to the bedroom. I locked the door and crawled under the bedclothes with my clothes on. She seemed determined to prove that, indeed, she was hard: she didn't follow. I stayed there all night, waking once when she tried to get in to go to bed at about midnight. I didn't let her in.

Nineteen

Leaving work, I ignored the bus stop and instead trotted to a nearby taxi rank. I was in a hurry because today was the first day my new band - no name yet - was practicing with a full line-up. Our keyboardist was taking part in his first rehearsal. As usual, I rang our flat from the phone box across the street to make sure Jenny hadn't got a client in there, then I went up the stairwell two at a time. When I tore into the kitchen I found Jenny bemusedly holding out a foil-wrapped package.

"What's this?"

"Sandwiches," she said.

I smiled. She'd known I'd be in a hurry tonight. "Thanks". I leaned down to kiss her and she put her arms around my neck and tiptoed to respond.

"Go on," she said when her lips came away.

When I turned toward the living room, she playfully whacked my arse with her palm. I heard the phone ring in the bedroom while I was collecting my amp and Strat. I tucked my sandwiches into my guitar case and carried amp and guitar out to the hallway. I was just in time to hear Jenny say into the phone, "Yeah. I'll speak to you later."

She replaced the receiver and got off the bed. She started when she found me in the bedroom doorway.

"Who was that?"

"Just Linda."

I stared at her. "What was that about then?"

"What?"

I was still staring at her but hesitant to spoil the good mood between us.

"I was just saying I'll call her back," she said.

"Why? You could've spoken to her then."

"Well..." She stopped.

"Why didn't you speak to her then? Why does she have to call you back?"

She pulled her lips in, looking into my eyes in impatience and weariness.

"Well?" I said and was surprised by the harshness of the demand. But it didn't stop me. "Why don't you want me to hear what you're saying?"

"Because it's private."

I tutted. "You don't know what private is."

She lowered her eyelids. I turned away and, without saying anything more, took my stuff out onto the landing.

On the tube, I stared grimly at the floor. My spirits had plummeted, the excitement of the coming rehearsal forgotten. After a while, I covered my face with my hand. I shook my head.

Things just weren't the same anymore. I'd never gotten over what she'd done. I'd gotten from Jenny - gradually, because she was so embarrassed about it - that she'd told Linda everything there was to know about me. My suicide attempt, my insecurity about my looks, my visits to prostitutes before I'd met her. All those things I had literally never told anybody before. It was worse than I'd thought. When I remembered now how Linda had been polite and pleasant to me whenever we'd met, I felt sick. I couldn't help feeling that she'd been laughing at me. Acting all innocent, asking me innocuous questions about who I'd sold guitars to, while her brain was busily mulling over the intimate bedroom details she knew about.

Linda was now the bane of my life. Jenny didn't invite her round when I was there anymore because I'd asked her not to, but of course they still met at other times and spoke on the phone.

I knew it would be unreasonable to demand that Jenny break off all contact with her but I felt I could never relax because of Linda. I hated Jenny going into the bedroom to take her calls from her. If an evening went by without contact from Linda, I felt relieved. And the days when Linda did ring, I felt queasy. Jenny had promised me she'd never discuss anything personal about me with her again and I knew she was sincere but I just didn't think she could keep the promise. Surely, it would be so tempting to let slip something if Linda had just done the same about her boyfriend? Plus she might tell her something that she didn't know I wanted kept between ourselves.

I was miserable. It was like having a worry that you could never really rid yourself of.

What made me even more furious was the fact that Jenny was getting fed up with my attitude. After her initial dismissiveness, she had become very apologetic when she realised how hurt I was. There'd been a period of several weeks where she was incredibly meek with me, and it was touching. But now she would snap back at me if I had a go at her. At times, I got fed up being obsessed with it myself: I didn't want to spend half my life brooding on it. But I couldn't help it. I had worshipped her and she had given me the feeling she had worshipped me - even as behind my back she was being considerably, meanly, less than reverential. It was devastating to find out that our love wasn't what I'd revelled in it being. But just because I wearied of my attitude, it didn't mean she had the right to weary of it. How dare she be irritated with me when it was her own hypocrisy that had started all this?

So we argued frequently when before we almost never had. At first I'd enjoyed the novel pleasure of being able to call someone I loved all the names under the sun but it palled when I realised the bliss it had replaced.

One good thing had come out of it all. I had finally been given the impetus to get up off my arse and start that new band I had been vaguely planning for ages. It was partly a gesture of defiance to Jenny. I wanted to have something else important in my life, prove my life didn't completely revolve around her. The shyness that had inhibited me up to now in getting a new band together just wasn't a factor anymore. I would never be an extrovert but I had to admit that Jenny had brought me out of myself.

I had a head start with the band. Adam at work had mentioned a guitarist he knew who wasn't in a group but who wrote songs. At that point I still had only vague plans but when Adam brought this bloke in one day I was immediately fired with an enthusiasm I hadn't felt since the best days of the Ragamuffins. Mick was a year younger than me but like me - and most musicians I'd met of my age - had a great knowledge of 'Sixties and 'Seventies music. He was Italian and his name was actually Michele - pronounced Mick-ay-lee. He was about a head shorter than me and quite good-looking in a swarthy sort of way. He spoke very good English, although he had a habit - which I found endearing - of opining on records he didn't like: "Is shit". He was a Beatles fanatic and we stood there chatting for nearly an hour about them and about how any prospective band we formed would be aspiring to their brilliance. A customer interrupted our conversation only once. When I was called upon to demonstrate the merits of a model (a Gibson) to the customer I used the opportunity to show off, playing sophisticated string-bending stuff for Michele's benefit as he hovered in the background.

When we resumed our conversation, Michele told me that I was a good guitarist but said that if we formed a band together there shouldn't be long guitar solos. "The best music is pop, not rock," he said. "All good pop music has great structure. Guitar solos spoil the structure."

I was amused, suspecting he was jealous of my superior technique. We discussed our band some more. He had a Small Faces-type set-up in mind: guitar and organ. I had been thinking more along the lines of The Clash's melodic, riff-driven rock but I loved the Small Faces myself and found myself getting interested in the idea. While we were discussing how the Small Faces' *Tin Soldier* was an all-time classic, Mick idly reached out for the Gibson I was still holding. I got a shock when I gave it to him and he started distractedly playing. He was better than me. His long, thin fingers formed chords at exceptional speed as he demonstrated a lovely, fluid style that also had a nice raspiness to it. If I said he sounded like Mark Knopfler, I'd be doing him an injustice because Knopfler has a MOR sound with much less of a bite to it than Mick's style. It was the first time I'd ever heard someone my age who was better on guitar. And he didn't think we should have solos!

I went round to his place in Kilburn that night with the Ragamuffins' demo. He said he liked half the stuff, and especially the acoustic stuff, but he said it sounded too ordinary. "Too many guitars. You need keyboards to make something sound more colourful."

Then he played some of his songs to me on his acoustic. His tunes were brilliant, with a classic pop structure of verse-chorus-middle-eight and a very 'up' and happy feel. The lyrics sounded a bit dated to me, the type of moon/June, boy/girl material the Small Faces could get away with but which audiences were too sophisticated for nowadays. Maybe it was because he was writing in his second language. Yet I realised immediately that our band was going to be far better than the Ragamuffins had been: we had two strong songwriters (or, at least, tune-writers) and two exceptional guitarists already, and that was just the two of us.

We had a bass player within days. His name was Jason. He was an eighteen-year-old Scot doing his 'A'-levels in London. He was very friendly and mature for his age and a real bass player, not a guitarist grudgingly doing that job because he'd been in bands with people more talented on guitar than him. We advertised in the *Melody Maker* for the rest of the crew. It took us hours of discussion and argument to come up with the final wording, which read:

DRUMMER AND KEYBOARDIST WANTED. WE ARE A BAND WHO LOVE THE CLASH BUT ALSO ADORE THE SMALL FACES. YOU HAVE AS YOUR HEROES MITCH MITCHELL/KEITH MOON OR IAN McLAGAN/MIKE GARSON. RING PAUL ON..

Mike Garson was the keyboardist on David Bowie's *Aladdin Sane* album. His gorgeous, elegant playing on *Lady Grinning Soul* was the best piano I'd ever heard on a record. We had worried

that maybe people wouldn't know his name but in the end decided
that a keyboardist probably would, and even if they didn't, they'd
know the name of the Small Faces' keyboardist. It turned out it
didn't matter because although we received three phone calls from
drummers and one tape in the post that the *Melody Maker*
forwarded to us, not a single keyboardist replied to the advert.

The drummer's tape we received was what sounded like a
maniac trying to murder a giant kit. Just like Keith Moon and
Mitch Mitchell, in fact. We decided to go with him and not bother
auditioning the other three. The sender of the tape turned out to
be surprisingly old at 36. We weren't worried about age, however,
merely glad to find an old-fashioned drummer who knew how to
play with proper frills instead of click-track metronome patterns.
His name was Doug and he looked even older than he was,
especially his teeth, which were either gnarled and yellow or
missing. I found out why his teeth were so bad and his face so
lined a couple of days after he'd joined. He was a former heroin
addict. He had been on it for twelve years. He - and the others -
were surprised to learn I'd once been addicted.

Doug played with both matched and orthodox grips, which
was unusual. I'd never heard of a drummer being able to switch
methods according to the song, or at least not one who could
employ either method equally well. His playing style was like a
jazz drummer's, only on a mega scale: it had a much looser, more
adventurous quality than the majority of drummers, but - because
of his heavy action - one that still had a lot of umph.

When we started rehearsing, it was a strange combination:
my hard rock stuff and Mick's pop. Within a few days, though,
Mick and I were influencing each other. He was suggesting
changes to some of my arrangements, making them sound more
sprightly. I was beefing up his numbers, making the lyrics less
gooey and adding bluesy chords. On top of that, Jason's melodic,
nimble bass playing and Doug's wide-screen drumming were
lifting the quality of the material even further. Often, I'd had to
carry the Ragamuffins but this was a band of equals, able to make
even ordinary songs very interesting. Jason was the best singer -
he had a nice quavery style - so he joined the ranks of the likes of

Paul McCartney, Sting and Phil Lynot by becoming bassist/ vocalist.

We'd obtained our keyboardist through an ad in the front window of Strings. He was a quiet, intelligent black bloke called Errol. At first, I'd been alarmed when he said he didn't like the Small Faces much (he'd also never heard *Aladdin Sane*) but I was extremely impressed by the fact that he liked Billy Preston. In fact, when Errol's mentioning his name reminded me of how much I loved Preston's sweet, classy electric piano on the Beatles' wondrous *Don't Let Me Down*, I kicked myself for not mentioning his name in the *Melody Maker* ad. I gave Errol the job after he took me to one of the keyboard shops in Denmark Street and dazzled me with his talent. Mick was pissed off by that. Tonight would be the first time he'd heard him play.

I had missed all this creativity. It felt great to be among musicians again. This time round I could enjoy it more. I was no longer too shy to contribute lyrics or self-conscious when band members' girlfriends came round to watch us rehearse. As for all the rejections the Ragamuffins had suffered - I put it out of my mind. Partly this was because I could already see we were going to be even better than the Ragamuffins: the Ragamuffins may have been unjustly denied a contract, but there was no way this band could fail to be signed. And partly it was because my ambition had come back now that it often felt like Jenny and I were no more than friends. Until recently, I was glad to be alive because I was in love. Now I didn't really know whether I was in love anymore.

Twenty

"This the best you got?" asked the teenager with the leather jacket and black Levi's. The item he was being sniffy over was a Stratocaster.

"What kind of model are you looking for?" I asked.

The kid, long black hair hanging in his face, plucked aimlessly at the strings with one of the shop's plectrums. "Dunno really."

I sighed very, very lightly. I went over to the racks and hefted an identical model out. Swinging its strap across my shoulder I casually said, "Well, it's the one I use," and picked up a plectrum from the box on the counter. I reeled off the guitar break from the Rolling Stones' *Sympathy For The Devil*. I could see the kid's attitude immediately begin to change. He had heard the instrument sound good. The fact that his fingers might not be able to make it sound good didn't occur to him, which was the way with most customers his age. Within five minutes he had signed a hire purchase form.

"You're like a cat on a hot tin roof."

Steve had been watching me.

"Like a cat 'oo's got the cream, more like," said Adam, grinning, from where he was tidying the display of songbooks.

Steve looked at Adam. "Paul's not interested in us lot anymore. He just wants to get out of here as quick as he can."

Adam smiled benignly. "Why should he be? He's gonna be a star. He doesn't wanna know us nobodies."

"Us wankers," Tony said

"Don't forget where you came from, willya Paul?" Steve said.

"Soon as I bloody can, mate," I said.

I stood there idly, my hands in my pockets. All of them were smiling indulgently. None of them came out with any of the expected smart-alec retorts. They were pleased for me. I was the talk of the shop. Every customer who came in somehow ended up leaving with the knowledge that one of the assistants was in a band that was about to sign a recording contract. Although that information had been imparted by me a few times - to regulars who I knew well - it was far more often the case that one of the others would be the one to tell. They were proud of me. I basked in their admiration.

With the shop quiet, I went off to the toilet, taking someone's *Daily Mail* with me. As usual, I skipped most of the home news section as it was almost all party political propaganda. Right or Left, I couldn't stand it. In the women's section, I found an article called GIRL TALK: WHAT EVERY WOMAN DOESN'T WANT ANY MAN TO KNOW. In a smirking tone, the article discussed the culture of the coffee morning. To a woman, it sniggered, the details of what was discussed behind closed kitchen doors were as sacred as the secrets of a confessional. Should men ever discover how their intimate secrets were laid bare, it would create a collective temper tantrum that would be the equivalent of ten thousand eruptions from Mount Vesuvius.

I threw the newspaper at the floor, my face twitching. Because of the toilet's confined space, my knuckles hit the wall. I made to kick the now splayed paper but my bunched trousers and underwear yanked my foot back. I sat there rubbing my face, seething.

These days it seemed that everywhere I went the callousness of women mocked me. I'd never really noticed it before - maybe it was a new phenomenon - but in every magazine, in every paper, on every TV or radio programme there seemed to be some smirking female bragging about the way her sex spoke contemptuously about men behind their backs. Not just any men. Their husbands and boyfriends. It had destroyed me because it had gradually made me realise I could never be in love again. Having moved out of Jenny's a couple of months ago when I came to the conclusion I would simply be happier not being there, I couldn't console myself with the thought that there'd be a future girlfriend to take away the pain of the memory of the last one. What was the point of another relationship, knowing that every embarrassing detail of my life would become public knowledge, whether or not I wanted it to, whether or not I gave my consent?

It made my head spin. On the face of it, you would think that women were more decent than men. They were so personable. Yet behind their gentleness and pleasantries, their hypocrisy was incredible. They demanded standards from men which they not only failed to meet themselves but which they - as could be seen from the article I'd just read - felt absolutely no conscience about not meeting. Not some women. Not a majority of women. All women. Women who you would never suspect such nastiness of. Jenny, for instance: I had thought she was the nicest person I'd ever met. All women seemed to have this blind spot, an aspect of their behaviour which they couldn't apply any self-criticism to.

A lot of them implied it was because of feminist principles, which made me even more angry: the kind of female journalist who spewed her hatred of men over the press in articles like the shit I'd just read were all middle-class. None of them had grown up on the 19th floor of a shithole in Battersea, none of them had ever gone hungry, none of them had ever gone through the day-to-day petty humiliations of working class life.

When I was finished in the toilet, I went to the staff kitchen to get my can of Coke out of the fridge. Adam was in there making tea.

"Paulie! You megastar." He held up his palm for a high five.

I was shocked. I felt so weary, it seemed a thousand years had passed since I'd gone into the toilet, yet here was Adam, frozen in time, still expecting me to be as happy as I'd been all morning. All I could do was raise my eyebrows at him before moving past him and his upraised hand to the fridge.

* * * *

Not long after the group started, we'd given ourselves a year to get a contract. Not that we had any plans to split up if we hadn't been signed by then. It just seemed good to have a target. It also allowed us to relax, giving us twelve months to create and integrate at our leisure. In the end it was fourteen months before a label showed definite interest but there was no panic after the first twelve months were up because it had become quite clear after eight or nine months that we were going places. During those fourteen months the band went through three name changes. First of all we were called The Cheated, the title of a book Doug remembered seeing. Then it was The Clan very briefly. We hastily changed that after realising it could be misconstrued as a reference to the Ku Klux Klan. We finally decided on The Coronets.

In our first few months together I was amazed at how hard it was to get gigs. The live music scene seemed to have died in the couple of years I'd been away. The pubs seemed to have all gone upmarket, trying to attract the Yuppie crowd, and the universities and colleges seemed to want guaranteed crowd pullers, probably because they were terrified of making a loss now that they were being forced to tighten their purse strings. Nobody seemed to want to know about new bands. In the beginning, the only gigs we could get were ones I almost literally begged off managers of venues the Ragamuffins had played, and some venues that Doug had played in his previous bands. All of them were unpaid gigs except for a couple Doug got us. We all, therefore, had to stick with our day jobs.

Part of our set was comprised of old Ragamuffins material. Or, rather, Ragamuffins material Mark II. I was a much better musician and composer than two years ago and I was re-writing stuff like *Don't Let Them Grind You Down* and *Golden Days*, streamlining them and augmenting them with bits and pieces cannibalised from other, abandoned, numbers. Those songs would have to be credited to both myself and whichever Ragamuffins had written the lyric when we made a record. The thought of Andrew and Aaron enjoying an unexpected windfall from the Coronets' record royalties years after they'd quit the music business was an interesting one. I was also, of course, writing new material but I had a block when it came to lyrics. It wasn't the old problem - being too shy to show my feelings - it was just that I had few things to write about. I couldn't write love songs because I didn't believe in love anymore. I didn't write political songs either, as I wasn't interested in politics. What did that leave? There were few passions I had that could be transferred to the rock medium - you can't, after all, write a song about your favourite novelist or favourite book. That only left rock and roll itself. I started writing songs about other musicians. One of them - called *Glam Slam* - was a tongue-in-cheek number about the days in the early 'Seventies when everybody on *Top Of The Pops* had platform boots on their feet and glitter on their faces. Another one was called *You Gave Us It All*. The latter, mid-tempo and acoustic with a dreamy quality courtesy of continuous arpeggios, was a tribute to the Beatles and a thumbed nose at those who were indulging in what seemed to me to be a trend of dismissing them. (This was ages before Oasis and the *Anthology* series made them hip again.) They were the two best things I'd ever written.

Mostly, though, I left the songwriting to Mick. Firstly because he wrote love songs. I may not have believed in love but I wanted them in our repertoire because I knew love songs were the most powerful kind there were. They were powerful enough to still touch me, although perhaps more for their vulnerability than anything else. The main reason, though, was that Mick just left me standing when it came to melody. He would probably have left me standing for lyrical content too were it not for the fact that he was writing in his second language. There'd been no use fighting it: I'd just had to accept that Mick was the most important member of the band.

When I got used to that idea, I somehow felt more comfortable. I liked the idea of pouring all my craft and energy into perfecting what were for the most part someone else's ideas. It made me feel really committed to the group, putting aside my own ego for the collective good. Or most of my ego, anyway. Because despite his prolificness, my best numbers were better than Mick's were. None of his stuff was 'special'. He was a craftsman at what he did, but what he did - the love song - was, when it came down to it, run-of-the-mill. *You Gave Us It All* and the old moody Ragamuffins piece *Golden Days* were unusual and memorable. I sort of felt like I was the Mick Ralphs of this band. Mick Ralphs had been the lead guitarist in Mott The Hoople and been completely overshadowed by the main songwriter Ian Hunter, yet the one track he would write on each album would either be the best or else so different that it gave the album a much greater breadth than it otherwise would have had.

Not that we sounded much like Mott The Hoople. We were more Fleetwood Mac crossed with the Small Faces: very melodic rock based around acoustic guitar and organ. It was a very commercial sound. That was why, when we started getting reviews, there was often a patronising tone to them. The likes of the *NME* and the *Melody Maker* were suspicious of anything they thought within a million miles of mainstream. They all admitted we were pretty good, though. After eight months together, *The Face* said we were destined to be stars.

Mick was already home when I got back. As usual, he was sitting on the sofa playing guitar. Since I'd left Jenny, we'd rented a two-bedroom flat together in Leytonstone. It was a measure of how good-natured Mick was that he had never once asked me the reason why when I'd told him she and I were splitting up.

He looked up. "Okay, are you ready?"

"I've been ready about eight years, mate."

* * * *

I knew that record companies were no longer run by squares in suits and ties with no interest in rock music but I had still been surprised the first time we'd gone to S&H Records to talk about a contract. Because S&H were one of the majors, I'd assumed their offices would be some kind of gleaming high-rise full of human worker ants. In fact it was a string of terraced houses that had been knocked together in a quiet street in Kensington. Apart from the receptionist, none of the staff wore formal clothes and Carmen, the Artists and Repertoire person dealing with us, had an office decorated with pictures, wicker chairs and hanging scarves that could make you believe you were in her living room.

It was Carmen who had first become interested in us at S&H. Not by hearing a demo: we hadn't even made one after a year together, even though we had begun building up a following in London and Essex. Instead, she'd heard a tape of Mick's songs that he'd sent to the company just before I'd first met him. He'd actually forgotten he'd sent it by the time she contacted him and said she was impressed. He told her his songs were now being performed by a band - instead of solo with acoustic guitar as on the tape - and to come and see us live.

Today everything we had been doing for fourteen months, and everything I'd done musically since Carol first taught me the chords to *Day Tripper*, was coming to fruition. We were signing a three-album deal.

The receptionist recognised Mick and myself from our previous two visits, the second of which had been to negotiate aspects of the rough draft of the contract.

"Hello. They're all waiting for you in Desmond's office."

We went through the door that led down a flight of steps which in turn took us into a winding corridor at the end of which was the office of Desmond Smith, contracts manager of S&H. Desmond was a friendly man in his late-thirties with thinning black hair. He was slouched in his chair, wearing a leather jacket and jeans, chatting with Carmen, Jason, Errol and Barry as we entered. I wasn't surprised to see Doug wasn't there yet.

"Here they are," Desmond hailed us. He stood up and extended his hand as though he'd never met us before. I accepted it, knowing what was behind it. He knew what a momentous day this was for us. There was also something else there, something I recognised more fully as the meeting went on. It was respect. We were about to become an S&H act. Artists the label was going to invest thousands of pounds in.

"I've just been telling Des what a couple of tough negotiators you and Paul are," Barry said to Mick.

"Got yourself a good publishing deal, didn't you?" Des said.

"That's right," Mick smiled.

I sat down in one of the chairs arranged around the desk. It looked like extra ones had been brought in for our signing. "Well,"

I said. "The Teenagers didn't make a penny out of *Why Do Fools Fall In Love.*"

"Are all your acts so on the ball?" Desmond asked Barry.

"Oh, I'm not a manager," Barry said. "I run a studio. Paul just knows me from when his last band recorded a demo at my place, so somehow I got roped in to help them with their contract."

"Oh really? Well maybe this is a new career for you."

I turned at the sound of the door opening with a bump to see a very smartly dressed man in his fifties entering carrying a bucket containing a bottle of champagne.

"Ah..." Desmond stood up. "Guys, this is Nicky Jones, managing director."

Nicky Jones went round the room shaking hands, the champagne bucket held in the crook of his left arm. His accent was American as he said "Nice to meet you," to each member of the band and Barry. He then put the bucket on Desmond's desk and sat in a chair.

"Is everything okay now with the contract?" he asked.

"Now it is, yeah," Barry said. "Now that we've got rid of clauses about breakages of 78's."

Nicky Jones smiled. "Standard practice."

"Yeah, well as your friend was just saying..." Barry indicated Desmond. "This is a band that's really on the ball."

It had been Barry who was on the ball: none of us had thought anything of the clause that said we would be responsible for reimbursing the company for breakages of 78rpm records. After all, they didn't exist anymore. But Barry recognised it as a scam by the label that other people - at other record companies - had told him about. It was also him who got rid of a clause which allowed S&H to require three more albums from us after we'd made the first three. When we suggested that them activating that clause would be a good sign because it would mean we were successful, Barry said "Yeah - and after you've become successful they can fucking well bid for you like all the other companies."

So asking Barry to look over our contract - as opposed to becoming manager, which he didn't have time for - was already paying dividends. He had been my idea. With a contract imminent, we didn't have somebody who could guide us. Both Mick and I knew how important it was to avoid falling into the trap artists of the past had in just signing any piece of paper waved under our nose by a record label. I didn't want to end up like Eric Burdon: countless hits, sell-out tours, classic records and absolutely nothing to show for it at the end of the day. Unfortunately, I'd long ago lost contact with Chris Smallwood, the Ragamuffins' agent. Barry was the next closest thing I knew to a manager. Remembering the knowledge he'd displayed that time he'd given myself, Andrew and Aaron advice when the Ragamuffins were in the doldrums, and remembering especially his candour about how cruel and arbitrary the business was, I'd decided this was the kind of person we needed to help us avoid the pitfalls.

We had to sit around making conversation while we waited for Doug to show. He was very unreliable because he'd become an intermittent heroin user again. I couldn't imagine he'd fail to turn up, though: he'd been waiting for this moment even longer than me.

"You have any preference when it comes to a producer?" Nicky Jones asked.

"Yeah," Mick said. "We were thinking of George Martin."

Jones, Desmond and Carmen displayed amusement.

"George Martin doesn't produce new bands anymore," Desmond said. "He always gets new bands wanting him to produce them."

"Does he?" I said, surprised. I had assumed newer bands would see him as a bit of an old fart. We wanted him because of the lovely clean, shining sound he gave everything he produced.

"Yeah. You've also got to remember that the production costs come out of your royalties. People like George Martin don't come cheap."

"We thought they all cost about the same," Jason said.

Desmond snorted, shaking his head.

"I'd like to have Ian Hunter," I said. "He's a brilliant producer. If you listen to the sound on those Mott The Hoople LPs... Just massive."

"That was down to Bill Price," said Desmond. "The engineer."

"Was it?" I said doubtfully.

"Oh yeah. I know Bill. You ever listen to *London Calling* by The Clash?"

"Yeah, 'course."

"Well he engineered that too and he did the same thing with that. Now *him*, you might be able to get."

Doug turned up when we were in the middle of a discussion about what a great band Mott The Hoople were. Jones was introduced to him and then the business got underway. Desmond read aloud the contract we'd finally agreed on, with the rest of us - including Jones - sitting there reading copies. The contract had nine pages. I was listening to Desmond's tone with interest as he read out the clauses that stated that no product could be released without our written permission and that cover artwork and promotional images and wording must be approved by us. They were clauses we'd had to fight for. Desmond's tone remained neutral. Jones gave us his own fancy silver pen to sign the last page, then added his own signature to each one.

"Thank you," he said. "You are now S&H artists. Welcome to the company."

Desmond reached over and picked up the champagne bottle. Allowing it to drip into the bucket, he said "Carmen - there's some glasses in that cabinet, thanks."

Meanwhile, Jones was now going around the table shaking everybody's hand again. I felt the skin of my cheeks tingle and my neck rasping against my collar. It was happening, it was happening. I was crying. Not flowing tears, just little stings at the corners. Embarrassed, I didn't move to wipe them away, hoping no-one would notice as I shook hands with Jones and accepted a glass of champagne from Carmen. Jones was giving everyone an envelope as he went round. I didn't even wonder what it was as I tore mine open, merely glad of something that gave me an excuse to lower my face. Inside was a cheque made out to me. As agreed in the contract, an advance against royalties of £20,000.

* * * *

I was standing with Doug on the steps of the S&H offices watching as yet another round of handshakes took place amongst Barry and Carmen and Desmond. A few minutes ago we had even been shaking hands for the camera: a staff photographer had been sent for so that pictures of our signing could be circulated to the music press. Mick, Errol and Jason emerged from the building and, after having weathered the sea of hands, walked over to us.

"Paul, Doug, we're going to the Aerial. Are you coming with us?"

The Aerial was a club we'd played in a few times. I realised that it wouldn't be just us going, but Jason and Mick's girlfriends too. I couldn't deal with anybody's girlfriends anymore.

"Nah, it's alright."

Mick looked at Doug.

"No," Doug said. "I've... gotta meet someone."

"Okay. See you later, then."

As the three turned toward Barry who was waiting for them at the kerb, I felt a gentle sinking sensation. I was back down on planet earth. I might have just achieved a lifetime ambition and I might have a cheque for twenty grand in my pocket, but I'd just gotten a reminder of how lacking in happiness my life was.

I turned to Doug. "You going to score?"

"Yeah."

"I'll come with you."

I said it on the spur of the moment. I didn't want to go back to the flat and sit watching television on my own on a day like this. My mouth almost watered at the memory of the sweet mellowness of heroin. If I couldn't indulge myself today of all days...

We set off together to a bloke Doug knew in Notting Hill. That day, we must have become the first people ever to go to score some smack in a taxi.

Twenty-One

I gasped, jerking my head up, as something connected violently with my shoulder. I squinted through bleary eyes. It was Mick, shaking me awake. I exhaled heavily, and slumped my face back on the pillow.

"Quickly, Paul. It's eight o' clock."

My brain bellowed at the thought of getting out of bed. I twirled my cheek around on the pillow. It felt lovely and warm, so comfortable it was almost erotic.

I was gasping again as, once more, something hit me. Mick.

"You'll have to be quick if you want any breakfast." With that, he walked out of the room.

I looked at the clock. Slowly, I realised that twenty minutes had passed since he'd woken me. The fact that it didn't even seem two seconds made me comprehend how shattered I was. My head fell forward on my neck, my eyes closing. I felt sick. I also felt battered. And my mouth tasted like I'd been licking out a toilet bowl in my sleep. I wanted to go back to my pillow. I couldn't, though. Fuck, fuck, *fu-u-u-uck*! The fact that I went through these hangover blues every single morning never made it any easier for me. Every day, the journey from mattress to carpet was an almost unbearable ordeal.

The solution was a shower. Immediately. No dithering, no languid, gradual waking. Not even a piss first. I just had to dive into the bathroom and get under a hot jet before I had time to think about it. This I now did, flinging the covers back, striding across the floor, locking the bathroom door, pulling my underpants off and stepping onto the anti-skid bottom of the shower unit. Water hit my grimacing face.

* * * *

Everyone was already gathered in the hotel's breakfast room. Mick indicated my place at the table for me at the same time as Eric, our manager, handed me the itinerary. Mick had ordered my usual two croissants: the thought of food in the mornings made me nauseous but I had to eat something for energy. I poured a black coffee from the jug as I looked at the handwritten photocopied sheet in my hand. It revealed we had a radio interview first of all, then the soundcheck at the venue we were playing tonight, then press interviews, then our gig. The thought of all that activity felt horrible. I sipped at my coffee.

The interviews were boring by now. We'd all started scrapbooks when we'd begun getting press coverage but by the time our first album came out and we were in every music paper in Britain, seeing our photographs and our opinions in print didn't seem anything special anymore. However, after every interview we had the satisfaction of knowing that it had helped shift more albums. Maybe thousands, maybe dozens, maybe only two or three - who knew? - but it all added up. Every piece of promotion we took part in took us another step toward where we wanted to be as a band. Next year we would almost certainly be touring as headliners. Not that we were doing too badly on this tour. We'd be breaking even at the very minimum. We'd be earning precisely what we'd spent on coming over, plus the proceeds of a very small merchandising situation (tee-shirts, etc.). Plus we might have left audiences with the desire to buy current or future record releases

My hangover had been reduced to a vague throbbing by the time we got into the cab to go to our radio interview. However, the sound of Eric's voice grated on my ears.

"This is a good one," he was saying. "An hour-long interview."

"An hour?" Mick said. "How did you get that?"

"They've got a policy of playing a lot of indie stuff and new bands."

Eric really knew his stuff. Barry had recommended him to us when we'd been about to embark on our first tour of Britain last year. Eric was a good-looking bloke in his late-forties with white hair and a very calm and patient manner. It amazed me how he arranged all the radio interviews. There were thousands of stations in America and all of them seemed indistinguishable from each other because they all had acronyms of four letters for names. It was surprising any of them had any regular listeners, it was so difficult to remember which was which.

When we got to KBWN or whatever it was called, we were introduced to a fat man with a beard and a colourful shirt called Bob. He was the host of the programme we were on. The five of us were placed around a large round table in one of the studios. Eric was given a seat in the control booth. Bob seemed rather shy with us but changed completely when we went on air, adopting a fast-talking, zany character. However, each time he played a track from our album and found himself with only us to address again, he was almost squirming as he tried to think of things to say. We were all embarrassed for him - except Doug, who never had much sympathy for anyone - and made small talk with him to help him. On air, though, he was a total pro.

"You're over here supporting Pride And Sense," he said after playing *Glam Slam*, our LP's opening track, "a band we had in here last year. How're you getting on with those guys?"

"Great," I said.

"They giving you a lot of good advice?"

"Well, there's not a lot of advice they can give us 'cos we're actually a better band than they are..."

Bob laughed. "Not quite as successful, though."

"We're getting there, Bob," Jason said.

"Well that's no lie. Your album *Kind Hearts* is one of the Albums Of The Year in *Rolling Stone* magazine. That musta lifted morale?"

We all replied in the affirmative. Mick added, "We were going to play small clubs on our own until that happened. Now we're playing support in big halls."

"It was a big turning point," I said.

"With no disrespect to you," Bob said, "It must be the lowest-selling of *Rolling Stone*'s albums of the year."

"Yeah," Jason said. "We were unknown here until that. We were amazed, actually. It was only available on import then. We were amazed anyone on *Rolling Stone* knew about it."

Later on during the hour, he asked us if we considered ourselves stars yet.

"Well, it's weird," I replied. "We're living the lives of rock and roll stars without being rich. You know: all the trappings - the interviews and the gigs and the fan letters and that - but without making much money. Not yet, anyway."

* * * *

Our venue that night was the Ochre, a 15,000-seater. When we arrived for the soundcheck, Pride And Sense were just finishing theirs. Pride And Sense had been a tinny little indie act three years ago. Two years ago they'd signed to a major. Their second album for their new label had recently come out and was in the American charts, number 26 last time I'd looked. Maybe it was partly because it had been produced by Andy Rhodes, the lead guitarist with Enervation, who'd had two number one albums in America. Their gradual but unmistakable progress was an encouragement to us. Our music was so commercial that I had thought we'd be a mass-market band. It was a bit of a shock to find us selling to basically the same audience who bought records by acts on independent labels. Our album was slick and lush (thanks to Frank Wilson, an S&H staff producer - we couldn't get Bill Price). What did it have in common with all those stark, stroppy LP's you found on the indies? Pride And Sense proved, though, that you could cross that bridge into real success no matter how modest the start.

Rob, the lead guitarist with Pride And Sense, was leaning against the PA eating a sandwich. I'd become close to him in the six weeks since the tour had started. He was a thin, straw-haired bloke with a gentle and extremely polite disposition.

We stood around chatting until Eric called me over to do our own soundcheck. We were using Pride And Sense's sound system. We went through our usual three numbers. There wasn't that much point, because Pride And Sense had always ensured the levels were okay. Doing a soundcheck in an empty 15,000 seater was quite painful. Your music roared out of the speaker stacks with no audience to absorb it. When we'd finished, we had the PA turned off and began working on a couple of our newer compositions. We'd written four new songs since the tour started and were using soundchecks and gigs to rehearse them. The idea was that by the time we came off the road, the one hundred and seven gigs we'd have done and the work we'd put into the new stuff would mean we would be ready to go straight into the studio for our second LP. We were definitely building up an artistic momentum: as an ensemble, we were becoming tighter and tighter.

The rehearsing came to an end when the first journalist arrived for the interviews Eric had arranged. We settled ourselves on amps and chairs to be asked how we got together, who our influences were, how we liked American audiences, how we felt about our album being voted one of the ten best of the year by *Rolling Stone* writers. It was always surreal: a human being we'd never met before asking us questions we'd been asked by dozens of other human beings. Luckily, we had in Mick and Jason two permanently good-humoured band members who could be relied on to answer every question as though it was the first time it had ever been put to them. Although I tried to remember the journalist as an individual had not asked us these questions before, my patience was thinner than Mick's or Jason's and it was sometimes really difficult not to be flippant or short with them. One thing that worked to keep me humble, though, was a realisation I'd made when we'd first started getting reporters from local papers coming to talk to us. Every town, every state, there'd be someone from the local rag who it was obvious had no knowledge of rock music but was just fulfilling an assignment. They were just earning their wages. We might find their questions boring but it was clear they found our answers equally uninteresting.

With the interviews finished, we had a free couple of hours. Mick was anxious to get back to the hotel because Julie, his girlfriend, was coming over for a holiday and was arriving tonight. I thought of passing the time with Rob but one of the roadies told me he'd gone for a meal. When I found that out, I couldn't think of anything else to do so I killed time by wandering around midtown Manhattan. I liked walking in New York because it was impossible to get lost in a city laid out like a grid. It made London, where an A-Z was essential if you didn't know the street you wanted to go to, seem ludicrous. I looked at some guitars in a shop on Fifth Avenue, then went into a record shop.

One of the things I'd noticed almost immediately about America was that they were really going for CDs. They were still very much a minority, luxury thing in England but over here - because they were half the price - they were a craze. The shop I was browsing in illustrated that: there were rows and rows of the things. The rows looked quite different from displays back home because - then - American record companies packaged CDs in 'long boxes' that were twice as big as the contents. Despite the growing popularity, I couldn't see CDs ever over-taking vinyl. They weren't as good. Mick had bought a CD player with his advance and I was amazed at how clinical and robotic they made music sound. If you put on a Rolling Stones LP, for instance, there was nothing of their trademark earthiness and thumpiness left. I had genuinely thought there was a fault with the bass control on Mick's machine until I heard Frank Wilson's - our producer's - and realised they all made music sound like that: glaringly bright and anathematised and with almost no bottom.

I got a nice surprise coming out of the shop. A couple of teenagers were about to walk in and stepped aside for me. Looking at the chest of one of them, I found myself staring at my face. He wore a tee-shirt bearing the band photograph that was on the cover of *Kind Hearts*. Automatically, I found myself looking into his face, smiling. It didn't register at first and he looked puzzled. Then he clicked.

"Paul Hazelwood! Jesus Christ, I don't believe this!" He turned to his friend. "Paul Hazelwood of the Coronets!"

The other one smiled and said "Hey!"

"We're gonna see you tonight!" the first one said excitedly.

"You're going to see us - or Pride And Sense?"

"No - you!"

"Pride And Sense!" the other sneered. "No way, man."

"I don't believe this!" the first one repeated. "Oh, man! *Kind Hearts* is one of my favourite albums!"

"Yeah?" I smiled, loving this as ever. "You didn't buy the CD version, did you?"

"No, vinyl. You like CD?"

I shook my head. "Hate it. Never buy the CD."

"Say, Paul," the second one said. "Can we have a backstage pass?"

"Well, I tell you what - go round to the stage door after the gig and tell them who you are. What're your names?"

"Garth and Michael."

"Okay, well I'll put you on the guest list. Just give your names and they'll let you in."

"Al-*right*!"

We shook hands and I set off for the hotel, glowing. This was what it was all about. Way beyond merely the live followings the Ragamuffins had had. People who bought tee-shirts and posters and records. I could still hardly believe it: we had *fans*.

* * * *

Garth and Michael weren't the only ones who had come just to see us. When we walked out on stage at the Ochre at seven o' clock it wasn't to the sight of groups of subdued people and huge patches of visible floor that is the usual lot of the support act. The place was already almost full. A cheer arose. I plugged in my Strat and looked out. A rippling sea of heads before us. Higher up, tiers of darkened balconies from which emanated the firecracking sound of applause. I was getting used to sights like this but every so often it still felt like I'd stepped into a fantasy.

"Good evening New York," Jason's Scots tones boomed around the hall.

An answering roar came back from thousands of throats, hundreds of times louder than the sound of even the most enthusiastic audiences when we'd been top of the bill at the Ariel or Marquee in London.

Doug counted in and we launched into *Tomorrow's Looking So Much Better*. Although it featured on *Kind Hearts*, it hadn't actually been part of our set when we signed to S&H. It was my lyric and middle-eight, Mick's tune. I'd written it in the couple of weeks after signing for the label, remembering all those times - especially with the Ragamuffins - when it had felt like I'd never get anywhere no matter how much ability I had. Many, many people had told me it was their favourite of our numbers.

In fact, despite me being a less important part of the band than Mick (lead guitarist and chief songwriter) and Jason (vocalist and therefore focus of most attention) I could boast chief responsibility for those parts of the concerts that seemed to mean most to the fans: *Golden Days* created an emotional interlude that had people holding their lighters up and *Glam Slam* had them slam-dancing to its riffs like maniacs.

It was quite strange playing these kind of venues insofar as I had to force myself to not be shy. The stage was just vast, so you couldn't really simply stand there. You had to move about a little bit, fill up the gaping spaces. I was never going to be Pete Townshend in that department but I tried to look like something more than a mannequin nowadays.

We did two encores. After the first one, I noticed Pride And Sense drifting back to their dressing room. They'd have to leave a gap after we'd come off. They knew the audience might find them a disappointment after us.

We had shower stalls in our own dressing room and I quickly stripped off and washed my by now steaming, slimy body. I was the first out, as usual. I didn't like the way women, especially groupies, thought they could barge into the dressing room anytime they liked. Dressed in fresh clothes, I gathered my things - basically a bag with my just-divested clothes - and made my way to the stage door. I found the door locked and had to go and find one of the staff to open it for me.

It was now dark outside. This was always the most melancholy part of the day, threading my way back to the hotel through the hubbub of crowds making the most of their evenings. The rest of the group would now be getting ready to go and get a drink at the bar or watch the headliners or just go and talk to fans. I couldn't face doing any of that. It would mean having to talk to women.

Back at the hotel I strummed, while watching television, the battered acoustic that I carried around as hand luggage. After awhile I fell asleep. I was woken up by Mick putting his key in the lock. He put his head round the door, checking to see if I was decent before Julie stepped in with him. He had come to collect his stuff. He and Julie were moving into Jason's room - which had a double bed - while Jason was moving in here.

While Mick went to get his stuff from the bathroom, Julie sat down in the armchair next to my bed and said, "How are you?"

"Fine." I rubbed my eyes.

She smiled at the guitar still balanced across my chest. "Writing songs?"

"Yeah."

Julie was a short-haired girl of about twenty who was at university studying journalism. She had a very soft voice and a sweet nature.

"Me and Mick are going to see The Ramshackles tomorrow. Do you want to come with us?"

Tomorrow was our day off. After that we had two more gigs in New York before moving on to New Jersey. "Nah, it's alright."

"You sure?"

"Yeah. I don't...feel like it."

She gazed at me. "You live a lonely life, really." She immediately got embarrassed. "I mean..." She hissed a laugh. "You know...You keep to yourself a lot, don't you?"

I was embarrassed myself and couldn't think what to say in reply.

"You should get out more." She hissed a laugh again. I thought that she, knowing she'd embarrassed both of us, would leave it there. But she went on. "We worry about you sometimes, me and Mick. I mean, you've got to have some pleasure in your life, haven't you? It's... If you've had a bad experience, you can't hide yourself away ..." Instantly, she tried to rectify what she clearly thought was a harshness in her tone. "I mean ... I ... It's better not to ... It's better to get out and start living again soon as you can ... "

I wanted to say something to make her understand I was grateful she was showing this concern. All of a sudden, I wanted to confide in her about Jenny and how socially crippled I was. It would be such a relief to pour it out for the first time. I'd never told anybody before. I stopped myself. Trusting a woman was what had messed my life up in the first place. Their manner made you think there could never be any situation other than the one you were in at that time: the two of you speaking intimately, alone in a room. But, of course, they had a life outside of that room, outside of that moment, and in that life they used the details of that supposedly special moment to spice up their poxy coffee mornings. Yet I found it impossible to connect the soft-complexioned face before me, transparently hoping for a positive response from me, with that fact. I still found myself wanting to tell her.

Mick re-entered the room. It jolted me back to the real world. I turned away from Julie and put my pillow over my head.

Jesus Christ. She was a nice person and she wanted to be helpful. But you just had to harden your heart and not respond. It was like *Invasion Of The Body Snatchers*. They might seem convincing but *don't trust them.*

I grunted from beneath the pillow when they said goodbye to me.

As soon as they were gone, I started getting angry. I got angry because the incident made me think about women and I always got angry when I thought about women. I could just see her and Mick now, being lovey-dovey in their room. If only Mick knew that what he thought was so beautiful and sacred was a hoot to Julie's female friends. Women had no consciences. They pissed all over the concepts of love and trust every day of their stupid, gossiping, giggling lives. And you weren't even allowed to criticise them for it. I'd learned that. If you demurred from the general belief that men were terrible, terrible oppressors and women perpetual victims, people assumed you were making excuses for a sexual inadequacy.

I got up and fetched the bottle of Scotch from my suitcase. I'd only started drinking six months ago but it was now a real problem. Each morning that I woke up feeling like death I resolved to cut down. But come evening, I had a gap to fill. No company, the gig over, a new hotel room. In fact, God knew what I'd do tomorrow: a whole day without the distractions of work. Still, at least I'd be able to sleep through my hangover for once.

Not for the first time, I wished for something that could give me oblivion without complications. You didn't get a hangover from heroin - the best artificially induced experience I'd ever had - but there were even worse complications. Not just the possibility of becoming an addict. I hadn't touched the stuff since Doug had told me of the dilutants dealers put in it: talcum powder, flour, even strychnine. Dealers killed people just so they'd have more to sell. Also, the thought of drifting back into taking drugs seemed obscene to me now that the band was doing well. One bust and you could say goodbye to the American market - they refused entry to anyone with even the most piddling conviction.

Even as I knocked back the first shot of whisky, I knew it was futile. It would take the edge off a lonely evening but it didn't do anything for all the lonely evenings that stretched ahead of me - for the rest of my life as far as I could see. I remembered now one of those moments of sweet, post-coital mellowness between Jenny and I. We were lying snoozing on top of the bedspread. My mouth was resting against her warm, smooth shoulder. My arm was across her flank, the palm of that hand on a cool corner of sheet. Below, my genitals glowed with that gorgeous sensation that lingers after orgasm. My right leg, meanwhile, was wrapped around Jenny's thigh, a position that parted my buttocks pleasurably. As I breathed quiet, long breaths through my nose, the thought came to me that nothing in the world could possibly be better than this. It was a thought that made me want to jump up and rejoice loudly. Yet doing that would spoil the moment. So I just snuggled further into her and settled for rejoicing in my brain.

Remembering hurt me like a knife stab. I poured from the bottle again.

Twenty-Two

It had been a bad idea, coming out. Inside the flat, I'd got the notion that turkey was worse within four walls. The activity on the streets would provide enough distraction to make me feel a little better at least. Also, the idea of pulling fresh, clean air into my lungs was a lovely one. Maybe the idea would have been sound if I'd had a shower first. I was awfully self-conscious, knowing that my sweat-drenched skin - crawling over my muscles as I entered the worst stages of withdrawal - must stink to heaven. I felt inferior, shameful, as I carefully steered clear of the people I passed on the pavement.

Still, I couldn't see how I could have done anything differently: even my current leisurely pace made my bones ache so much they felt like they were grinding together at the joints. The effort of lifting myself into the bath and soaping myself would have been agonising.

A white railing appeared in my vision. I moved over and leaned against it. I stared at the zigzagging white lines painted on the side of the road as I waited for some sense of relief at the fact that I'd stopped moving. Before it could come, I was hit by another attack of chills. Wrapped in my heavy coat, on a pleasant spring day, sweating profusely, I suddenly felt like I was freezing to death. It was a different kind of cold than the one you feel in winter. It came from inside, a cruel, numbing feeling that set you shaking almost instantaneously. I closed my eyes and hung my head, waiting for it to pass. It was irritating the way my teeth started chattering. It was like the hiccups, an involuntary thing that felt so comical and stupid but which you just couldn't get rid of.

I pushed myself off the railing. It would be better when I got home. At least I could lie in bed and go through it away from the noise of traffic and people and without being stared at. I had to check myself after a couple of determined steps. My leg muscles had groaned at the swift movement. I stopped and waited for the wrenching sensation to subside, then continued at a more cautious pace. This was much worse than the last time I'd gone through cold turkey. My tolerance had become sky high. The comedown was proportionately worse. I was definitely giving it up. I was on the waiting list for a detox unit. All I had to do was get through the days 'til then.

Mind you, I might not have to go through detox. I wouldn't have any money until next week. By then I could have turkeyed it all out of my system. I winced and pushed aside the thought of four or five more days of what I was going through now.

It took me ten minutes to shuffle my way through the handful of streets that led to the flat. Around a quarter of the way there, I realised I had another problem. My intestines were churning violently. Surely I didn't need to go again? I'd been to the toilet three times today already and each time endless foul-smelling watery shit had erupted. How much crap could a human body contain? I hadn't eaten a thing for about three days, either. You never had much of an appetite on smack. Okay, I'd also been constipated a lot lately, which was another side effect of using, but every time I felt as though I'd emptied myself, more would appear from nowhere. Christ. Another fifteen minutes sitting on the toilet when I got back, trying to keep my trousers covering my legs because the chills were happening again.

I put a picture of my bed in my mind to gee me up. It had seemed seedy and oppressive earlier today as I lay sweating and tossing in it, trying to put off getting up and the full consciousness that went with it as long as possible. But now the thought of its cool sheets was blissful. With effort, I maintained that thought as I felt a sudden wetness at the back of my trousers. I clamped my buttocks together and kept walking. Not far to go now. Another few minutes and I could rest my throbbing limbs on that soft mattress. It would be the most fabulous contrast to the concrete that was pounding through the soles of my shoes right up into the bones of my skull. I clamped my buttocks together again as I experienced an insistent bubbling sensation. The sensation didn't become less insistent. Instead, a dribble forced its way through and made its heat felt under my buttocks and at the back of my left thigh. I stopped dead in dismay.

The people walking around my immobile form made me feel even more pathetic and sick than I would have done anyway. If only they knew what was happening to me now. This was the pits. I started walking again, a little gingerly. As I'd feared, the new motion caused the hot dribble to continue its journey down my leg. I'd *have* to have a bath now. Maybe the soak would bring some comfort.

Abruptly, I realised I couldn't do it: I couldn't go through turkey anymore. This was only the beginning of it. It was already horrible and filthy and painful enough, but I knew enough to know it got worse. I couldn't do it.

I needed money. I was going to get it. I didn't care what I had to do for it. I'd hold up a shop if I had to. Suddenly, I didn't feel inferior to the clean-living people around me. I felt angry towards them. They were all pathetic nine-to-fivers, spending their lives tugging their forelocks. I was better than them. I had talent. The only reason I was on smack was because my talent hadn't got me anywhere. They didn't know what it was like: to be gifted but to go unrewarded for it. I'd tried to make something of myself. I had nothing to be ashamed of.

I was going to sell a guitar. They were the only things I had that were worth anything. I'd buy a replacement when I could. All I had to do was get through this bad patch. As soon as I was clean I could start earning again. Losing one of my four guitars wasn't the end of the world. I tried not to think of the fact that a few days ago I'd sold Mick's silver disc for *Glam Slam* to get some smack, just as I'd done with my own one long ago. I still hadn't told him yet. I didn't know whether he'd mind or not. I didn't see why he should. We always used to laugh at the story we'd heard of how Mick Jagger had taken a Rolling Stones gold disc out of its case and put it on the turntable to find it was a Mantovani record.

By the time I got back to the flat, I was feeling deliriously happy. I'd soon be over this agony and the way I'd found to get over it was a painless one. I felt stupid for not having thought of it before, preferring to go through withdrawals rather than contemplate parting with a possession I already had more than one of. I ran to the toilet to get the crapping over with. By now I had hot dribbles down to my socks but it didn't bother me too much. It also didn't bother me as my bowels exploded for the umpteenth time that day, splattering the rim of the lavatory bowl. I usually felt embarrassed that my shit ended up in places nobody else's did but, then, in an hour or so that problem wouldn't apply: I'd have the glorious constipation that goes with being wasted.

A sharp, involuntary clenching of my stomach made me gasp. I bowed my head, closing my eyes. There was a very brief respite, then they came again, twice as savage: cramps hitting my abdomen as though someone was in there grabbing fistfuls of my intestines. It was so painful I cried out. Tears filled my eyes. I'd had these attacks yesterday and all this morning. It was shocking that anything could be so painful. Suddenly, I was hit by a double attack of cramps and diarrhoea - my anus rasping another hot stream simultaneously with my gut rolling and retracting. My entire body shot forward then back on the toilet seat, reacting mindlessly to the chaotic happenings inside me. When the cramps subsided once more, my head collapsed toward my knees. I groaned in exhaustion. The groan echoed off the room's tiled walls. And yet... Deep down, I still felt happy. Before, these attacks had stretched in front of me into the distance. Now I knew this would probably be the last.

I decided to sell my Gibson Les Paul. It was the one I played least. I'd only bought it because Mick Jones of The Clash had used one.

Only it wasn't as simple as that. After bathing - I'd have had a shower, if we had a shower hose - and throwing my dirty clothes in the washing machine, I took my Gibson to a shop in Notting Hill Gate that bought and sold instruments. They only offered me £45 for it. I'd been hoping for at least eighty. That way, instead of going through all the palaver of having to score again, I'd be able to buy enough to last me four or five days. I'd take it in diminishing quantities over those four or five days, at the end of which I'd be virtually clean and any withdrawals would be minor. Then I could go back to a proper life.

When the assistant at the shop told me what he was prepared to give me for the Les Paul, it was as though he'd physically struck me. The thought of having to go back home to get a further guitar to sell him was ludicrous: I was leaning against the counter because I was now at the stage where I couldn't stand up straight. Every muscle I had felt slack. I wouldn't be able to make it home and back here. It was like telling me to swim to America. I stared at him, completely frozen. I could have wept. It was only when I realised that the assistant had glanced uneasily at his colleague behind the counter that it occurred to me that I must be presenting a strange sight. I bowed my head in embarrassment, hardly believing that I'd been standing quivering and on the point of tears before a complete stranger.

In trying to recover I was too hasty, stammering my words. "Er, I... Er... Can't you - It's... "

He was staring at me almost fearfully. "Right," I said firmly. When I saw that he didn't understand me, I elaborated: "I'll take it." Unfortunately, those words barely came out, my throat managing only a hoarse whisper.

The assistant's colleague had to explain: "He says 45 quid's okay." I could feel the both of them staring after me as I walked out with my 45 pounds in my hand.

* * * *

I went to a dealer who was fairly nearby in a block of flats in Holland Park. I didn't know him personally but I knew the address because Doug had stopped off there on the way to rehearsals with me about three months before. A harsh-faced blonde girl in her twenties opened the door. I found myself not really knowing what to say to her. Up until fairly recently, I'd always acquired drugs in a quite informal manner, buying off acquaintances or else letting Doug get them for the both of us. The girl wasn't perturbed by my slack-mouthed confusion, though. She opened the door for me to step inside. It was probably blindingly obvious why I was there. Even freshly bathed, I must look as big a wreck as I felt. She was used to them.

She walked barefoot through a carpeted hallway, leading me into a living room that looked as though it belonged to any respectable member of society. In there, a longhaired man in his late-twenties was talking on the phone. I sat in an armchair without waiting to be asked. I'd have fallen down otherwise.

The man was finishing his conversation. As he pressed the button on the cordless phone, he looked at me, raising his eyebrows. "What you after?"

"Smack."

"How much you got?" His manner wasn't warm but wasn't unfriendly either.

"45 quid."

"Right. You get half a gram for that."

It was about what I'd expected. I handed over the money while his girlfriend watched, drawing on her cigarette. When he briefly flipped through the edge of the notes and then tossed them on the table without counting properly, I got a strange feeling. I could have kissed his feet. It just seemed an act of such kindness. It was what withdrawal reduced you to: anybody ending your turkey seemed like a god, let alone somebody who communicated that he trusted you not to con him. I made big, dopey eyes at him to convey my heartfelt thanks as he gave me a small wrap of paper.

I stood up and uncertainly asked, "Can I use your toilet?"

"Nah, not in 'ere, mate," the girl said.

"Oh, okay... Thanks, then." I turned toward the hallway. The girl followed me to let me out.

I was shocked at the bright light and city noise when I was back on the landing. I wandered down to the far end of the landing, looking for an alternative stairwell to the one I'd come up. I found it - a fire escape that was likely to be quieter than the stairs at the main entrance. I walked down a flight and sat down, pulling my gear from my pockets. My needle was blunt but had only ever been used by me. It would have been nice to be able to sterilise it but I wasn't going to wait a second longer than I had to. I was seething with impatience as I waited the few seconds for the smack - mixed up in the spoon with my saliva - to dissolve from the heat of the maximum flame of my lighter, hissing at it, "Come on, come on!"

I raised my head, but not particularly quickly, when I heard footsteps on the stairs. It didn't seem as though I was in the same world as the sounds for several precious moments. By the time I realised this was still real life, I was looking at a tall black bloke slowly descending the flight I was sitting on. His eyes moved from my spoon to my curious face. His expression was knowing and contemptuous. Behind him were two other blacks, both, like him, in their early twenties. He sneered at me: "Junkie!" One of the others sucked his teeth.

I tried to ignore them as the first one sauntered past, eyes still on me. They'd be gone in seconds. Just concentrate on your stuff. The smack was now a steaming, brown puddle, exactly the state for injecting. I was torn between being self-conscious and unashamedly ravenous as I started to draw up the liquid through the sodden cigarette filter that floated in its middle. Suddenly, a hand whipped out of nowhere and sent the spoon spinning into the air, its contents splashing on the stone steps. I jerked my head sideways and found myself looking into the mischievously smirking face of the second black. The cruelty of what he'd done - the deliberate wastage of what had taken me physical agony and my own property to obtain - was beyond belief.

Staring into his eyes, I literally wailed: an elongated, shattered moan. The three looked at each other in amazement and amusement. In slow motion, my open-mouthed face turned to look at the scattered smack. It was now almost nothing but dark dashes over several steps. The one exception was a small pool below one of my knees. Immediately on seeing it, I erupted up, span and tried to pull it up into the syringe. Somewhere in the distance, I registered the laughter of the three but all I could really concentrate on was the devastating fact that the most I could draw into the needle was a millimetre of liquid, none of which could be guaranteed to be free of the impurities that a cigarette filter would usually keep out.

Tears were rolling down my cheeks. Incredibly, though, what they'd done was not enough for them. The first one grabbed hold of my collar and wrenched me backwards.

"You got any smack for me, man?" he mocked.

"*No!*" I screamed.

The others laughed at my hysteria but within a microsecond their laughter receded into distance because in attempting to wrench free of the first black I experienced an attack of exhaustion and dizziness that made everything sparkly. When the sparkliness faded, I found myself on all fours, my head bowed and one of my palms resting in another small pool of liquid smack that I hadn't noticed. Out of the corner of my vision, I saw the group trotting down the next flight of stairs. I was already oblivious to them, hastily putting the needle tip to the newly discovered puddle. It didn't improve the level in the syringe by much. I jacked up what there was. After that, I lowered my body and licked at the pools and dashes of the spilled smack.

After doing that, I sat there with my arms around my shins and my forehead resting on my knees. This was unbelievable. After all I'd gone through today, I still needed to find a way to score.

* * * *

I went round to Doug's. It was something that wouldn't have occurred to me if I hadn't been desperate. Doug had been sacked from the band about six weeks ago for not turning up for a gig. This had been the final straw after he'd repeatedly missed rehearsals. We'd voted on it and Mick had been the only dissenter. I hadn't felt sorry for Doug, firstly because he wasn't a particularly pleasant person, secondly because I didn't see his using as an excuse for inconveniencing the rest of us. I was just as addicted as he was but it would never have occurred to me to miss rehearsals. As for failing to turn up for a gig, I just found that shocking.

He lived in a squat in Notting Hill Gate. The journey back there, which I walked, wasn't as bad as the one to Holland Park because the smack I'd managed to consume had taken the edge off the turkey. I was feverish and aching so much it was an effort not to whine out loud but I didn't quite feel on the cusp of death anymore. I was rehearsing what I'd say to Doug all the way there. I hadn't been around when he'd been told he was sacked. I'd deliberately arrived late that day so I wouldn't have to see him. I knew that the others had told him there'd been a vote on it. I was trying to work out a conversation-opener that would suggest that I hadn't really had much to do with the decision.

It turned out that Doug didn't seem that bothered by being sacked. When he came to the door of the flat after one of his fellow squatters opened it and went to get him for me, he simply nodded and motioned me inside. I followed him down the hallway, engulfed by his intense sweaty smell. His room was large but extremely bare, with no proper bed, carpet or decorations. I noticed his drums, packed in their black PVC cases, stacked against a wall. Doug sat on a mattress covered in a few blankets on the floor below the room's window. I didn't want to sit next to him or touch his dubious-looking blankets so instead walked over to the window and pretended to look at the view.

"You lot still togevver, then?" he asked.

His lack of visible resentment had made me decide to get straight to the point and ask him if he had any stuff, but he had spoken as I was preparing to frame my question and it threw me off balance. "Er... Yeah. 'Mean, we're waiting to see what's happening at the moment. We're not really rehearsing or anything."

He nodded.

"Doug... You got any smack? I'm really fucked. And I haven't got any money'

"Ain't got any smack..."

I grimaced.

"Got some dikes, though..." He walked over to a cardboard box that seemed to contain his clothes. I had heard the term before but didn't know what it referred to. He produced a small brown bottle from the folds of a jumper.

My heart sank. Some puny ordinary medicine from a chemist's shop was not what I needed. "Haven't you got anything else?"

He shook his head. It was such a typical gesture from him - abrupt and unconcerned in the face of somebody else's discomfort - that it reminded me of how much I couldn't stand him. "Fucking hell, Doug!" I said. However, there was a slight rein on my anger. I didn't want my tone to be too harsh because he still might provide access to something or someone that could stop my pain.

It bounced off him anyway. Expressionless, he walked over and held the bottle out to me. I looked at the two-colour, printed label: "Diconal".

"What is it?"

"Dikes. They're painkillers. Take away the withdrawal pains."

"Really?"

"Yeah. I was into them before I was into smack."

I looked at him. "What do you do - inject them?"

"Yeah. Crush 'em up."

The thought flashed through my mind of the dangers of injecting oral drugs into my bloodstream. Then I remembered the stuff I'd been in danger of injecting - and possibly had - every time I'd taken smack over the last few months and the misgiving seemed ridiculous.

I opened the bottle and poured some of the pills into my hand.

"Oi, *oi!*" Doug said. "You ain't 'aving that many." He took some back and reclaimed the bottle, leaving me with four tablets in my palm.

I didn't feel irritated. After all, he was giving me something that would help relieve my pains without asking anything in return. Maybe he wasn't as bad as I'd always thought. The tablets were little pink things with the word WELLCOME stamped into them. Doug showed me how to dissolve them in water and then inject them. They didn't make me feel great in the way a hit of heroin did. But they did make me feel normal again - able to think about things other than my creaking body.

Afterwards, we sat around hatching plans to get more Diconal or maybe methadone off a doctor. We talked for a couple of hours about it. While we were talking, I felt optimistic and excited at the thought of getting stuff without having to flog my possessions or be humiliated in the way I was outside that dealer's flat today. Walking home, though, I started to feel depressed. I was living the lifestyle that had seemed so pathetic to me only a few months before when I'd observed that Doug seemed to spend every minute he wasn't playing trying to work out ways to score. It was stupid. Empty. And a total waste of money. And yet, I didn't have any choice but to go along with his ideas. How else was I going to get through the next few days? I never, ever wanted to go through another day like today.

Christ, we needed to do some gigs. There was still enough of a market for us to fill out venues like The Marquee. If we could arrange a few gigs quickly, then we'd all have money on our hands. And I'd have enough to get a steady supply of smack and wean myself off it. But we didn't have a drummer and everybody was apathetic at the moment.

When I got back, I was glad to find Mick wasn't in. I knew I'd have to face him some time and explain about his missing silver disc but I didn't want to do it today. I just wanted some sleep. The thought of going to bed was a wonderful one. An end to another terrible day.

Who would believe that three years after signing a major record deal I'd be in this position? Life was no different. Well, yes it was. It was worse. Not the fact of being a junkie. Just the general sense of having achieved nothing. It was worse than that depressing and frightening period when the Ragamuffins had started to drift apart because of the rejections. It was worse because this time we'd almost made it and we'd seen it slip away. When you were going through the depression the second time round, you had both the depression and the deja vu to deal with. The deja vu made it seem like a sick joke. Plus there was the knowledge that you'd had the chance. They didn't come around too often. It was difficult to keep up your hope sufficiently to have any more goals when you knew you'd already had opportunities most people never did.

If someone had told me three years ago that the level of fame and acclaim we had achieved would not improve our lives one iota, I wouldn't have believed them. When I say fame, okay we weren't talking about household names. But videos on *The Chart Show*, seven *Top Of The Pops* appearances, Single Of The Week in *Melody Maker* and *NME* more than once, one of the Albums Of The Year in *Rolling Stone*, spreads in *The Face, Q, Time Out...* In three years we'd made three acclaimed albums. We'd done four British headlining tours of anything up to 5000 seaters - all sold out. It was success by anybody's standards. I remembered one particular day when I'd sat revelling in the sight of our video for *Glam Slam* on *The Chart Show* then went down the road for some shopping and found that the S&H promotions people had done their work for the single: my face was plastered over every derelict shop front I passed.

And what was the tally at the end? I'd never earned more than £150 a week. I was living in a shared flat whose rent was cheaper than the one Mick and I had shared three years ago. And I, like all the others, now owed the record company £30,000. And that was just the financial cost.

There was no way we could complain about the support S&H had given us, though. Yes, they were now dropping us, but only after several years of losing money on us. During that time, they'd never once interfered with our music and never once asked us to do anything ridiculous to promote it. The first album hadn't recouped the recording costs or the advertising budget, but they told us not to worry. I remembered Desmond Smith telling us that he was going to make the public realise how good we were. We were nurtured by S&H. They gave us a much bigger budget for our second LP, *Revelation*. We hired a famous producer, Vic Steven, and recorded it straight after coming off tour. It was brilliant and it got great reviews. Even when that failed to take off, they didn't do what they could have done: let us go. We were already in so much debt to them that it was obvious that if we didn't have a big success with the next album, it was unlikely they'd ever recoup what they'd spent. Letting us go would have meant cutting their losses. But they believed in us and gave us another chance. Only to find that no matter how many times we appeared in the music press - and the American music press absolutely loved us - and no matter how many small-to-medium gigs we could sell out, we were never going to be the platinum-album, stadium-filling act they had imagined we would be.

Doug and Mick were pissed off with the fact that we were left in debt because acts had to pay their own recording costs. Writers didn't have to pay for their books to be printed, did they? (If S&H had dropped us after the second album, we wouldn't have owed them anything because they would have broken the contract.) I didn't really agree with them. S&H had invested literally millions in us. I'd met an advertising guy from S&H once and he'd told me that one of our British singles alone had cost £60,000 to promote. The record company had put their money where their mouth was.

It was what I'd told that radio interviewer on our first American tour: we were living the lifestyles of rock stars without the financial rewards. Tours and records and videos and press cuttings and recognition in the street could make you feel you had made it but, in reality, we had never had genuine success. I was still the same working class nothing who assistants in hi-fi shops could humiliate by refusing to prove to me that my player had been fixed properly. I was still down with the unwashed bloody masses.

Of course, I had something the unwashed masses didn't have: a talent and the residue of the small amount of fame we'd achieved. Record royalties were out of the question but there would be a trickle of publishing royalties. And we could still make a moderate living playing live in British cities. That was all it was though: a living. Without a recording contract, we'd be playing to an audience that would gradually diminish, milking past achievements for their last drops. Eric had said we might be able to find an indie label prepared to sign us. But what could a small independent label do for us that a major couldn't? The production would automatically be inferior on any album we made for an indie: none of them had the money for a good budget. We would at least still be creating, still doing what we loved, but it was small comfort. I'd seen other bands do it: hanging on grimly to a

SEAN EGAN

recording career for a few more years in the pathetic belief that if they had one more try they'd make it. Bands came and bands went. If you were switching from a major to an indie you were already on the way down. We only had more disappointment ahead of us.

I'd drifted back into smack. I'd just wanted something occasionally to take away the dreary sense of anti-climax of my life. I'd begun using every few days. On smack, if taken irregularly, there were no severe after-effects. I couldn't deal with any more hangovers. But what at first had been once in a while became every other day. And then I'd begun to tell myself that even if I did shoot up on two or three consecutive days, abstinence over the next week would prevent me getting addicted. Trouble was, I never could abstain so long. I was bored, now that we weren't playing live and had nothing to record or promote, I was lonely - still celibate and solitary - and I was so, so disappointed. So then I'd told myself that okay, I was becoming an addict, but it was no big deal because when the time came I could just wean myself off it gradually. In fact, that thought had become very attractive to me. It meant I didn't have to agonise about becoming addicted anymore: as there was a relatively pain-free way to stop, I could allow myself the luxury of being a regular user for a while. I'd knock it off when things got a bit better. Things getting a bit better always seemed a vague "in a few months" in my head.

PART FOUR

Twenty-Three

The keyboardist and the bassist were arguing. The bassist was called Aaron, although he didn't pronounce it like Aaron who had been in the Ragamuffins. He was a blonde American with film-star good looks, which he spoilt slightly - I felt - with a poncey earring. He said it: "Arron". He was telling Justin, our bespectacled, skinny, black-haired keyboardist, that his playing was "baroque". Doug, sat behind his kit, was, like me, trying to keep out of it.

"What the fuck's that?" Justin asked.

"It means elaborate. Over-elaborate. You're going over the top. It's supposed to be a quiet love song and you're drowning it."

Justin turned to me in exasperation. I always got the feeling he would be proud as punch if I backed him up in a musical dispute. He'd been a big Coronets fan and had been disbelieving when he answered the ad in the *Melody Maker* and found that the band he was applying to join was my new one. It so happened that today I agreed with his point of view so no doubt he was ecstatic when I turned to Aaron and said, "No, it sounds okay. It sounds... rich. It sounds good."

"I don't want it to be 'rich'. I want it understated."

I opened my mouth. I closed it again. I wasn't going to get into any arguments in this band. It wasn't worth caring. I'd learnt that from the Ragamuffins and the Coronets: you could agonise over every last note but that didn't mean the band were going to end up any better off. As the two of them continued to bicker, I lifted my strap over my head and went off to the toilet.

Getting to the toilet meant climbing the stairs of the house Aaron rented with three other Yanks. It was back to the days of rehearsing in living rooms. As I stood peeing, I suddenly hoped that the tiff downstairs would lead to the rehearsal petering out, as they often did when two or more people who were supposed to be creating together abruptly couldn't stand the sight of each other. Then I could slope off early to go and see Bruce. Meeting him yesterday had been a Godsend. Maybe he would give me some free drugs again today.

Unfortunately, the argument had more or less been resolved by the time I went back down. Justin had decided, if somewhat sullenly, to refrain from playing his baroque patterns while Aaron tried to follow his train of thought, so I had to stick around another hour or so. After which, I went back to the bedsit I had over Mr. Case's shop to dump my stuff before setting off to Bruce's. Though I'd told Doug about re-meeting our mutual acquaintance yesterday, I didn't tell him I was going back to see him today: Bruce might not have enough drugs for three and if he didn't I wanted to make sure that he was sharing with me.

Bruce greeted me with a silly, giddy warmth. "Paaaul! Alright, mate?"

"Alright?"

"Come in..."

My heart sank when, leading me to the living room, which loud music was emanating from, he said, "I've got a few mates round..." It meant no opportunity for the sense of intimacy that us being alone had generated yesterday. That might reduce my chances of getting any more smack off him.

I knew at a glance that his friends were all druggies. It was five or six blokes and a couple of girls. They were lounging around on the floor and the furniture. All of them had that junkie air: unhealthy, slightly scruffy, and with a part-hostile, part-shattered attitude. Some had pupils that made them look like David Bowie in *The Man Who Fell To Earth*. Not one of them said hello when

Bruce introduced me. Their eyes just flicked my way and then looked away or else followed me almost suspiciously as I sat on the wooden chair Bruce offered me.

Bruce then disappeared without a word to the kitchen and I was left sitting extremely self-consciously with nothing to do. I felt like an intruder. I was a bit ashamed: sitting amidst people who were his genuine friends, me only here to scrounge. I stared at a spot on the wall, trying to appear as though I was deep in thought and oblivious to them all. The fact that they weren't saying much to each other made me even more uncomfortable. Like any gathering of junkies, they weren't exactly a lively bunch, talking desultorily amidst much scratching and blowing of noses. Whenever another silence came along, I was sure everyone's attention was on me.

"Oi, mate..."

I looked up, trying to locate the person who'd spoken. It was a bloke with curly black hair and a black beard, dressed in jeans and a denim jacket. He was sitting in a group of three over by Bruce's stereo. The two blokes with him were looking through Bruce's album sleeves in a disinterested fashion. The bearded man made to say something more from where he was but after glancing at the doorway moved closer to me, shuffling on his knees across the carpet. He rose slightly to put his elbow on the arm of the sofa next to my chair.

"So how long you known Bruce then?" he said in a low tone.

Immediately, I knew there was something going on. "Not long," I said guardedly.

"What... When you say not long, 'ow long're you talking about? A few weeks, like?"

"'Bout that," I lied.

"So you're not, like, a good friend of 'is? You don't know 'im that well?"

I looked across at his two companions. They were no longer pretending to look through the record sleeves but were following our conversation. "No," I replied.

"Oh, right. 'Cos we don't eever..." The bearded bloke looked down. I got the feeling he was trying to work out what to say next. His friends were moving across now.

"I mean," the bearded one started again, almost whispering now. "It's not like... You know, you're not friends, right? So..."

One of his two companions, now both kneeling beside him on the floor, came to his aid. He was a weaselly-looking bloke with red hair. His manner was more impatient than the bearded one's. "You're only here for the drugs, right? Like us."

I couldn't really deny it. Embarrassed, I shrugged.

"Fing is," the red-haired one continued, and his voice now went so low I could hardly hear it, "this bloke's got sixty grams of smack..." The conspiratorial nature of his voice made me feel guilty and caused me to glance up at the others in the room. Only one person was paying attention to us - a blonde girl lying full-length on her side on the floor, a cigarette in her hand - but even she glanced unconcernedly away when my eyes met hers. The red-haired one looked round too and, satisfied, carried on. "We're gonna get it. 'E don't need it - 'e's giving it away to people." He paused. "Are you in?"

I'd worked it out. The rest of the people in the room were Bruce's real friends. These three were, like me, just people he'd offered some of his stuff to when he'd been feeling lonely.

"What d'you mean?" I said.

"You know," said the bearded one. "Fuckin' take it. 'E don't need it."

Sixty grams split four ways was fifteen grams each. Enough to last me two, three weeks. And four people could overcome one person - especially one pathetic weak junkie who had to offer drugs to get company - with very little effort.

I looked into the face of the weaselly-looking redhead, whose red-rimmed eyes were eagerly awaiting my response. Like me, he hadn't shaved for a couple of days. I could see flecks of dried food in the ginger bristles on his chin. Bruce had already presumably given him some of his stuff for nothing. I'd never, ever known a junkie who had been prepared to give drugs away with no conditions. Bruce might be a boring, pathetic lonely person but he didn't deserve what they were thinking of.

The bearded one must have seen the look of distaste on my face. He slapped the shoulder of the redhead and rose. The three of them withdrew to the corner where Bruce's records were. I could sense them glaring at me during the next few minutes. It didn't make me feel any superior to them, though. I'd been tempted.

Bruce finally reappeared. He beckoned me into the kitchen from the doorway. He had some freshly boiled smack laid out for me on the kitchen counter. There was even a needle placed beside the bowl for my convenience, although of course I'd be using my own.

"Oh, thanks Bruce," I said, and I meant it. I looked up from the delicious-looking brown puddle into his face. I wanted to give him a warning. Wanted to tell him that some of the people in the other room were out to do him harm.

Before I could, he had replied, "Oh that's alright, mate", slapped me on the arm and left the room.

I hesitated a moment, then turned to the drugs, digging my needle out of my breast pocket.

* * * *

I heard shouts and hurried footsteps and urgent commands a thousand miles in the distance. My eyes flickered open. They were the sounds of panic. I allowed my eyelids to descend again and continued to enjoy my drowsiness.

I could have shouted in outrage when I realised that the rocking my body was experiencing was somebody trying to shake me awake. I sprung to my feet, snarling.

A male face that I recognised from the living room earlier sprung back when its owner saw my aggressive posture. Backing toward the kitchen door, he explained, "Better get out, mate. There's been two OD's." With that, he turned and joined a couple of others hurriedly exiting through the front door. I caught a brief glimpse of one of his companions: the blonde girl who had been smoking a fag on the carpet earlier.

I put a hand on a counter while my brain tried to come to the surface. After a few seconds of laboured breathing and still unrelieved grogginess, I went and sat down in the chair again. I put my hands to my face, rubbing slowly.

A picture appeared in my head of a weaselly-looking redhead with food flecks in his stubble. I sprang to my feet so fast the chair legs squealed and clattered on the lino. Bruce. That bloke had said overdose. Jesus - don't say they'd... I was stumbling through the hallway and into the living room. The first thing I saw was Bruce lying on the floor, his eyes closed, his mouth open, his head flopped to the side.

"*Fuck!*" I screamed.

It was only when the girl leaning over Bruce flung her head toward me in surprise that I realised there was anyone else in the room. In fact, there were three people apart from Bruce and me. One was the bearded bloke, back propped against the settee. Kneeling over him was the weaselly-looking redhead.

"You fucking-" I started, glaring at the redhead. My outrage and fear were so great, I couldn't get anything else out. Then the fear took over and I ran to the kitchen to find a weapon. I saw the syringe Bruce had provided for me where he'd left it on the counter beside the cooker. Instinctively, I grabbed at it, ready to stab with it. Then I realised what a pathetic knife that would make and looked desperately about for a proper one. I spied a drawer and dived over and tore it open. There was a huge bread knife in there. I was turning toward the doorway even as I wrenched it out. The expected attacker wasn't there. The knife in front of me, I stepped carefully toward the hallway. I realised I was crying. They'd done it. I'd known they were going to. I should have said something. The thought brought my anger back and I wasn't scared anymore. I marched back into the living room, perfectly prepared to kill.

The scene was as I'd left it. My eyes went from the bearded one and the redhead, still beside the sofa, to the girl kneeling over Bruce. I was trembling, my breaths shuddering out of me. I realised the redhead and the girl were looking at me in alarm, or rather at the blade I was holding unsteadily in front of me. Several seconds of silence followed, during which I switched my eyes back and forth between the two couples. During those seconds, I became aware of a few things. One was that Bruce's head was in the girl's lap and her demeanour when I'd originally come in had been one of concern. The other thing I realised was that the redhead might be staring at me, but his bearded friend's eyes were closed. So many explanations for what I was looking at flashed through my head. My heart hammering away, I was imagining the bearded one and his friend trying to take Bruce's drugs from him and Bruce and the bloke with the beard being injured in the fight. No longer concerned about the girl, I turned all my attention on the other two.

"You fucking arsehole!" I barked at the redhead.

His eyes were wide. I revelled in his fear, imagining the terror Bruce had experienced when he and his friends had put their plan into action. The only thing was, I wasn't sure now what to do. Even in the state I was in, I wasn't going to stick the blade in him - not if he wasn't attacking me. Plus I was desperate about Bruce. My head swung back to him. His eyes were still closed, his head still turned away in that alarmingly lifeless manner. I looked from him into the girl's face. She was crying.

"Is he alright?" I said.

She didn't answer.

I shouted it at her. "Is he *alright!*"

She shook her head, biting her lip.

I turned back to the redhead, stepping toward him, knife before me, suddenly once again angry enough to be ready to use it. He got hurriedly to his feet and walked backwards slowly.

"You cunt! What did you do to him?"

He shook his head, his mouth hanging open.

"You fucking little arsehole!"

"I ain't done nuffin'..."

"Fucking knew you- You bastard!"

"What?"

"What did you do to him?"

"Nuffin'! 'E overdosed!"

"Because of you!"

"No! Tony's OD'd an' all - look!" He indicated the one with the beard. I glanced at his friend. He still had his eyes closed. "It was too pure, that stuff."

I looked into his weaselly, red-rimmed eyes. The thing about weaselly junkies was that they were convincing liars - they had no shame about wheedling and whining to try to fool people. But... It was possible. I had just come out of being wasted. I wasn't thinking totally straight. Maybe I was jumping to conclusions.

"Look at 'im," the redhead said.

I tightened my grip on the knife as I stepped over and peered into the face of the one with the beard. I also kept glancing at the redhead. You just couldn't drop your guard amongst the scum you met in junkie circles. I jabbed the tip of the blade into the bearded one's face. There was a brief muscle spasm and blood abruptly sprung onto the skin but otherwise there was no reaction. I looked up at the redhead.

"'E's dead," he said. Then added "They bofe are..."

I looked at Bruce. The girl's face was shiny with tears. I went over and felt for a pulse in Bruce's wrist. I couldn't find one. I held the blade of the knife under his nose but when I took it away it wasn't steamed up.

"Come on," the redhead said. "Let's get out of 'ere."

It was a sensible suggestion but instead of rising, I slumped from my kneeling position into a sitting one. I was exhausted. I was also embarrassed at having accused the redhead - whose own friend was dead. And I was disoriented, part of me still inhabiting the other world heroin took you into. I also felt sick. Not exactly grief stricken - after all, I hardly knew Bruce. But he had shown me kindness.

The girl tried to get me to leave with her but I ignored her. The redhead stayed behind after she left, looking for Bruce's hoard. He was justifying himself to me, saying there was no point in wasting it, but he needn't have bothered. I didn't have the energy to get angry. I twisted over and lay on my back beside Bruce, my hands over my eyes.

* * * *

I'd been sitting on a bench on Eel Brook Common for at least an hour. It was cold and the happy couples passing by made me feel melancholy and alone. I could have gone back to my bedsit but the thought of the hairs and soap and piss in my sink seemed to sum up the sick mess my life was. So I'd stayed here. I wasn't going to rehearsals tonight. Couldn't imagine wanting to go ever again. Or anywhere else. I was sick of being me.

There was somebody standing over me. A male face was smiling at me. I knew him from somewhere but I also knew he couldn't be anyone important because I wasn't able to put a name to him. His smile irritated me, even frightened me a little bit. It seemed almost as though he was leering at me. I looked down at a small shape hovering below my chin. It was the top of the head of a little girl who was gazing blankly at me. My eyes were drawn to the bright red of her big woollen mittens. I looked back into her face. I wasn't irritated or frightened anymore: she was with the man so he couldn't be any danger. Something about the girl's face was compelling. She had faint dark rings around her eyes and a slightly flat nose. They rang a bell far, far back in my mind. I looked up into the man's face and was gazing at the same dark rings and misshaped nose. I knew those features, I was certain. The man was still smiling, waiting for something from me. In another second, I realised what he was waiting for was recognition as my brain finally yielded up the information that this was my cousin Andrew.

"Oh," I said.

Andrew sat down beside me and pulled the little girl between his knees. "Didn't recognise me, did ya?"

I was shaking my head but not in answer to his question. It was a way of trying to tell him I couldn't cope with this. I wasn't in the mood for reunions. Plus there was something else. I didn't want him to see me like this. I hadn't seen him since the Ragamuffins split up seven, eight years ago but I had spoken to him on the phone when the Coronets were touring America the second time round. If I spoke to him now, it would be obvious how far I'd fallen since then.

"You look different yourself," he said.

Self-conscious, I looked into the distance. There were a lot of things about me I didn't want him to notice, chief amongst which was the fact that if you looked closely you could see - surreally -

a tinge to my skin that you would just have to describe as yellow. I didn't know if he'd know what that meant.

"You in a new band?" he asked. "Couldn't believe it when I 'eard the Coronets 'ad split up".

Jesus. He would have to say it. Absolute confirmation that I didn't need this at all. I was literally about to get up and walk off when he added, "Wish you 'adn't. Fantastic band."

I remembered the phone conversation we'd had when the Coronets were in Illinois. It was an armpit of a place but to Andrew - back in dreary, drizzly Tooting - it sounded exotic. Just like all the other places we were gigging at the time. He'd been so pleased for me. I'd come away from the call slightly sad because he'd sounded regretful that he'd given up on the Ragamuffins. He was the manager in a press cuttings agency at the time. I could tell he was thinking It Could Have Been Me.

My hostility dissipated. He wasn't like that weaselly redhead. I was with one of the good, normal people in life now. I wasn't able to smile but I raised my eyebrows in acknowledgement of the compliment.

He looked into my eyes and snorted, surprised and pleased that we'd met again after all this time, waiting for me to express the same feelings. My face wandered away from his.

"This is Louise, by the way..." I looked at the girl, whose blonde hair he fondly tousled. "You've never seen 'er, 'ave ya?"

"No".

"She's nearly four now." He bowed to look into her solemn face and said, "That's your uncle Paul."

She looked up into his face. "I seen 'im on telly."

Andrew laughed. "No. 'E's your uncle. 'E's my cousin."

"'E plays the guitar."

Andrew looked at me in puzzlement for a moment. Then he said, "Oh, that's right. She's seen Coronets videos. She knows you."

I was somewhat surprised to say the least. A second ago Andrew had confirmed my worse suspicions by telling me I looked different. It came as a bit of a relief that his kid could still recognise me from images of two or three years ago.

Andrew sang a few bars of *Glam Slam* to her. It looked like he was waiting for her to join in, as though she usually did. But she got shy and turned her face away from me, burrowing into his chest. Andrew snorted and turned back my way.

"You've got a fan there, I tell ya. She loves *Glam Slam*."

I didn't respond. I was gloomy again.

"So what you doing these days? In a new band?"

I nodded.

"What they called?"

I kept my mouth closed for a couple of seconds. I opened it and, after a pause, said "No name yet."

"You got a deal yet?"

I shook my head.

"What kind of music you play?"

I didn't answer, looking at the teenagers playing football on the pitch on the other side.

"I saw Philip not long ago. He's working in telesales. Sells magazine subscriptions."

Despite myself, I looked at him. I remembered Phil and his gormless way of speaking and endless effing and blinding. "Telesales?"

"Yeah."

"Who'd buy a magazine subscription off Phil?"

Andrew laughed, nodding. "I know."

I finally managed a smile. I looked at my shoes. I looked back at Andrew. "What about Aaron?"

"Oh 'e's making a lot of money actually. Labouring jobs, but a lot of money. Ten pound an hour sometimes."

"You still manager of that cuttings agency?"

He shook his head. "My girlfriend works. I play with an oldies band, called Crawfish. Make a bit of money doing that. I look after *her* in the daytime." He gazed at his daughter for a few moments. "Best job in the world."

Louise, her forehead still pressed against Andrew's chest, was examining me out of the corner of her eye. Her suspicion of me was so blatant that it actually managed to bring another smile out of me. Suddenly, I felt better. Andrew's love for her and her own innocence were endearing. I asked "You seen my Dad lately?"

"Yeah, saw 'im at my Mum and Dad's place a couple of weeks ago. You ain't seen 'im in years, 'ave ya?"

I shook my head.

"How many years? Two? Three?"

"About that," I said sheepishly.

We said nothing for a while, both watching the footballers across the way. Then Andrew asked, "You wanna come back to our place? You're not going anywhere this evening, are you? Have dinner with us if you like."

The thought struck me straight away that to spend an evening with Andrew and his girlfriend and kid - discussing our family and talking about old times - would be so refreshing. Like stepping out of the dark - junkie life - into the light - normal life. "Yeah," I said. "Okay."

* * * *

I'd never met Lisa, Andrew's girlfriend, before. She came home from work to find me on the sofa with Louise sitting on my lap watching cartoons while Andrew prepared the evening meal in the kitchen. The three lived in a second floor flat in a pretty nice council estate in Fulham. Lisa was slightly older than Andrew, in her thirties, and I was a bit wary of her. She worked as a manager in a student canteen and I assumed a career woman like that would be even more contemptuous of men than I knew all women already were. Yet when someone is genuinely interested in you - as she, being a Coronets fan too, was - you can't help being disarmed by them. The fact that talking about the Coronets made me uncomfortable these days didn't really come into it. I revelled in the novelty of two people hanging on my every word instead of dismissing me as a scrounging piece of junkie trash. And Louise was just as star-struck as them. Her shyness had faded away and she'd taken a shine to me based on my many appearances on her family's television screen.

At eight o' clock we were gathered round the circular glass dining table in their living room, the Small Faces playing on the stereo (I'd asked them not to play Coronets stuff), eating a nice chicken dinner. There was a fifth place set for Chester, Louise's teddy bear. Lisa was asking me why I left the Coronets, which fact had been reported in all the music papers a few months before the entire band had split up.

"Well, I just wasn't as enthusiastic anymore. 'Cos we lost our contract with S&H and they were talking about signing to an indie label and I just didn't see the point. We were never gonna get back to where we were before. So I just lost enthusiasm."

All of that was true, although it wasn't why I'd left the band. Mick said to me one day, "Paul, I've got some bad news." He looked me straight in the eye as he explained: "You're too unreliable. I'm sorry, mate. We took a vote."

I'd been kicked out for exactly the same reason that I had helped kick Doug out: I was too often off trying to score when I should have been at rehearsals. It was a sickening feeling. Not just the irony but also the knowledge that colleagues and friends couldn't stand me anymore. Mick, of course, had been very sorry about it but I'd had a couple of warnings before. And suddenly my lack of enthusiasm was thrown into perspective: an over-the-hill band with the chance of a modest contract with a small label was a better prospect than being an unemployed guitarist.

Andrew said "I was really surprised when I saw one of the Coronets say in the NME that the Coronets never made any money, apart from the publishing royalties."

"Everyone always is."

"Yeah, but even I made some money from 'em." When I'd spoken to him from Illinois that time, he'd been over the moon that we'd recorded some Ragamuffins songs. "Even today, I still get cheques for Kind Hearts. And I didn't have to do anything. It don't seem right that you didn't make anything."

"Are you in a new band, Paul?" Lisa asked.

I nodded, speaking around a mouthful of sprouts. "We're trying to get some gigs at the moment." Saying that - the suggestion of activity - made me feel a bit better about my life.

"Must be really bad - having made all those albums but not having earned any money from it," Lisa said.

"It is. Especially when people recognise you. You know: 'What are you doing here, you're a star'."

"D'ya get recognised a lot then?" Andrew asked.

"Quite a lot. Not so much lately, 'cos it's been ages since I left, but about... I dunno, once every few months. And usually they don't quite know who I am. It's just: 'Haven't I met you before?' or 'Haven't I seen you somewhere before?'"

A few minutes later, Lisa was telling us about something that had happened at her work that day. She'd picked up the phone to make a call and found herself on a crossed line, listening to a phone call between two businessmen.

"I put the phone on loudspeaker and we were all sitting there listening to it, then Richie - one of the blokes there - came along and he picked up the receiver and started making animal noises. He was going 'Mooo!' or 'Baaa!' and every time he did it, these two blokes would stop for a second and then carry on talking. They were wondering what the hell was going on but they never mentioned it."

We all laughed together. A small voice echoed the "Moo!" and we turned to it. It was Louise, grinning and waiting for us to congratulate her.

* * * *

A couple of hours later, I was in the bathroom taking a pee. My facial muscles felt strained from the hilarity of the evening. I'd been drinking endless cups of tea as a result of a dry throat stemming from the similarly unfamiliar quantity of conversation. My spirits were bubbling. I couldn't remember when I'd last had such a good time. Doing up my flies, I noticed a bottle of green mouthwash on a shelf. I picked it up and untwisted the cap. I didn't pay too much attention to hygiene these days but I thought I should make the effort tonight. As I poured some mouthwash into the bottle's cap I felt a very faint nausea, more in the chest region than the stomach. Signs of withdrawal. I ignored it and tilted back my head to take in the mint-smelling liquid. Turkey was a problem I could deal with tomorrow. Tonight, I was going to be a normal person.

Twenty-Four

The evening spent with Andrew, Lisa and Louise put me in a strange mood for several days. The simple pleasure to be got from being in the company of a happy ordinary family took me by surprise. It was a change from junkies. And a change from the band, who fatigued me both as people and as a concept whenever I remembered it was my third time around at trying to make it.

I suppose it would have had a similar effect even without those horrible events at Bruce's place, but what happened there really emphasised how terrible my life was compared to Andrew's. When I thought of how I'd run around in hysteria with that knife in a room containing two dead bodies and then thought of little Louise sitting on Andrew's lap singing *Glam Slam* at me, it just made me feel like a primitive life form living in sludge.

I couldn't get over how happy Andrew was. He hadn't got much in life, not when you considered what his ambitions had been when the Ragamuffins were going, but from what I could see he was blissful. He hadn't even got a profession with his degree, let alone become a millionaire rock star, but it didn't occur to him that his life had come to nothing. As far as he was concerned, he had everything he wanted.

Long, long hours were spent in the days after bumping into Andrew thinking these things over. I felt sad, but in a mellow kind of way. It somehow seemed inappropriate to be depressed or bitter. Just as you don't shout in a church, so the lack of trauma or conflict in Andrew's family's life made it feel as though I would somehow be transgressing by feeling any extreme feelings. So I was mellow when practicing with the band, mellow when doing my round in the mornings, even mellow when trying to score, calmly settling for some valium a friend of Doug's had conned his doctor into prescribing instead of what my body really needed.

* * * *

The doorbell rang. Aaron went to answer it. It would be Doug. He was always the last to arrive. That didn't annoy me anymore. I was more tolerant of him these days. In fact, I always felt embarrassed when I thought of how I'd gone along with the plan to sack him from the Coronets. I'd been impressed by the fact that he'd never said to me that I'd got what I deserved when the same thing happened to me.

When Doug entered with Aaron, there was a person with them who I didn't recognise. It was a handsome bloke in his early twenties with short black hair and designer stubble. He wore a flash brown PVC jacket and had a gold chain hanging outside his black sweatshirt. He looked briefly around the faces in the room before Doug murmured something to him and pointed at me. The bloke moved toward me.

"Er, Paul..." Doug said. "You know Bruce? Well this bloke wants to ask you something..."

My head started spinning. A friend of Bruce's? He must think I had something to do with his OD. Laughably, when Doug had indicated me, my first thought was that the bloke was a fan of the Coronets who had asked Doug to introduce him to me. One half of me was embarrassed by my assumption, the other was shell-shocked at what it turned out he did want.

"Can I 'ave a word, mate?" the bloke said in a flat tone.

"Yeah," I said, very quickly and with too much emphasis, anxious to communicate that I was perfectly prepared to co-operate, had nothing to hide.

"We can talk in the kitchen," Doug suggested.

The bloke turned to see where Doug was indicating and, with a glance at me, followed him out of the room. I could feel the others looking at me as I leant my guitar against a chair and went with them.

In the kitchen, the bloke slowly turned to me with his hands on his hips and said, "You know Bruce Smith?"

I hesitated, simply because I'd never heard his surname before. "Yeah," I said, and knew the pause must have made me sound suspicious. I tried to recover: "Yeah," I said again.

"You know where he got the smack 'e 'ad?"

"Well, I don't know who from, exactly..." The bloke's brown eyes gazed levelly into mine. "It was too pure, wasn't it?" I added.

He continued to gaze at me. I moved my eyes to the kitchen table, then back at him. It was almost like being in front of a teacher.

"How d'you know it was too pure?"

What he'd asked felt somehow like a trick question. I hesitated again, unsure that I could say anything that wouldn't incriminate me, at least in his eyes. I could see Doug - who was leaning against a cupboard - trying to be non-committal, quietly looking over at the window on the far wall. After several seconds, I had done nothing except flick my eyes several times away from his stare. I closed my open mouth and shrugged. I made to say something but he cut me off.

"How'd you know it was too pure?" he asked again.

"Well, that's what some bloke there said. I mean, I -"

"Who?"

"Eh? Oh, some bloke who was there... That day..."

"What day?"

My heart was lurching as it occurred to me that he might not even know Bruce was dead. I shrugged. "The- You know..."

His eyes were boring into me. "The day 'e died?"

I didn't know whether or not to be relieved that he did know. "Yeah," I said weakly.

"So 'oo was this bloke you're talking about? What was 'e doing there?"

I tried to ingratiate myself. "Oh he was just some hanger-on. I knew as soon as I saw him. He wasn't a friend of his or anything."

"And 'e was the one 'oo told you the smack was too pure?"

"Yeah. I mean, I don't know whether he was right or not 'cos I'd had some smack off him that day and the day before and it was alright. But two people died that day, so... Maybe it was a different batch..."

"D'you know 'is name?"

"No. I just met him that day."

"And you don't know 'is name?" he said in a tone of mocking disbelief.

"No. I mean, I hardly spoke to him." Yet again, I shrugged. This really was like standing quaking in the presence of a headmaster. I had an amazing feeling of smallness and nervousness.

"Doug told me you goes to 'im Bruce give you free drugs."

I nodded. "Yeah..."

"So why'd 'e do that?"

I had been about to shrug again. I stopped myself and instead it came out as just a twitch of the shoulders. "We were friends." Even saying that made me tremor. If this bloke had been a friend of Bruce's he could easily ask me why we'd never met and I wouldn't have an answer. I could already picture myself shrugging if he did.

"You ever work wiv 'im?"

"Sorry?"

His eyes appraised me for a couple of seconds before he repeated the question. "You ever work wiv 'im?"

"How d'you mean?"

"I mean, did you sell for 'im?"

"Sell? What - drugs? No. No, Bruce wasn't a dealer. 'Mean, he gave smack away."

The bloke suddenly flared up. "'Course 'e gave it away! 'E 'ad sixty fucking grams, didn't 'e?"

I looked at Doug. Wordless, looking as sheepish as I felt at all this, he turned his eyes back on the bloke.

"So what 'appened to the drugs?" the bloke asked.

"What - Bruce's drugs?"

"They *weren't* 'is drugs! What 'appened to 'em? 'Oo's got 'em?"

"I dunno. That bloke was looking for 'em. After Bruce overdosed."

"What - the one you were just talking about?"

I nodded.

"Yeah - and where do I find 'im? You don't know, do ya?"

"No, but I don't think it was his fault Bruce died. 'Cos one of the blokes who died was his mate, so..."

The bloke tutted. "I don't give a fuck about Smith. I wanna know where that smack went."

Perhaps because I had been so apologetic about what had happened to Bruce, I was truly shocked at the words the bloke had just come out with. My mouth opened. Suddenly, everything was different. All of the reasons for me being nervous and deferential to this person disappeared. I didn't know who he was but he obviously wasn't a friend of Bruce's.

"Who the fuck *are* you?" I said.

A mean look came over his face. It telegraphed what he was going to do and I was pushing at him even as he rushed toward me. He'd been going to grab hold of my jacket and my palms deflected his hands and sent him backwards a little way. He sprang back, his face even more livid. I was kicking and punching as he did. There was no fear in me now, partly because I'd discovered he wasn't some vengeful friend or relative of Bruce's and partly because a benefit of being a junkie is that you don't feel pain as much as straight people. I'd found that out in a couple of punch-ups - one of them with Doug - in recent times. That knowledge made you far less nervous of fights. The bloke and I were turning in small circles around the cramped kitchen, letting off short punches and kicking at each other's legs. Doug meanwhile was trying to stop it, his palms up, following us around, mouthing soothing words that I couldn't make out. I did register, though, that he mostly seemed worried that this violence might upset the bloke.

The bloke had grabbed hold of the shoulder of one arm of my jacket in all the scrabbling and was clinging to it as he tried to land punches with his opposite hand. It was serving to keep his face within range and I repeatedly bashed at his nose and cheek with my knuckles. His blows were landing too, of course, but it only produced a faraway discomfort. Even the pain of the bruises left by it would be swept away the next time I jacked up.

The bloke let go of my jacket and pushed me back. He shuffled back a couple of steps himself. It gave me the opportunity to kick out at him. He barely paid attention to my foot as it thudded into his hip, merely swaying away to lessen the impact. He was busy getting something out of an inside pocket of his jacket. I only really noticed when he held it up, pointed at the ceiling. He glanced at it and, satisfied, held it toward me. It was a Stanley knife. It was then I realised that the motion of holding it upwards had been to push the blade out.

There was a second where my brain was totally neutral about the sight, me neither alarmed nor dismissive. But as I found the bloke coming my way, I reacted with a fright that surprised me. I threw myself backwards. The blade danced under my nose. Without waiting for him to move again, I jumped further away. I was certain that it wasn't a bluff: he was obviously a nasty piece of work.

"Alright..." the bloke said, walking calmly in my direction. "You still gonna give me lip?"

Carefully, I maintained the distance between us by circling off. I realised I was now out of my depth. Even a junkie couldn't shrug off the damage a knife would do.

"Eh?" he asked.

My eyes were on the hand he held the Stanley in. He'd stopped in the centre of the room, cockily enjoying my sudden wariness.

Abruptly, I realised something. I was standing at the kitchen door. The thought that I didn't have to be frozen in this tense tableau, that I could just hop into the hallway and run away, was so hilarious I almost couldn't believe it was possible. I did it, swivelling and pelting down the hallway. The noise I made fumbling at the front door latch prevented me from hearing whether or not he was chasing. If he was, slamming the door closed behind me to hold him up would have been a smart thing to do but I wasn't calm enough for that. I sprinted down the path, tore open the gate and only paused to look round when I'd run almost to the end of the street. He and Doug were standing at the gate looking at me. I turned away, feeling exhilarated, almost laughing. I trotted down another couple of streets, then slowed to a walk.

* * * *

At Andrew's place that night, I heard Louise asking who it was from beyond the front door as Lisa looked through the spyhole. Lisa was telling her as she opened the door and before she'd set eyes on me Louise said with pleasure in her voice "'Allo Paul!"

"'Allo..." I cooed back, simultaneously raising my eyebrows at Lisa, who smiled a greeting.

Louise, who was dressed in pink dungarees, pulled at my hands as I stepped in. "Do your fing, Paul..."

"What thing?"

"You know."

I gripped her miniature hands and hoisted her up to my chest level, then let her down again. I repeated the action. She grinned with pleasure.

In the living room, Andrew was stretched out on the sofa, head propped in his hand, watching *Eastenders*. "Hi Paul. Dinner's nearly ready."

I sat in an armchair. Louise climbed into my lap. I was basking in the fact of other human beings being pleased to see me. The quality of my life felt like it had improved ten-fold since my regular visits to Andrew's place had started. I could now hardly believe that I'd ignored the benefits of human warmth for so long.

"You been in a fight, Paul?"

"Eh?"

Andrew nodded at my face. "Got a bruise on your cheek."

"Oh... Yeah..." I put my fingers up to the tender patch. "One of the blokes in the band..." I improvised.

"Yeah? What was that - artistic differences?"

I laughed. "Yeah!"

Andrew smiled. "We 'ad a few of those!"

That set off a bout of Ragamuffins reminiscing that took up most of the evening.

As I sat at the table eating the delicious lamb dinner Andrew had made, I was trying to think of a way to show how grateful I was to him and Lisa. I was dismayed when I found I couldn't. I couldn't give them any money to repay them for the hospitality because I didn't have any. I couldn't invite them to my place because it was a cramped bedsit with a urine-smelling sink. I couldn't even express it verbally: I'd just get embarrassed if I tried to tell them how much their company had meant to me recently.

I noticed Lisa gazing at me across the table. I turned my lips up in a small smile, gazing back. As though she understood what I was thinking, she returned my smile. In my vulnerable state, maybe I was reading more into it than there was but the tiny exchange did give me some suggestion that she knew I appreciated coming here meant a lot to me.

Twenty-Five

After another lovely evening with Andrew's family, it came as something of a shock the next day when, preparing to go to rehearsals, I remembered that it might be dangerous to do so. Approaching Aaron's house, butterflies were going around my stomach. As I pressed the doorbell, I hung back a couple of steps. Aaron opened the door. He nodded at me casually enough and made to go back in.

"Aaron!" I hissed after him. He turned. I pointed silently toward the living room. "Anyone here...?" I whispered.

"Well your friend from yesterday didn't come again, if that's what you mean."

I stepped in and closed the door.

Doug, for once, had got there before me. "So who the fuck was that, then?" I immediately asked him.

"'E works for a dealer." He seemed embarrassed. "Bruce stole 'is drugs."

"Bruce?"

Doug nodded. "He never got given that sixty grams. That was bollocks. 'E stole it off this bloke called Tony Heald."

"That one yesterday?"

"No, that's Jimmy. 'E works for him. Tony Heald's a dealer. Bruce ripped 'im off. Jammy bastard."

"So what did he want with me?"

I was aware of the others rapt at the conversation.

"'E just wanted to know whether you knew where it went."

"What - you told him I might know?"

"Well, not really. I just told 'im you'd told me you got free smack off Bruce and 'e goes 'e wanted to see you."

I went and sat on the sofa and gazed at the wall, reflecting on that. Doug had probably been offered some smack for doing him that favour.

"Sorry, mate," Doug said. "I didn't know 'e was gonna get nasty about it. 'E's a right arse'ole."

I looked at him. "Does he still think I know where the drugs are?"

"I dunno. I told 'im you didn't. I dunno. 'E's an idiot."

"Fucking psychopath," I said. "Oi, I hope you haven't told him where I live?"

"I don't know where you live."

I realised it was true. He'd never been round and I'd never given him my address. There'd never been any reason to. And thank God.

Aaron interjected in a slightly self-righteous tone: "He isn't coming in if he comes round again."

"Well I didn't plan on inviting him in," I snapped.

That made Justin chuckle. Which, in turn, made me smile. The tense atmosphere leavened, we got on with some rehearsing.

We all looked at each other warily when, a few hours later, the doorbell rang. Nobody moved for a couple of seconds. Aaron lifted his bass over his head and, leaning it against an armchair, walked over to the window. He peeked through a gap in the curtains. "It's Randy."

Randy was his girlfriend. She was an American woman, although she hadn't come over with him. She sat and watched us as we went through the last few minutes of our rehearsals. It had been a productive session today. We'd worked out the arrangement on two songs already written and written a new piece of music - without lyrics yet - from scratch.

I was pretty pleased with myself but it can't have been just that which made me say yes when Randy, out of politeness, asked me whether I wanted to come to the pub with her, Aaron and Justin. I was still in my strange mood. It was like a state of limbo: Andrew's happiness had suddenly made me unsure whether what I'd been so het up about for so much of my life - women gossiping - was actually important. Randy must have been surprised when I took her up but she didn't show it. As we waited for Aaron to have a pee, she asked me how it had gone today.

"Pretty good, actually. Productive. Feels good to work hard."

She smiled. "Especially after what happened yesterday?"

"Christ, yeah. I'd just managed to forget about that."

Her smile broadened. I could sense her warming to me. This was the longest conversation I'd ever had with her. Like all friendly people would, she had been upset by my coolness toward her - and to tell the truth I'd enjoyed it: hurting members of the female sex in that small way was a mini-revenge.

"Aaron told me about it. Pretty hairy, huh?"

"I nearly *lost* hair over it."

She laughed. Aaron, coming down the stairs, looked curiously at me as he heard her.

At the pub, the other three ate the spaghetti dish that was on the menu. I stuck to liquids, as usual not trusting my stomach when I wasn't getting enough smack. I'd scored this morning after borrowing some money from Andrew last night and taken less than my usual half a gram to make it last.

I left around half-six. I was baby-sitting tonight: Andrew and Lisa were going to see a film. I was glad I hadn't told them I was a druggie. They'd never have let me baby-sit if I had. On the way there, I stopped into a mini-mart to buy some chocolate for Louise.

* * * *

Lisa was pulling on her coat as she opened the front door to me. Louise was standing in the living room doorway dressed in her pyjamas.

"'Allo!" I said to her.

"'Allo!" She was about to hold up her hands so that I could do my 'thing' when she saw the Cadbury's Creme Egg in my hand.

"Look what I've got for you."

Her mouth open, she slowly extended her hand toward it, not quite sure what she was being offered.

"Oh, look," Lisa said. "Uncle Paul's bought you some chocolate."

Louise looked from her face back to the egg, her face slowly lighting up in a smile.

"Say thank you then," Lisa said.

"Thank you."

I picked her up and took her into the living room. As I did so, I heard footsteps on the stairs. It was Andrew, pulling on his own coat as he came down. He nodded. "Alright?" I said as I continued.

I slumped down onto the sofa, Louise bouncing briefly in my lap as I did. She was picking puzzledly at the egg's foil wrapping. I took it gently off her and started to peel it away. Distractedly, I registered the doorbell ringing. As I was holding the unwrapped egg toward Louise, I heard Andrew say from the hallway "Who wants to know?"

A male voice said, in a harsh and unfriendly tone that made me jerk my head up, "Are you called Hazelwood?" It sounded like it was a question being asked a second time.

I couldn't see into the hall from where I was. I sat gazing at the door, ears cocked. There was a moment of hesitation, then Andrew's voice said "No..."

"Really?" a different voice said. "That's funny. Says Hazelwood on the poll tax register."

I felt a sliding sensation in my chest. I recognised the voice. It was the bloke called Jimmy. I rose to my feet, lifting Louise with me. Even as I was doing it there was the sound of scuffling in the hallway. Lisa gave an outraged "Hey!" The door I was staring at flew inwards. When it banged against the wooden armrest of the chair behind it, my heart stopped beating for a moment. Andrew came backwards into the room, propelled by a man whose hands were fixed to the front of his coat. The man was shortish but very beefy. He looked vaguely half-caste. The front door slammed closed. Lisa came stumbling in after them, clearly having been shoved by Jimmy, the next to enter.

When Jimmy saw me, his mouth fell open. "It's him! 'E's 'ere - look!"

The half-caste looked round. He pushed Andrew away from him and moved toward me. I stood frozen, Louise still in my arms. The half-caste looked toward Jimmy and, as if to make sure, said to him in a voice I could only just make out "He's the one?" When Jimmy nodded, the half-caste walked right up to me. His eyes flicked from Louise into my face.

"You know 'oo I am?" he asked.

"Er, Tony Heald, is it?"

"That's right. And you're the little wanker 'oo stole off me."

I shook my head. "I didn't steal off-"

His fist hit me in the face and sent me back onto the sofa. Louise tumbled out of my hands. Still stunned, I was pulled up by the shirt.

I could feel the blood crawling from my nose over my top lip as he said, perfectly calmly, "Don't fucking interrupt me you little drip of piss."

"I swear - I didn't steal anything!" I jabbered, cringing even as I said it because I was doing what he'd just told me not to do.

"So why'd you give me all that shit yesterday?" Jimmy said.

I looked over at him. He was leaning casually against the now closed living room door, blocking the exit. Andrew and Lisa were staring, uncomprehending, at Heald and me. "I didn't know who you were. I-"

"Bollocks!" Heald grabbed me by the hair. I yelped. This was hurting, smack addict or no. "You're gonna give that stuff back or you're dead!"

Louise, who had been left sprawled on the sofa when she fell out of my arms, was suddenly crying - the screaming kind of crying that children make. I saw Lisa move toward her only to be grabbed by the hair by Jimmy and pulled back.

"Jesus Christ," I said. "I swear - I didn't steal anything."

It was astonishing but the look on Heald's face became even more furious. He shoved me back and I was on the sofa again. "I ain't taking the fucking piss!" he barked. "I'll kill you!"

Suddenly, he stooped and lifted Louise up by the hair.

"I'll kill her an' all!"

"Ahhhh!" The elongated noise that came out of my mouth made it sound as if I'd just been stabbed: the sight of Louise suspended in the air, her legs kicking, her wails huge, was horrific beyond belief. My palm was held helplessly, beseechingly toward Heald. He was totally insane. The only way to calm him down was to say I *had* stolen from him. I was about to do so, trying to think up a story, when there was a flash of movement before me. Heald fell forward. His huge barrel chest covered my face for a second before he rolled off and flipped full-length onto the carpet. I lay there, staring at him, thinking that he had instigated some bizarre smothering attack. But he lay face-down and completely still.

"You better get the fuck out!"

I looked up. It was Andrew, addressing Jimmy. Jimmy glanced at his fallen friend. I looked at Andrew's right hand. It was clutching a pink, foot-long ceramic cat that usually stood on the shelf above the television. His fingers gripped it around the neck, the squared base held out threateningly. Louise, now kneeling on the carpet, was still crying. Instinctively, I reached for her and pulled her up onto the sofa. Her scream-crying was so massive it sounded like she might do damage to her throat. I held her face fiercely against my side, feeling my own tears on my cheeks. I looked up again. Jimmy, back still to the door, was groping for the handle. His handsome face was hateful as, still facing us, he pulled the door open. Then he turned and we heard the sound of him unlatching the front door.

Lisa, fingers steepled against her face, eyes narrowed in distress, was tip-toeing, bent over, toward her daughter as though she felt any faster motion might cause her more trauma. I tried to look into Lisa's face as I relinquished Louise but she just enveloped her and buried her nose in her hair. I looked at Andrew. He was standing in the middle of the room still holding the pink cat. My brain clicked back on and I caught up with what had just taken place. I went and stood gingerly over Heald. He still hadn't moved. I saw for the first time the small blob of red in his short curly hair.

Andrew was now standing beside me. I nodded at the cat. "You get him with that?" I asked superfluously.

He didn't answer, merely looked back down at Heald.

I used the old junkie trick. Going to the kitchen, I got a carving knife out of a drawer. Getting down on my knees, I had to turn Heald's head sideways to get access to his nose. The knife didn't steam up. My heart was pounding as I turned him over onto his back. This couldn't be happening. Not twice in five days. But even with unrestricted access to both nostrils, the blade remained shiny. I closed my eyes. The instinct came to me to get out of here. Then I remembered. This wasn't some shooting gallery. It wasn't some place I could just abandon. It was the living room of my cousin. I looked up. Andrew had now joined Lisa on the sofa. Louise was across Lisa's lap with her head buried in Andrew's thighs. Both of them were stroking at her, trying to soothe away the shock and the terror. Yet both of them had their eyes on me, staring at me. Their faces were frightful: both shiny from tears, both uncomprehending.

I'd never felt so guilty.

I looked back down at Heald. The blood was now fanning out on the carpet above his head. My head flopped down. My eyes closed, I knelt like that for several seconds.

"Paul?"

I looked up.

"Is 'e dead?" Andrew asked and I realised he'd asked me it a second ago too.

I nodded. Andrew, open-lipped, seemed not to know what to do with that knowledge. Lisa seemed to shrink away from it, closing her eyes, lifting her daughter and putting her mouth to the back of her shaking neck. Seeing their reactions made me get to my feet.

"I'll call the police," I said. It was my duty to start to sort things out: it was my fault that this had happened to them. Over the last few days I'd started to feel like one of the family. Now I'd besmirched their good, decent lives through my own dirty, nasty one.

Lisa looked up. "What did they want?" she said. Her teeth were pressed together, her eyes intense.

I couldn't answer. I could have told her, of course, about the incident yesterday at Aaron's house but that would have meant telling her about the incident less than a week ago when I'd been in a flat where two people died, which in turn would have meant me telling her that I was a junkie. It was information that I would have had no problem telling the kind of people I'd been knocking around with in recent years.

"I- It..." I stopped. I couldn't tell them. I shrugged and turned away, walking aimlessly over to a wall. Even as I did it, I was appalled at what would seem to them to be my casual attitude. I had to give them an explanation. But when I spoke what I said was "I- I mean, I don't know..."

It was utterly unnerving to be gazed at by two faces that were streaked with tears. I found I had to put my hand against the wall I was pointlessly standing near to steady myself. My next words came out in a rush. "Listen - I'll call the police but say I did it, right?" I looked at Andrew. "When the police come, I'll say I hit him with the..." I nodded at Andrew's hand: "...thing. Okay?"

I wanted to make some gesture to them. I owed them something. "Okay, Andrew? Don't tell them what happened. I'll say he was attacking me and I had to defend myself. 'Cos he was, really. You don't have to get involved with this."

They were both still staring. I shifted, horribly uncomfortable. "Okay?" I said, an edge of desperation in my voice now. Wanting some tiny sign of approval or forgiveness or something.

The logic of it came to me. "'Cos this bloke - the other one, I mean - came after me before. I mean, I've got witnesses to him coming after me before. Pulling a knife on me. So it'd be much easier to say he came after me again, with his mate, and I defended myself. You don't have to get involved at all. I'll take the blame. And... I mean, nothing'll happen to me because I've got witnesses to what happened before. The police'll know he was after me." I waited for a response but had to continue blabbering when it was obvious there still wasn't going to be one. "Alright? That'd be much better. No need to... It'll save you from..."

I had nothing left. I could now only shrug and look at them, waiting for them to answer.

Twenty-Six

The hum of the light coming on was barely perceptible but it woke me up as it did every morning. It was 6.30. I stretched for a while and then threw back the blankets and swung my legs onto the floor. I was in the single bed. Opposite me, Terry and Miguel lay snoozing on the top and bottom respectively of the bunk. I'd wake them in fifteen minutes. That was the arrangement. It suited me as well as them because it gave me privacy first thing.

I went over to the small wall-mounted table at the foot of my bed and dampened one half of my towel in my water jug. Then, standing up, I proceeded to wipe my body clean from head to foot. I didn't spend too long on my genitals, partly because I didn't want the others to catch me doing it, partly because you could never get rid of the stink of them anyhow. The faint aroma of dried piss was everywhere in prison. I merely whisked the towel in and out of the front of my 'bollock-danglers': the standard issue boxer shorts that gave you no support. The washing done, I switched the towel round and dried everywhere I'd wetted before pulling my shirt and denims on. I went through this routine every day because we were allowed one bath per week.

I woke the others when I heard the first cell door being opened on the landing. They leapt out of bed, anxious to be up and dressed when our cell was opened. We took our buckets out to the lavatories. The cell buckets were the most disgusting sight in prison: at the start of each morning they would usually contain an inch of piss, a couple of turds (covered with shaving cream to disguise the smell), tissues used to wipe backsides, a couple of dog-ends and the odd crumpled envelope or chewing gum wrapper. It made me sick to look at one, even my own. After emptying my bucket and carefully washing it, I came back to the cell to fetch my bowl and my jug for the day's shaving and drinking water.

While I was shaving, Terry and Miguel went to do their applications, either for their letters or visitor's order. They were each allowed one visit from one person or a group of people per month. As a remand prisoner, I was allowed a visit every day. Ironically, I had hardly any. I hadn't had many friends or much close family before coming in, of course, but those who were inclined to come I tried to discourage. Mick had been twice, Andrew - with or without Lisa - came once every fortnight or so, my Dad every few weeks, sometimes with my uncle Reg, Justin every week. I never got much pleasure from the visits except for those of Michele and Justin. I didn't have anything to feel guilty about with regards to them, unlike with my Dad who I'd not even bothered to see for years before landing here. Andrew I felt guilty in the presence of for obvious reasons but, even worse, he felt guilty about me being in here instead of him. It was terrible trying to make small talk with him.

Breakfast was squares and circles of egg and meat plus toast and tea without sugar. We ate off trays in our cell. Afterwards, unlike the others, I brushed my teeth. I'd let them go a bit when I'd been using. I was now brushing them after every meal, using the gritty, sweet tooth powder we were provided with, or ordinary soap when that wasn't available.

The mail came round half-an-hour later. Miguel got two letters and Terry none. When I saw the jiffy bag that had come for me, though, I knew I could cheer Terry up. It would be the tobacco my dad regularly sent.

"Tel..." Terry looked over from one of the room's two tables, where he was still sitting after eating his breakfast. I tossed, one after the other, three packets of Golden Virginia to him.

"Oh, cheers Paul..."

Convicts weren't allowed to have stuff sent from outside. They also weren't allowed to buy more than a certain amount of tobacco from the canteen at any one time. Remand prisoners, therefore, were given money and asked to have their friends send in stuff to them which could then be passed on. My dad always sent in more than I'd asked for - probably because he knew tobacco was currency in nick - and I was quite happy to give it out. Other prisoners thought I was mad not charging for the service but I enjoyed the generosity. It wasn't just a case of merely changing back to the person I'd been before smack, either. When Terry refused to have the window open when smoking, I didn't do what would have been almost anybody's first instinct, i.e. threaten to cut off his supply. I was a more patient individual than I'd ever been.

The next hour and a half was spent reading. I always found it hard to concentrate as Miguel had his radio on most of the day. Another reason I couldn't keep my mind entirely on the words before me was that I was struggling to control my bowels. I never felt like taking a crap right at the beginning of the day so after breakfast I had to hold everything in until exercise when I could use the toilets in the yard. It didn't bother me too much as it was now part of a regular routine.

When we were called for exercise, I grabbed the wad of tissue I'd collected this morning: there was never any paper in the yard toilets. Outside, it was fairly cold but the breeze whipping at my hair and clothes was a huge relief after 23 hours of the smell of farts and sweat inside. When we came round to the toilet block, I asked the nearest officer, Mr. Harris, for permission to use it. I laid two pieces of tissue across the toilet seat before sitting down. My crap was fairly noisy, as it tends to be when you've been bottling it up, but it didn't embarrass me too much. It was better than the alternative of squatting over a bucket in front of two other people.

Exercise was something you could never truly say you enjoyed. It gave you fresh air, the chance to talk to people you knew from association periods and the ability to move your body without fear you'd bump into your cellmates or an object, but it always had you bored well before the end. Walking again and again around a featureless yard, always in pairs, was just so stupid and tedious. It might help if you could do it for a shorter period but it was an hour or nothing. Most of the people here didn't even have the nothing option: convicts had to do it whether they wanted to or not. Mind you, I doubted there would be many absentees even if it was optional and even if it wasn't the only chance of taking a crap in private. The terror of being in my cell without a break the entire day had made me grit my teeth and brave every exercise period for seven months.

Back in the cell, it was my turn to sit on one of the two chairs. As usual, I exploited the chance to play guitar. I could do that on the bed, of course, but sitting hunched over for long periods without a support gave me backache. The guitar had been given to me by Mr. Harris. He was the wing officer and, like everyone else here, knew I'd been in a semi-successful band. This was through press coverage of my arrest: as a man in his fifties with silver, thinning hair I rather doubted he owned our albums. My case had attracted a lot of publicity, such as the story from an inside page of The Sun pinned on the notice board in our cell by Miguel: POP IDOL ON MURDER CHARGE. He'd cut that out of a two-day old paper when he'd learned I was going to be his cellmate. Loved the "idol". The guitar belonged to the prison drama department. I would have to surrender it whenever they needed it. It might be thought loaning the guitar to me was a kindly act but it didn't come across to me like that. Harris was a punishment fiend - not sadistic but a real believer in being made to pay for one's sins. However, in my case he knew I'd protested my innocence to the assistant governor in my meeting with him on my second day here, plus I also thought he just found it refreshing that somebody with talent should be here amongst the normal deadbeats.

My cellmates considered it a nice novelty, too. Miguel would turn his radio off when I played and they would often both sit there listening to me. Occasionally we'd have a raucous singsong lasting a couple of hours. I wasn't writing songs, however. Like heroin, that was a drug I was finally finished with.

There was a sudden explosion of yells and jeers. They were coming from the other cells but because they were being issued from the windows were audible outside as well as along the landings, creating an effect like a group of demented people screaming in an echo chamber. The cons in this block had noticed the nonces taking their exercise. Miguel and Terry jumped up to join in.

"You fucking perverts!" Terry screamed, hands gripping the bars. "You're the scum of the earth, you bunch of cunts!"

"You're fucking dead when we get you!" Miguel called out.

Then they both joined in the menacing, monotonous chant that had built up across the block: "BEASTS, BEASTS, BEASTS, *BEASTS...*"

I continued to noodle. A couple of people had told me I was lucky my case had got the publicity it had: anyone else declining to join in the baiting of sex offenders would have been suspected of being one himself. At first, I'd tried to explain that I felt amazed that convicted murderers - such as Miguel - thought themselves better than rapists but I'd given that up now. Using that argument was futile, even with minor offenders: when cons talked about the people on Rule 43 they were so beyond reason it was frightening. There was a total hatred in their eyes, a complete unwillingness to hear any view other than the common one on the subject. It was obvious why. Life in here was so miserable you could almost taste it: letting it all hang out by screaming at the nonces was the closest you could ever come to joy. And if, like Miguel, you were considered by society to be beyond forgiveness, it was nice to tell yourself there were people who had done something 'worse'. The collective screaming was continuous until the nonces were out of sight behind the toilet block. When they reappeared, it started up again.

Aside from exercise and nonce-baiting, the only other distractions in prison were the video shows/association periods we had twice a week, chapel on Sundays, the weekly bath and the weekly visit to the library. Even the thrice-daily journey to the food tables seemed a form of entertainment: anything that got you out of the cell for a few minutes. We were all jealous of the nicks where prisoners worked. When I'd first been remanded, I'd spent two days at Middlesex prison before being transferred here. We'd been employed sewing mailbags four hours a day. It had seemed monotonous to me at the time but now I would have loved the chance to be doing something - even that - in a different room for a significant chunk of the day. The funny thing was, even though we weren't given work here, we still got our £3.11 weekly wages.

I wouldn't even be in prison now if I hadn't fucked up at the police station the night Andrew clobbered Tony Heald.

When the police arrived, I was surprised at how calmly they took the sight of a man lying dead on the carpet. Although there were a lot of them - two arriving first, followed by another group of four five minutes later - they didn't over-react. The first thing they did was to organise getting Heald into the ambulance we'd also called, even though they could see he was beyond help. Then one of the first group asked what had happened. Lisa and Andrew said nothing, looking at the floor, allowing me to speak. After they'd heard my story, they asked us all whether we would attend the police station voluntarily. Andrew and I said yes, but Andrew asked if Lisa could stay because she had Louise to look after. The police said she could. One of them stayed behind to interview her while Andrew and I were taken to the station.

When I was being interviewed, I spun the interviewing officer the yarn I'd planned to give about Bruce's death: Jimmy pursuing me and Heald and Jimmy coming round and causing havoc to an innocent family so they could recover their drugs in order to kill more people with them. Despite being shaken by what had happened, I didn't feel too nervous, although I was a little edgy insofar as I was wondering whether Andrew and Lisa were sticking to the agreed story.

The reason I wasn't nervous was partly because of the fact that it had been done in self-defence, even though not really by me, and partly because the knowledge of doing this to help someone else gave me such a righteous feeling that I couldn't imagine anything bad coming out of it. So it was over-confidence that led me to be careless about the exact details of Heald being struck. I should have stuck closer to the truth and said that I'd hit Heald with the cat when he'd grabbed hold of Louise. Instead, I said I'd done it while defending myself. The copper interviewing me let me go on and on before calmly asking me why, in that case, the injury was to the back of Heald's head.

The copper was very good at his job - he tied me up in knots. And once tied up, I couldn't untangle myself without implicating Andrew. When the police found out I had a criminal record for possession - I'd got a £50 fine a year before - that sealed it. I was formally arrested on suspicion of murder. Even worse, although they weren't remanded in custody, was the fact that Andrew and Lisa were charged with being accessories to murder.

Thankfully, that was dropped six weeks later. My solicitor reckoned it was because the police thought it might be difficult to secure a conviction against a mother and a househusband. Thank God I'd thought to wipe Andrew's fingerprints off the ceramic cat.

No matter how many times they begged me to, I wouldn't let Andrew and Lisa go back to the police and tell them what really happened. I was just as shocked as they were that the legal system could be worried about the death of a psychopathic smack dealer but I wasn't going to do anything that would complicate their position. They were now completely in the clear. If we all changed our story, that might change. I'd already caused them enough trouble.

My attitude to the chance of an acquittal changed from day to day. I'd been told I had more than an even chance of a not guilty verdict, and for the reasons I'd originally thought: the fact of Heald's profession and witnesses to Jimmy pursuing me. Also, he had convictions for assault and possession. My solicitor had even told me the jury would probably be impressed by the supposed glamour attached to a one-time recording artist. Yet nothing would surprise me now, not after having been charged in the first place.

Still, at least I was off smack now. The prison authorities took a humane, if brisk, attitude with detox: methadone maintenance for seven days then that was it. Smack was actually available in prison, particularly to those like me who could have unlimited stuff sent in to barter with. I was never too tempted.

It felt to me as though the eighteen months of my life before coming here had gone by without me actually thinking about anything at all. I'd been drifting along ever since being sacked by the Coronets, my life revolving around getting smack. That had been helped - or worsened, if you like - by the fact that I'd found the place over Mr. Case's shop. It was almost a dream come true to be able to live rent-free. It meant I didn't have any of the problems other junkies had: any spare money could be used to feed my habit rather than be saved for keeping a roof over my head. So I had disappeared into a heroin haze. I'd re-emerged at regular intervals, of course, as I tried to give it up, but there was nothing else to do so I had always drifted back into it. I'd had hepatitis (putting me in hospital for two weeks), I'd had boils on my thighs which when I cut them open with nail scissors poured a thick yellow and red liquid, I'd seen the veins in my right arm collapse one by one, I'd had a sore on my calf which looked - and smelt - like something you might find behind a fridge. One of the reasons I'd formed my last band was that I thought it would provide enough of a purpose and a distraction to keep me straight.

I'd been wrong, of course. Nothing had.

This time, I was off it for good. I knew what I wanted in life now. I wanted what Andrew had. Love. When Andrew and I were teenagers, we'd both been convinced that the highest form of happiness was making a living playing music. Well, I had never been happy when I had that. I had only ever been happy when I was in love with Jenny. And Andrew had been made happy by Lisa.

I knew love didn't exist the way men thought it did, but, Jesus Christ, wasn't what it was enough? Remembering the happiest moments I'd had with Jenny gave me a terrible feeling of loss. It had been so good. Contrasting it to what I had now, it just made me want to collapse into the loving arms of a woman, regardless of the knowledge of the regular betrayal that was their gossiping. In fact, the thought of that betrayal gave me a certain kind of pleasure. It was the thought of magnanimously accepting that injustice rather than opting for the alternative of a life without intimacy. I'd chosen the latter when I'd left Jenny. Looking at what had become of me, I knew I'd made the wrong decision.

Even if you weren't a successful rock star, there were things that definitely made life worth living. First and foremost, the pleasure to be had from sex and intimacy with a woman. Then there was the pleasure to be had from listening to a great record or reading a great book or seeing a great film. And there were the smaller pleasures, like your first cup of tea in the morning or the clean, fragrant, warm sensation after stepping out of a shower or the well-fed, comfortable feeling from pigging out on cod and chips and a Coke. On balance, life wasn't a pile of shit.

It was time I stopped sulking and revelling in misery. I'd had enough of it. If your life was bad, you should try to improve it. If the path you were on showed no means to improvement, you should get off it and get on another one.

* * * *

The day wore on. The trick was to keep devising ways not to fall asleep. If you slept during the day, you wouldn't be able to sleep at night and it was much better to be asleep at night because there was no light then so you couldn't read and your cellmates were asleep so you couldn't play music. So we would read our library books or our newspapers. Read each other's books or papers if we'd finished ours. Listen to Miguel's radio. Look out the window. Do exercises on the floor (though only one at a time because there wasn't space for more). The fact that I had a guitar didn't mean I had any more distractions than the other two. In my case it had to compensate for the lack of any real conversations. I had nothing much in common with Terry and Miguel. Or with any other prisoner. There might be another inmate with a degree to his name but I wasn't aware of him.

I also had a visitor today. I didn't see it as an enjoyable distraction, though. In fact, I didn't know what I saw it as.

When visiting time came, I was almost in a trance. As I walked to the visiting hall, my entire body was numb. The sounds around me seemed miles away and it was though I was looking through somebody else's eyes.

It was only because I knew what number table she was sitting at that I recognised her. Although I'd been wondering if she'd changed much, I couldn't help having the picture in my head of her when I'd been fourteen. The last time I'd seen her. Walking slowly over to her, it occurred to me to ask the woman before me if she was sure she was at the right table. When she rose upon seeing me, the absence of a smile on her face, strangely, made me less unsure. Her expression was serious, almost grim, but it wasn't one of puzzlement. She recognised me.

"'Allo, Paul." Now she smiled.

"Hi." I dropped my eyes, embarrassed, confused about what I should do. I covered my embarrassment by sitting down, a little too hastily. She sat down too.

She looked like a relative of my mother rather than the real thing. The features I could remember were still there but were blurred by a facial plumpness that was new to me. As were the lines around her mouth, nose and eyes and the general lack of smoothness of her skin. Her hair was only slightly longer than it had been fifteen years ago but it was completely grey.

The overall effect was shocking. The huge change brought it home to me that she was a stranger. I didn't know where to look. She might be my mum but I didn't know her.

"Long time no see," she said.

I could only manage a brisk nod. When she saw that, she hissed in self-conscious laughter. Which made me feel for her. She wasn't feeling too comfortable either. It brought me out of my stunned state of mind. I smiled at her and nodded again.

She took heart from that, smiling broadly. "You've changed," she said.

That surprised me. I hadn't thought of how different I might look to her. I was about to tell her she'd changed too but stopped in case it sounded critical of her appearance. I wouldn't have got the chance anyway because suddenly she was crying, covering her eyes and emitting a long gasp.

Quickly, I reached for her other hand, which was lying flat on the table. She squeezed my hand hard, still weeping into her other palm. I was sure then that I got a glimpse through her eyes for a moment because, following her comment that I'd changed, I was remembering that the man she saw before her had actually been a child the last time we'd been in the same room together.

She took her hand away and looked in her bag for some tissues, shaking her head in apology as she did. "Can't believe... It's been..."

I squeezed her other hand harder. "I know..." I said vaguely.

She dried her eyes but kept the tissue held up near her cheek. She looked into my face for a long time. I couldn't do the same. The eye contact was uncomfortable and I kept glancing around the room. I noticed with some relief as I did that none of the tables near us were occupied. The only person looking at us was Mr. Watts, one of the officers, seated across the room in his elevated umpire-style chair.

"Bet you were surprised your uncle Reg met me."

"He *would* have to meet you when I was in prison."

She laughed. "I was glad 'e did."

She continued gazing at me. I was afraid it was because she might be about to ask me about the case. I hoped she wouldn't. I didn't have the energy to go into it. I'd already explained and justified myself to so many people: police, solicitors, screws in here, my dad, Mick... Thankfully, it seemed as though the information my dad and Reg had given her was enough because she went down a totally different, and unexpected, route.

"So you went to university, eh?"

After a surprised pause, I said "Yeah. So did Andrew."

"I know. Right brainboxes we got in the family now."

I smiled, glad at the pleasure that seemed to give her.

"And a pop star an' all..."

"Well..."

"I couldn't believe it when your dad showed me your records. I mean, you've gone to university, you've made records and been on telly... You've really done well for yourself."

By now I was past being surprised that people thought having made records meant you'd made something out of your life so I just raised my eyebrows at her as though in bashful acknowledgment.

She was stroking my hand now. She smiled. "You were always playing that guitar you 'ad when you were little. You wouldn't let go of it."

"And you gave me my first electric guitar."

She looked down at the table. "And then I left you. Same day." She needed the tissue again, bringing it up to her eyes once more.

I hadn't meant it like that. "It's... Don't... I mean, I wouldn't have become a musician if it hadn't been for you buying me that..."

She brought her eyes up to look at me. They were bright with tears. "You musta been... I tried to explain it to you, in the letter... It wasn't 'cos of you."

"I know."

She dabbed at her eyes some more. This time she put the tissue away in her bag. "I'd never do the same again. I've got another son, you know."

"Have you?" I said, very surprised.

She was surprised too. "Yeah. Didn't your dad tell ya?"

"No."

"Yeah. And a daughter."

"Oh..." I was amazed. Although she'd loved me, she'd never been particularly motherly. "How old are they?"

"My son's nine and my daughter's seven. Michael and Julie, they're called."

"Are you married?"

"No. I never got a divorce from your dad."

"Oh yeah."

There was an awkward silence.

"So you've got a little brother and sister now."

I nodded and smiled. "Andrew's got a daughter."

"Yeah, your dad was saying. I'll 'ave to go and see 'er."

"You and dad are getting on alright, aren't ya?"

She grinned. "Yeah. Bit of a shock for bofe of us at first. But we get on great really. Tell you the troof, Paul, we never 'ad much togevver. 'E can't 'ave been too upset when I left. It was you I was worried about when I did." Her voice lowered. "I know you took it pretty hard."

I was thinking of making out that I hadn't but that wouldn't sound particularly flattering to her.

"It's..." I started. I shrugged and finished "...you know. All in the past."

"Oh God. All in the past. Jesus. Wish I could go back and change the past."

I snorted. "So do I."

"What... You mean... All this business?"

I nodded.

"You'll be alright, though. Won't ya? That's what they reckon."

"Yeah," I said, faking conviction. "There's not much chance I'll be found guilty."

She nodded, glad of the chance to be persuaded. "What you gonna do then?"

"Dunno."

"Gonna make more records?"

"Nah. Finished with that."

She was surprised. "What... you don't wanna do that no-more?"

"No. I'm fed up with it."

"You'll need a job though. I mean, you can come and stay with us, that's no problem, but what about... Y'know... What you gonna do wiv your future and that?"

"Well, the governor here has said he can get me a transfer to a prison with writing classes. I want to go for that."

"Ooh - yeah. You'd be good at that."

"Trouble is, it's in Kent."

"That don't matter. Long as you get the chance to do something like that. We'll all still come and see ya. You know what you should do? You should write your life story. Fings *you've* done."

I nodded. "That's what the governor reckons."

It was what had helped me make up my mind to give up being a musician. I knew I could never go cold turkey on songwriting. Writing would be the creative outlet that replaced it. It was perfect because, though I wasn't kidding myself I could be a great writer straightaway, I had an interesting and saleable story from the get-go. Maybe I could become a good writer by the end of the process of telling it.

"Yeah. 'E's right. Or you could sell your story to a newspaper, y'know. They're always interested in fings like this."

"Yeah, they've all asked me."

"What - the papers?"

"Yeah. *The Sun, The Mirror, The Star*. All of them."

"Yeah? That's great! You can get a lot of money from fings like that."

"Yeah, I know. *The Sun* offered £20,000. Providing I'm acquitted." I added, "Found not guilty," in case she didn't know what it meant.

"And you've said yeah?"

I shook my head. "My solicitor said wait until after the case and then they'll all offer more."

She opened her mouth, eyes widening. "That's great. So it won't be too bad when you do get out of 'ere, then."

I nodded.

She continued "'Cos your dad said you never made any money from your records. I couldn't believe that."

"No-one can."

"'E reckons people treated you badly. Accountants and that."

I smiled. "No. It wasn't people treating us badly. We just never sold enough records."

"Oh. Well... You deserve some luck, anyway. After what's happened to you."

"I was quite lucky coming here actually."

"What - here?" She pointed at the table.

"To prison." She was so puzzled she couldn't speak. "It's changed me," I went on. "I'm... calmer now."

"How'd ya mean?"

I paused. "It's hard to explain. You needed to know me before. It just gives you time to stop and think. I mean, for instance, if you'd wanted to come and see me before I came to prison, I would've said no."

I'd embarrassed her as well as puzzled her. She looked steadily down at her hand as it continued to stroke mine. But then she surprised me. She looked up and said "We've bofe done a bit of growing up since we last saw each uvver, ain't we?"

I looked into her wide brown eyes. I got a jolt suddenly. I was seeing again what had once been a fixture of my life, eyes I'd gazed into countless times when I was a child. It was as though it opened a gate. Everything else rushed in with that jolt of recognition, thousands of fragments of memories: our estate in Putney, the carpet with square patterns we'd had in our living room, the way my dad had used to shout "Wanker," when a politician or somebody upper class appeared on television, the way the books arranged on the windowsill in our living room were kept upright by a little statue of Buddha... Another lifetime.

I turned over the hand my mum was stroking and squeezed her fingers tightly. I had to dig my teeth into my bottom lip or else I would have needed a tissue myself.